VISION OF SEDUCTION

Also by Cassie Ryan

Ceremony of Seduction

VISION OF SEDUCTION

CASSIE RYAN

APHRODISIA

KENSINGTON BOOKS
http://www.kensingtonbooks.com

APHRODISIA BOOKS are published by

Kensington Publishing Corp.
850 Third Avenue
New York, NY 10022

All Kensington Titles, Imprints, and Distributed Lines are available at special quantity discounts for bulk purchases for sales promotions, premiums, fund-raising, and educational or institutional use.

Special book excerpts or customized printings can also be created to fit specific needs. For details, write or phone the office of the Kensington special sales manager: Kensington Publishing Corp., 850 Third Avenue, New York, NY 10022, attn: Special Sales Department, Phone: 1-800-221-2647.

Aphrodisia and the A logo Reg. U.S. Pat. & TM Off.

ISBN-13: 978-0-7582-2066-0
ISBN-10: 0-7582-2066-9

First Kensington Trade Paperback Printing: August 2008

10 9 8 7 6 5 4 3 2 1

Printed in the United States of America

*To my sister, Amy,
for being my first and biggest fan,
not to mention my unflagging cheering section.
This one's for you, Sis . . .*

Special Thanks

As with every book, the path from blank piece of paper to bound book on the shelves was a winding road that was only reached with the help of many. After all, it takes a village to produce a book . . . well, something like that!

First, huge and unflagging thanks to my wonderful agent, Paige Wheeler, who effortlessly traded fun and snarky e-mails with me, punctuated with encouraging phone calls. You're the best, Paige!

Thanks must also go out to my critique group, the ever-fearless and always supportive Butterscotch Martini Girls (www.butterscotchmartinigirls.com), who continue to add writing credits and pen names at an exponential rate, so you'll have to pop out to the site to see all eight of us as our various and sundry pen names and personalities.

Cheyenne McCray, you're amazing! Not only are you a writing machine, and an author I respect and look up to, but you're also a great friend. And huge thanks for the wonderful cover quote and all your encouragement!

Thanks to Audrey LaFehr, my editor, her assistant, Amanda, and the Kensington art and marketing department for all their help and support.

To my son and husband for being proud of me, and supporting me in all things!

A huge thanks to all my readers and fans who have supported the Seduction Series and have sent me great e-mails and fan mail! Please stop by and check out my newly updated Web site at www.cassieryan.com.

1

_____

"Is a little mind-blowing, no-strings-attached sex too much to ask?"

Katelyn Hunt gripped the display case so tightly she thought the glass might shatter and rain down upon the carefully displayed crystals and pendants as she stared at _him_.

Rita, Katelyn's business partner and best friend, shook her head, sending her bob of dark hair swinging. "No. I imagine every woman is entitled to a little toe-curling sex, but have you ever considered scratching that itch by actually finding a man you like and care about, rather than a one-night stand in between each case of batteries?"

Katelyn rolled her eyes at Rita's familiar argument. "Relationships are for women who can't function on their own." She glared at her friend before letting her gaze slide back to the hunk who had haunted their shop for the last few days. "I don't need a man for anything."

"Uh-huh—what about that mind-blowing sex?" Rita closed the display case with a _snap_. "But you're not even going to have that if you don't eventually talk to the man." She walked away and left Katelyn racking her brain for a good retort.

Damn! I hate it when she does that.

True, Katelyn had never actually met him, never even spoken to him, but he'd spent the last few days inside the store—totally oblivious to her, much to her irritation.

He bought chai tea in the coffee shop, sat in the overstuffed chairs, and spent hours reading an eclectic collection of books. In fact, the only part of the entire two floors of her new-age shop he hadn't frequented was anywhere she happened to be working.

Or maybe it just seemed that way.

His muscled arm reached for his chai tea, which was sitting on the small oak table next to him, and Katelyn's mouth literally watered as his long fingers closed around the cup and lifted it to his lips.

A surprised gasp slipped from her lips as a hot spurt of arousal arrowed through her, tightening her nipples and making every inch of her skin heavy with need.

What the hell is happening to me? For some reason this man made her react like a bitch in heat.

"At least he's a paying customer."

Katelyn jumped as Rita's voice sounded next to her.

"Don't sneak up on me like that!" Katelyn placed her hand over her heart, willing it to slow before it galloped out of her chest.

Rita laughed and shook her head. "I didn't sneak anywhere. You're just too involved in fantasizing over *him* to notice anything around you." Rita hummed as she padlocked the display cases and then bumped Katelyn aside with her hip to wipe off the day's smudges with glass cleaner and paper towels.

"What the hell are you so happy about?"

Rita's face blossomed, and her eyes sparkled with excitement. "I think Aedan is going to ask me to marry him tonight."

"That loser?" Katelyn grabbed her friend by the shoulders and glared at her, half tempted to shake some sense into her. "I thought you broke up?"

Rita rolled her eyes and ducked out of Katelyn's grip. "No, you were hoping we would. Just because you're terrified of a relationship doesn't mean the rest of the world is, too."

"I'm not terrified!" Katelyn's response sounded too defensive, and she wished she would've taken a deep breath before answering. Rita always knew how to press her hot buttons. "I just don't want you to get hurt. Every time you talk about him, it gives me the creeps."

Rita's eyes narrowed, and she pinned Katelyn with a glare. "Are you trying to tell me you've had a vision about him?"

"No," Katelyn reluctantly admitted.

"Then we're done discussing this." Rita, back to her overly cheerful self, gave Katelyn a quick hug and then stepped back but seemed just short of performing a pirouette. "Lock up for me, okay? I know it's my turn, but because you still need to go talk to Romeo over there, I figure you can handle it."

Katelyn shuddered as she watched her best friend and business partner bounce out the front door. The door chimes jingled merrily behind her, but for some reason they reminded Katelyn of a death knell.

She had asked Rita thousands of times to bring Aedan into the shop. If she could just shake hands with him, it might trigger a vision and give her more insight as to what bothered her about him.

No matter what Rita said, Katelyn's gut clenched whenever Aedan's name was brought up—and that definitely couldn't be a good thing.

The movement of her dark stranger picking up his chai caught her attention, and she swiveled her head to watch, even as she bit back a long sigh of appreciation.

His Adam's apple bobbed as he swallowed, and she watched,

transfixed, until he broke the spell by glancing her way and catching her staring again.

Damn!

His eyes reminded her of liquid amethyst, and each time their gazes locked, she felt as if she might drown in those deep purple depths. The corners of his lips curved, and then his attention returned to his book as he set the chai back on the table.

Once again, his gaze had held nothing but polite acknowledgement.

The loss of even that noncommittal attention made her feel suddenly chilly, and she rubbed her arms to chase away the gooseflesh.

She wasn't under any delusion that she was "model" hot, but she was a reasonably attractive woman, and there had definitely been men in her past—even though she hadn't allowed any of them to stay for long.

Hell, he could at least take one appreciative look before returning to his books, right?

Katelyn puffed out a breath that fluttered her bangs. "Men."

She'd found herself openly staring at him hundreds of times throughout the day, and although he'd caught her a few times, she was sure she'd made it look nonchalant. She hoped.

But how could she help it? This man was a walking wet dream. His dark mahogany hair gleamed with almost auburn accents under the fluorescent lights. The hair looked soft as silk, and her fingers literally itched to reach out and touch.

He'd gathered it back into a simple ponytail that hung halfway down his back. She'd always thought men with long hair appeared too feminine for her taste, but no one would ever think to accuse *him* of anything of the sort.

The harsh, unforgiving lines of his face made him appear aloof, and his jaw seemed carved from solid granite. But . . . those sensual lips. They softened him, which made him rakishly handsome, even approachable.

His broad shoulders tapered to a trim waist and down to muscular thighs Katelyn could envision tracing with her tongue. His wasn't the overly ripped physique of a bodybuilder which made men resemble plastic Ken dolls on steroids. Rather, he had the muscles that spoke of a male in his prime.

In fact, he oozed liquid masculine sex—something that, if bottled, would give spontaneous orgasms to every woman within a fifty-mile radius. A product Katelyn would definitely invest in for personal use.

She blinked and realized his intense amethyst gaze studied her briefly before returning to his book.

Damn! He caught me again. He's going to think I'm a stalker.

She squared her shoulders, yanked on the bottom of her low-cut vee-necked top to ensure "the girls" were shown to best advantage, and walked from behind the display case toward him.

Sexual awareness tingled through every pore as she neared him. It was as if the air around him was drenched in pheromones designed to draw her closer. Her steps faltered as she briefly considered that he could be using a spell of some sort to draw her. Enough magick practitioners frequented her shop that she knew such things were possible; however, she had never used them herself.

Her senses expanded, sampling the energy around him. When she found nothing amiss, she resumed her confident trek forward to stand in front of him. Katelyn cleared her throat before speaking. "Excuse me."

He looked up, and her breath caught as the full intensity of his gaze settled over her, causing her blood to heat and her libido to sit up and beg. He seemed to see deep inside her to places with dark secrets best forgotten. A sudden mental image of one of those long fingers tracing a line between her breasts and straight to her clit flashed through her, and she resisted the urge to shiver.

His lips curved. "How may I be of service?"

The deep bass rumble of his voice surprised her, and not just because it seemed to feather against her nipples, clit, and every intimate place she owned, but because of the formal way he spoke.

Where is this guy from?

Wherever he called home, the sensations his voice created made her realize just how long it had been since she'd had a man willing and naked. Every erogenous zone on her body tingled and ached—adding their input to the equation.

The deluge of arousal brought to mind a laundry list of ways he could "be of service." Katelyn breathed deep against the surge of lust before speaking. "I'm Katelyn Hunt, the owner. I've noticed you around the store for the past few days."

And Rita thinks I'm freaking insane for obsessing over you.

He continued to study her as though memorizing her every nuance. She resisted the urge to fidget as a surge of moisture dampened the insides of her thighs and her skin began to feel achy and heavy with need. She swallowed hard and vowed to crank up the air-conditioning as a trickle of sweat lazily traced its way down her spine. "We're getting ready to close. I thought maybe you'd like to go have a drink." *Or some kinky, mind-blowing, illegal-in-thirty-seven-countries sex.*

In one languid movement, he stood, forcing her to crane her neck to look at his face. He reached down and took her hand in his before placing a gentle kiss on the back, which sent shock waves of arousal straight to her aching labia. "I'm Grayson—"

"Hello, Grayson." An older woman pushed her considerable bulk between them, cutting off his words, forcing him to drop Katelyn's hand and making Katelyn take a step back. "I'm Ethel Harding, and you're the sexiest man I've seen around here since my fourth husband, Earl."

Katelyn glared at the interfering woman who had pressed

her ample bosom against Grayson's arm while one hand caressed his chest. There was no way Katelyn was going to lose him to some woman who was ninety if she was a day—especially after she'd finally worked up the nerve to approach him. "I'm sorry, Mrs. Harding, but this is a private conversation between myself and Grayson."

Ethel batted her fake eyelashes at Grayson, and Katelyn was surprised the poor things didn't crawl off her face like indignant black spiders that refused to do her bidding.

"It's *Ms.* Harding. The last Mr. Harding passed on last year." Ethel's drawn-on eyebrows disappeared into her overdyed hairline. She waved a fleshy hand liberally dripping with gaudy rings and bracelets that clacked together like discordant wind chimes.

Katelyn narrowed her gaze and wished she could shoot lasers from her eyes and fry Ethel where she stood. She dropped her voice to arctic-chill levels. "All right . . . *Ms.* Harding. Again, this is a private conversation, and the store is now closed. It's time for you to leave."

Ignoring Katelyn, Grayson raised Ethel's beefy hand to his lips. Katelyn harrumphed and crossed her arms in front of her.

He brushed a gentle kiss across the back of the wrinkled skin, and Katelyn resisted the urge to turn her glare on him.

A heavy sigh escaped Ethel, and Katelyn knew the woman was lost.

"Perhaps I can be of some assistance, Ethel." Grayson had the gall to toss Katelyn a saucy wink.

"Aren't *you* the charmer?" Ethel blushed like a virgin and licked her thin lips as her whole manner became . . . predatory. Ethel's hungry gaze raked over Grayson, and his brow furrowed for the first time.

Sensed the danger a tad too late, huh? Katelyn resisted the urge to smile at his predicament.

"Actually, Ethel, a woman of the world, such as yourself, deserves a man with more means and the ability to take care of you properly."

Katelyn clenched her fists and tried not to make retching noises in the background of Grayson's "performance."

Oblivious to Katelyn's sarcastic thoughts, Grayson continued. "But let's consult the gods, shall we?"

He placed Ethel's hands between his own and closed his eyes as if waiting for enlightenment. Out of curiosity, Katelyn let her senses expand to sample the energy surrounding him again.

As a Seer, she was used to reading people's auras, and she'd always been fascinated by people who were true psychics as opposed to Seers, who received visions only as needed. She'd been a Seer since birth and had spent many years trying patiently to educate the populace about the difference.

Grayson's aura was definitely different from anything she'd ever sensed—he buzzed with power, whereas most people possessed only a faint hum.

Katelyn stiffened in surprise. This power intrigued her more than his handsome face and his killer body. He was either an old soul or an actual practitioner who knew how to harness and use energy. In either case, this made Grayson a rare and interesting man.

However, when his energy didn't change, she immediately saw him for the fraud he was. She allowed her shoulders to slump as disappointment and a thin tendril of anger flowed through her. In order to receive impressions or messages, psychics needed to change their energy levels. As a Seer she didn't get a choice—the vision came whether she wanted it or not, and her energy not only changed but usually sucked her under.

Grayson's deep voice broke the expectant silence and caused goose bumps to march over her skin. Something about that voice slipped past all her shields and reached deep inside her, exciting her and scaring her at the same time.

"Apparently, the next Mr. Harding is right at this moment sitting down to lunch at the Phoenix Resort. I see a gray, pinstriped suit and a large garnet ring on his right pinkie finger."

Ethel's wide eyes and sudden intake of breath told Katelyn she'd been totally reeled in. "No one has ever been able to give me such detail in a reading before. You're truly extraordinary!" She cast a condescending glare in Katelyn's direction before turning her adoring attention back to Grayson. "What else can you tell me?"

He closed his eyes once more, as if seeking enlightenment from the universe. "I see lots of money in your future and . . ." His voice trailed off, and he pursed his sensual lips.

"What? What?" She slapped her other hand over his and shook it as if the jerky movement would spill the answers from his lips.

He opened his eyes. "I'm loath to speak of something so private in front of such cultured women as yourselves, but because the gods are giving me this message for you, I suppose I should share it."

Ethel shook his hands some more and seemed in danger of exploding on the spot if she didn't hear his next words. "Share! Share! We can't disappoint the gods."

He sighed as if deciding whether to override his better judgment. "Well, it seems the future Mr. Harding is rather . . . well endowed, and enjoys using his . . . equipment."

Ethel's mouth dropped open, and Katelyn thought the woman might drool on the floor like a bulldog. "I mustn't keep him waiting. Thank you! Thank you!" Quicker than Katelyn would've given her credit for, Ethel grabbed Grayson and mashed her fleshy lips against his. Then she reached into her purse and thrust a wad of bills into his hand.

In seconds, the whirlwind who was Ethel Harding left the shop, the chimes on the door tinkling to show Katelyn she hadn't imagined the whole thing. Then her gaze again found *him*.

"So, are you a professional con man?"

He shook his head, still recovering from Ethel's kiss—though he did stop short of wiping any remnants of the deed from his lips. "She obviously didn't know the difference between a Seer and a psychic and didn't care, as long as she received the answers she sought. So I gave them to her."

Katelyn resisted the urge to be impressed that *he* knew the difference. "And what happens when Ms. Harding gets to the Phoenix Resort and realizes you lied to her? You'll be long gone, and she'll be back in my shop screaming bloody murder."

Anger and frustration roiled in Katelyn's belly. She stalked to the front door to flip her OPEN sign to CLOSED. Then she strode behind her display case, putting distance between her and Grayson.

Why are men so high-maintenance? I only wanted a hot night, and now I may have a pissed-off retired debutante on my hands.

Grayson followed Katelyn but stayed on the customer side of the counter. He laid down the wad of money, obviously an offering for her, and then placed both long-fingered hands on the case and leaned forward, invading her personal space.

Her gaze was pulled downward like a magnet. Katelyn tried not to dwell on how those large calloused hands would feel gliding over her body.

Heat flowed through her, causing her nipples to harden against her bra and moisture to gather between her thighs. Her calf-length peasant skirt swirled around her suddenly sensitive skin, making her wish she had worn jeans.

She huffed out a breath. If he wasn't a good candidate for her one hot night, she should just move on. But her body had different ideas. She couldn't explain why, but she was drawn to this man like a drug. In fact, she'd never reacted to a man this way before.

Grayson leaned forward, the well-defined muscles of his forearms flexing with the movement and threatening to turn her into a needy puddle of hormones. His amethyst eyes danced with mischief as he spoke. "When she reaches the Phoenix Resort, she'll find the owner, Mr. Fowler, who when I left him a few scant hours ago said he'd gladly trade his entire fortune for a doting wife to share his life and lavish vacations in someplace called Boca. Somehow, I think that's exactly what she will be more than happy to offer."

Katelyn reached forward, intent on removing his hand from the top of the display case—but leaning closer only brought those sensual lips way too close to allow her to think clearly.

When her hand made contact with his arm, she gasped. Her sight grayed, and the familiar disorientation that accompanied her visions assaulted her.

She tumbled into a lush wilderness—no, it was too manicured to be wilderness . . . a park or garden perhaps. Fragrant plants of every type surrounded her while a massive white stone mountain that glittered almost pink in the distance rose off to her right.

Mist from the waterfall made the air heavy with moisture, but the air was sweet with the scent of gardenias, lavender, and all manner of growing things. Thick grass rose under her bare feet, and she realized she wore only a skimpy cotton half top and some boy shorts that sat low on her hips.

Katelyn searched the clearing, and joy suffused her as Grayson walked toward her. She enjoyed watching the play of his muscles as he moved. His gaze was predatory and hungry, and her skin tingled in anticipation.

When he reached her, he folded her into his arms. She melted against him, their mouths fused together as if they'd done this a thousand times. His tongue delved inside her mouth, and those wonderfully large hands slipped under her half top to cup her aching breasts. She moaned against his lips as her body screamed for more.

She clawed at his clothes as each touch of his hands spread electricity and mindless need through her entire body. When they'd bared each other, she moaned as he guided her gently down to lie in the sun-warmed grass.

Katelyn sighed as the grass tickled her sensitive skin and the scent of lush vegetation, lavender, and a fragrance uniquely Grayson filled her senses. He swallowed the sound as his weight settled over her, his body cradled in the vee of her open thighs. He braced himself on his forearms and continued to explore her mouth while his thumbs stroked her cheeks and neck.

His crisp chest hairs teased her engorged nipples with every movement, and she writhed under him as her arousal spiraled higher.

He pulled back enough to look into her eyes. "Katelyn . . ."

Her name on his lips sounded exotic, forbidden, and a sudden orgasm slammed into her. She dug her nails into the muscles of his back as her world spiraled.

Katelyn blinked as blood slowly returned to her brain and she realized she still stood inside her shop with a death grip on Grayson's arm. Her legs wobbled, and she held on tighter to keep from collapsing.

He gently pried her fingers off his bare arm, wincing at the deep indents her nails had left. "Katelyn, are you all right?"

She nodded, amazed she didn't have another spontaneous orgasm when he uttered her name. As if a large weight pressed down on her, Katelyn leaned heavily on the counter and concentrated on slowing her ragged breathing and pounding heart.

"A vision?"

She closed her eyes against the sensual assault of his deep

voice as she continued to concentrate on bringing air into her lungs while her body screamed at her to throw him to the floor and ride him until neither of them could move.

What the hell is wrong with me? Something isn't right.

When she looked up, expecting to see a calculating gleam in his eyes or, even worse, distrust and pity, she was stunned to see genuine concern. His reaction both shocked and warmed her. Most people didn't understand her visions, so, therefore, they feared them and reacted accordingly.

Without a word, Grayson walked around the counter and steadied her. She recoiled, afraid she'd have a repeat vision and become a puddle of goo on the floor at his feet. But when his warm hand closed over her shoulder, nothing happened except for the enticing scent of man and chai that filled her senses.

He led her from behind the counter to the overstuffed chair he'd spent the last few days in and gently helped her sit.

In no condition to object, Katelyn sank into the cushions.

Grayson cupped her cheek and ran the pad of his thumb over her bottom lip. "I'll try to find you some bread or sugar. Stay here."

Her skin still tingled where he'd touched her, which did nothing to help her shake the effects of the vision. Katelyn fisted her hands in her lap, resisting the urge to bring her fingers to her lips.

Grayson slid behind the café counter and rummaged through the fridge and cold case. He returned moments later and pressed a cold bottle of water into her hands.

Her hands shook as she gripped the bottle to twist off the cap—and realized he'd already done it for her. A small surge of gratitude warmed her.

Maybe chivalry isn't quite dead—just severely crippled.

When she'd taken a large drink and swallowed, he pressed a muffin into her hands. Katelyn stared down at the pastry, surprised he knew how to counter the effects of a particularly strong vision. And even more surprised that she appreciated the gesture.

Okay, possibly men were useful for more than sex. Maybe she'd start slow and find a male friend first, and then work up to the rest.

She'd already determined Grayson was either a practitioner or a very old soul, but even with that, he continued to intrigue her.

"Eat, Katelyn. You'll feel better." He knelt in front of her, those liquid amethyst eyes concerned and watchful. "Then we can discuss that drink you mentioned before Ethel intruded on our conversation."

Embarrassed, she took a bite of muffin and chewed. The carbs should equalize her system. She kept a drawer full of Milky Way candy bars for just this reason, but she was too embarrassed to ask him to go raid her stash. The muffin would have to do. She swallowed and chased it down with a swig of water before meeting his gaze. "I was asking you out for a drink, but I'm not sure I'm up for it after that vision."

The sensation of her nipples grazing against his muscular chest while they lay on the fragrant grass surged through her, and she resisted the urge to whimper as her body screamed for a repeat performance.

"What the hell are you doing to me?" Katelyn closed her eyes and let her head fall back against the chair. She had fantasized about men before, but somehow her body was stuck on overdrive with this one. Even stranger was the fact that he felt like a future déjà vu waiting to happen.

The few times she'd had visions that gave her this same impression, those moments had always come to pass—even if they weren't exactly what she'd thought when she'd first seen them. Though how she could misinterpret the steamy sex in a lush park, she didn't know. Yet a big part of her couldn't wait.

"What did you see in the vision?" Grayson's hand engulfed hers, and everywhere his skin touched hers, sexual awareness burned. Apparently, her palm had turned into a large erogenous zone while she hadn't been paying attention.

"Katelyn?" His thumb feathered over the back of her hand. "Can you tell me what you saw?"

Heat rose from her gut to suffuse her neck and cheeks.

Goddess! I haven't blushed since high school.

"I see." His voice sounded smug and possessive. "Would you like to have that drink first, or jump straight into the contents of your vision?"

Her eyes flew open, and she pulled her hand from his grasp as her anger and self-protective instincts flared to life. "I don't remember sharing with you the contents of my vision, and even if I had, you're getting awfully cocky and sure of yourself, aren't you?"

His grin widened, sparking her anger and she opened her mouth to let him know what she thought of conceited men.

The front door slammed open.

Katelyn startled and spilled the remaining water on her skirt. As the cold liquid hit her, the chimes hanging on the back of the door flew off to land on the floor.

Five attractive blond men filled her doorway—their pale skin gleaming, their gazes narrowed and hostile.

Their eyes turned murderous when they saw Grayson.

"Fucking Klatch! The Seer is ours."

2

Grayson de Klatch, the Seventh Prince of Klatch, cursed as five pale Cunt warriors filled the doorway. The traitor race that had caused a civil war on his home world of Tador had been banished, and their name had become something of an epithet on Earth and on Tador ever since.

Grayson stood with his back to Katelyn, shielding her from any attacks. "Leave or die, Cunts. There are no other choices. The Seer will be safe from you regardless."

Katelyn gasped behind him, most likely misinterpreting his use of the term, as it was usually only applied to females here on Earth—and incorrectly, at that.

She bolted from her chair and ran behind the glass counter, surprising him, since she was no doubt still weak from her vision.

Grayson took advantage of the distraction and raised his hand to send a bolt of deadly pink energy sizzling from his fingertips across the room toward the Cunts. The leader blocked the bolt with a hastily thrown energy field, but Grayson's beam bounced away to hit another Cunt squarely in the chest.

A hint of relief rolled through him. If the Cunts couldn't control where their energy beams bounced, Katelyn was still safe hiding behind the display counter. Energy would automatically go toward the next easiest target, but couldn't bend around corners.

The affected Cunt groaned as he slumped to the floor.

Four blue beams sizzled toward Grayson from the remaining Cunts. He dropped into a crouch, tossing out an energy shield with his left hand, and shot anther pink beam toward them with his right.

Their blue beams sizzled against his shield, slowly draining his energy and showering him with blue sparks.

Every hair on his arms stood at attention, and a smell like burned electrical wires filled the air. He strengthened his shields and shot another quick bolt toward his enemies.

Sizzling pink energy caught one Cunt in the calf, dropping him on top of his downed friend.

A growl of rage rolled out from one of the Cunts before he and the other two sent a concentrated blast of blue toward Grayson.

Grayson dove to the side, not willing to risk his shields in a head-on assault from the mingled energy beam.

Burning heat prickled over his hip and then receded as his body hit the hard shop floor.

His shoulder slammed against a display shelf. Sharp stabs of pain lanced through him as muscles tore and tendons popped.

He bit back a groan, but allowed himself a few curses. Now he was injured, and his ill-advised dive had taken him farther from Katelyn.

Before Grayson could recover, the Cunt closest to the Seer bolted toward her and disappeared behind the counter.

A band of panic constricted inside Grayson's chest. Katelyn was at the mercy of the Cunt.

Grayson had to disable the two Cunts in front of him before he could help her.

He poured more energy into his shield as he shot quick bursts of pink power toward the pair in front of him.

Blue sizzling energy crackled from behind the counter. Grayson ground his teeth. What had the Cunt done to Katelyn?

Surprise filtered through him again when she stood up. She held a small black instrument in front of her. It crackled blue energy of its own between two small metal tips.

Her green eyes blazed with anger as she glared from one Cunt to the other. She looked like a queen defending her castle.

A blue beam caught her in the stomach, and she screamed—an angry sound rather than one of pain or fear.

Red-hot rage seared Grayson's insides, fueling his powers. If his future mate sustained any permanent damage, he would hunt down every last member of the Cunt clan.

He poured the energy born of adrenaline into the twin pink bolts he sent hurtling toward the remaining two attackers. The beams sliced through their shields like a knife through tissue paper. The bolts hit them squarely in the throats and their screams sent warm satisfaction through him.

The last two Cunts dropped to the floor in boneless heaps, and Grayson resisted the urge to kill them. He needed stamina to survive the trip *between* and to make sure Katelyn was safe—especially now that he'd have to use precious energy to function with his injuries.

Grayson's shoulder throbbed, but the adrenaline racing through him numbed it enough so he could manage to cross the room. He circled around the display case and stepped over the downed Cunt to kneel next to the Seer.

Katelyn's mane of unruly red hair was latticed over her face, and she groaned. He gently brushed the locks away before lifting her with his good arm, and hefting her over his shoulder.

He bracketed his arm behind her knees to keep her from sliding, the thin material of her flowy skirt allowing him to feel every warm inch of her.

Her soft curves pressed against his chest and shoulder, causing his cock to spring to life inside his tight jeans. He groaned as he shifted to a more comfortable position. He didn't have time for this. He had to get her to safety, then he could worry about the rest.

Gritting his teeth, Grayson raised his injured arm and drew a large portal in the air with his hand, using his last reserves of power. The air shimmered, and the portal expanded until it was an oval large enough for him to walk through.

He took one last look to ensure none of the Cunts could follow, and then stepped forward into the bone-chilling cold that was the *between*.

The air around them crackled with energy, sending a march of goose bumps over his skin.

Grayson shivered as the dark, still air surrounded them, making it difficult to breathe. He inhaled deeply, trying to find every last bit of oxygen in the thin air, and took a few minutes to let his body adjust to the vastly different environment. It was obvious why it had been named the *between*, but he still hated each and every trip through the portal.

The Seer groaned, and he laid his good hand on Katelyn's shapely ass to keep her in place. Even in her unconscious state, she shivered and cuddled against him.

The tang of mold on the back of his tongue burst inside his senses and he pushed forward even as his stamina leached out into the abyss. He cursed the Cunts for causing him to expend all his energy before this trip *between*, and then cursed again when his voice was swallowed by the oppressive air surrounding them.

Each step became harder than the last, like walking through taffy.

Grayson's limbs, suddenly heavy, dragged him down, each step forward harder than the last.

Then a small spark of light appeared just in front of him, signaling the portal point in the clearing just beyond the castle.

He reached out to draw another portal in the air in front of them, gritting his teeth against the blinding pain from his injured shoulder. The shimmering oval illuminated the blackness in front of him and then widened until it was large enough for him to step through.

As soon as he cleared the portal, the warmth of the Klatch sun began to chase away the cold, even as the portal snapped closed behind him. He slumped to his knees, careful not to jostle Katelyn, who lay limp over his good shoulder.

"Prince Grayson, are you hurt?"

It took a moment to make sense of the words after the muted sounds within the *between*. When he did understand what was said, he had to gather strength just to be able to nod.

Grayson's vision blurred around the edges.

He was still coherent enough to recognize the speaker as a member of the Royal Guard, several of which stood in a line before him.

Grayson swallowed hard before he spoke. "I've found the Seer. Guard the portal so we aren't followed by the Cunts who attacked us."

The guard who had spoken and wore the dark purple livery of the royal family reached out to take the Seer's limp body from him.

Grayson growled at the man. "Stand down. I can take care of my future mate without your help."

The guard bowed and stepped back, his dark hair falling over his brow.

"Don't be a damned fool, Grayson. Let them help you before you fall over and crush the poor woman. Then she'll never get to discover what an ass you are." King Stone stepped forward through the line of guards to stare at Grayson. His lavender eyes studied Grayson as though assessing injuries and damage.

Stone had recently become king when his wife, Alyssandra, had ascended the throne as queen. But Grayson would always think of Stone as one of his two oldest friends. He didn't think he'd ever get used to calling Stone "King."

Ever since he could remember, Stone had been one of the three—himself, Stone, and Prince Ryan—who were always in trouble or about to be. Wherever there was destruction or mayhem around the castle, all eyes turned toward the "Trio of Disaster," as Stone's mother, Darla, had called them.

Stone must've taken Grayson's silence for assent because he reached out and lifted Katelyn from Grayson's arms.

As soon as Stone held her safely, Grayson allowed himself to slump onto the warm grass, careful not to land on his injured shoulder. He closed his eyes and breathed deeply, allowing the nourishing energy of his home world to seep into him. Even with that comfort, he knew it would take several days to heal if he didn't seek out some sexual sustenance soon—especially with the ripped muscle and torn tendons.

As a Klatch witch, sexual energy was as much a needed sustenance as food or water. His race could survive for a while on only food and water, but they needed sexual energy to thrive and even to survive.

In fact, the reigning queen's job was to maintain a symbiotic relationship with the planet of Tador—the home world of the Klatch. The king helped her build her sexual energy, and she in turn healed the planet, which sustained the Klatch people.

Grayson acknowledged he'd pushed himself too far, but it wasn't like he'd had much choice. The Cunts would have taken the Seer if Grayson hadn't acted.

The thought of replenishing his energy with some random Klatch maid when his future mate had finally been found didn't appeal to him. In fact, it felt like a betrayal to her. That left Grayson with something of a dilemma.

"Guards." Stone's stern voice filled the clearing. "Pick up Prince Grayson, deliver him to the baths and have several of the maids attend him."

Grayson tried and failed to push himself off the grass to tell Stone he'd have no maids attending him, but his friend spoke again.

"Because Grayson's mate has finally been found, I don't think she'd appreciate him receiving sexual sustenance from anyone but her." Stone smiled down at Grayson, his expression amused. "Clean him up, renew his energy as best you can, and put him to bed. I'll deliver the Seer to the queen. I'm sure Alyssandra will find some lady's maids to attend her."

Grayson opened his mouth to thank Stone, but gave up when no sound emerged other than a croak.

Stone's chuckle filtered down to Grayson through his exhaustion. "Consider it a returned favor for everything you've done for myself and for Alyssandra. I'm looking forward to watching you settle down with just one woman."

Grayson pushed himself up in bed so he could lean against the headboard. Pain stabbed through his shoulder and down his back and arm. He cursed and tried to shift again for a more comfortable position, while his valet shoved pillows behind him.

"I still think you're being unreasonable, Grayson." Queen Alyssandra waved away his valet and arranged the pillows herself. "You need to heal, and you haven't even kissed the Seer yet, so how can that be considered cheating?" Sunlight streamed through the open balcony window of his bedroom to glint off Alyssandra's tumble of mahogany hair and the lavender beads decorating her scattered braids.

Grayson relaxed back against the pillows and flashed her a

grateful smile before he turned his thoughts to putting into words something he couldn't explain even to himself.

"Leave him be, Alyssandra," King Stone added from a nearby chair.

The queen rounded on her husband, her hands fisted on her hips. "Are you telling me that from the time you understood we were betrothed until a few months ago, when you found me on Earth, that you didn't find sexual sustenance with anyone?"

Heavy silence suddenly filled the chamber, and Grayson almost felt sorry for Stone for walking into such a self-made verbal trap. Almost.

"Well, no. . . ." Stone admitted.

Over the past few months, Grayson had become used to their familiar banter. Even the kind they did only through telepathy, which left everyone else in the room feeling like they were watching an Earth television show with the sound off.

Stone had definitely changed when he'd finally found Alyssandra, but the changes were for the better. He was happier and more content somehow. Grayson envied him that.

"What have I missed?" Prince Ryan, the third leg of the Trio of Disaster, burst into the room and immediately made himself at home. He plopped onto the overstuffed ottoman and snatched the goblet of ale from Grayson's untouched dinner tray.

Grayson smiled. "Alyssandra was winning another argument with Stone."

"It wasn't an argument," the king and queen said together and then laughed.

Ryan downed the ale and then pantomimed a large yawn. "So, in other words, I haven't missed a thing."

Alyssandra shot Ryan a mock caustic glare, and he grinned at her, obviously unrepentant. "I was trying to convince Grayson to let one of the maids help him heal his shoulder before the Seer wakes up."

"Are we going to talk about what to tell her, or are we going to argue over my health and welfare?"

The queen gave him a meaningful look, clearly communicating that she would drop the subject . . . for now. However, Grayson had no illusions that she would give up permanently. She was one of the most tenacious people he'd ever met.

Alyssandra poured a new goblet of ale for Grayson and laid the dinner tray on his lap. "If you refuse to find sexual sustenance, then you need food, so eat." Her voice was firm and told him this was the price for her dropping the earlier subject.

He smiled, picked up a piece of bread, and bit off a corner.

Ryan refilled his borrowed goblet of ale. "From what you've said, Gray, the Seer is an independent and very stubborn woman. She has her own business and a life back on Earth. We can't just huddle around her bed and when she wakes up tell her she's been chosen to give up her entire life, move to a different planet, and participate in a triangle that resembles Earth's Roman orgies so we can save our planet."

A dull throb started behind Grayson's temples and slowly radiated outward until the pain in his shoulder throbbed with the same rhythm. All his energy had been focused on finding the Seer. He hadn't given much thought to breaking the news to her about what they hoped she would give up, and do, for a planet she knew nothing about.

A quick glance around the room assured Grayson he wasn't the only one who had put off that particular line of thinking. Everyone's faces darkened with concern.

The queen sat on the foot of Grayson's bed, careful not to jostle his food tray. "We've found her—we can't just give up now. There have obviously been women in the past who were willing to do this—from what I can tell from the queen's archives, the triangle has been instituted at least three times in our history."

Alyssandra had been kidnapped when she was an infant and taken to live on Earth with the losing faction of a quarter of a century old civil war. The kidnappers had raised her ignorant of her true heritage, and Alyssandra's mother, Annalecia, had slowly weakened on Tador from grief and strain. Annalecia's symbiotic relationship with their home planet had deteriorated until Tador had slowly begun to sicken and die.

Luckily, Alyssandra had been recovered and was able to ascend the throne in her mother's place, but now the planet was too far gone for only the queen and king to repair through their generation of sexual energy. Their only hope seemed to lie in some obscure references in the queen's archives—something called the triangle.

Unfortunately, time was extremely short. The Seer had to be taken through the Klatch coming-of-age ceremony on her twenty-fourth birthday, which was just a handful of days away. Only then could the triangle ritual be completed.

Alyssandra chewed her bottom lip and shook her head, the beads in her scattered braids clinking together softly. "I think we need to convince her to stay for a while and get to know the planet, the Klatch, and Grayson, and hope she falls in love with all three enough so she will want to stay here with us and perform the triangle."

Grayson let the idea roll around in his mind for a minute. "She'll be angry when she finds out we lied to her." A large fist closed around his heart at the thought of starting a relationship on omissions and lies. But even if the civil war hadn't happened, he would've been slated to marry another full-blooded Klatch and produce heirs, regardless of his personal feelings. How was this different, except that he had found the woman himself?

Ryan leaned forward, setting his goblet of ale on a nearby table. "True, but once she calms down, she'll understand why we had to omit a few facts up front."

"I'm not so sure about that." King Stone's expression showed nothing but doubt.

"It's not like we have much of a choice. Otherwise, we've lost before we've started." Ryan stood and gazed around the room. "We said we were willing to do whatever it took to save the planet and institute the triangle. Are we, or aren't we?"

Stone scrubbed a hand over his face, his appearance suddenly tired and sad. "It's up to you, Grayson. She's slated to be your mate. Do we tell her outright, or go with Alyssandra's plan?"

The weight of three heavy gazes pressed down on Grayson, and he looked away. They were right, this was his decision, and he would bear responsibility for whatever he chose.

His thoughts strayed to Katelyn as he'd seen her fighting off the Cunts in her shop.

Her fiery red hair had billowed around her, and she hadn't cowered or screamed. She had somehow attacked the Cunts with some type of energy from a handheld weapon. The sound of her scream of rage when the Cunt's beam had sizzled against her chest reverberated through his memories, and he smiled. "My Seer is a warrior, even if she doesn't yet realize it. If we tell her up front, she will try to keep the control of the situation firmly in her own hands." He glanced up, and his smile turned grim. "I agree that we don't tell her until the time is right."

3

Misty fog drifted around Katelyn's ankles, even as she recognized the vision for what it was. Twenty-three years of experience made it almost impossible for her to mistake a vision for anything else.

Yet, this one was more vivid than usual—less déjà vu and more *current* somehow. She couldn't pinpoint the differences, but she *knew*.

The air was heavy with water and ripe with the scents of plants and earth. Katelyn couldn't see anything past the mist even though the sun warmed her and shined off the soft green grass under her bare toes. From the smells, this place reminded her of the beautiful, grassy meadow in her last vision.

"Good morning, Katelyn."

The deep bass rumble that made her name sound like an exotic delicacy startled her, and she turned toward the voice.

Grayson emerged out of the mist, looking much as he had when she'd first seen him walk into her shop. A plain black T-shirt stretched over broad shoulders and down to a tapered waist.

Tight jeans molded over muscular thighs before covering the tops of well-worn black cowboy boots.

His dark hair gleamed with amber highlights in the sunlight. He'd pulled it back into a simple ponytail. It looked soft and satiny, and Katelyn's fingers literally itched to reach out and touch.

Grayson's chiseled jaw and sensual lips would be enough to make him handsome, but those eyes the color of deep melted amethysts made him breathtaking.

Unease skittered along Katelyn's spine as images of the battle inside her shop flooded back.

Shit! Did that actually happen?

It must've been another vision. Yet, it hadn't felt like a vision, but rather like something that had actually occurred. And why would she have a vision of something so bizarre when all her visions usually came true in some form?

A sinking sensation churned deep inside her belly, and she concentrated, attempting to crystallize the images inside her mind's eye.

Try as she might, she couldn't remember anything past the blue beam that had slammed into her chest like a sledgehammer. When the vivid memory of the searing pain made her wince, she knew she hadn't imagined the attack.

Katelyn squeezed her eyes shut, trying to block out the memory. Somehow, when the sizzling beam had struck her, she had known if the beam hadn't stopped draining her energy, she would have died. She brought her hand to her chest, wincing again as she touched the sore spot left by the beam.

"Am I dead?" Even in her vision, her voice sounded hoarse and unused.

Grayson's deep chuckle vibrated through her. She longed to press her body flush against his and ask him to laugh or even speak so she could see what those wonderful, low rumbles would do to her in close proximity.

"No. Far from dead, my beautiful Seer. Unconscious, or maybe even asleep but not dead." He stepped close, and Katelyn's breath caught in her throat.

Heat and energy pulsed between them, and every coherent thought fled from her mind as she gave herself up to this vision.

"I'm glad you are all right. I have come to help you heal—to help heal us both, actually." Grayson captured a strand of her hair and rubbed it between his thumb and first two fingers.

The innocent caress sent gooseflesh marching over Katelyn's entire body, followed by a tingling wave of heat just under her skin. A low moan escaped before she could stop it.

She nearly let her head fall back in surrender, but then his words and not his actions filtered to the front of her awareness. "Are you a healer?" she asked. "Your energy is very powerful, but it doesn't feel quite right for a healer."

Grayson laughed, and once again, the beguiling sound roamed over her like a verbal caress. "No, my beautiful Seer. I'm no healer." He traced a single calloused finger over her bottom lip, and she clenched her fists to keep from leaning into the light friction of his touch. "I'm a Klatch witch, an ancient line of otherworldly witches whose life force is sexual energy."

It was Katelyn's turn to laugh. "Wow, I'll be happy to lend any help in that arena you might need. Although, unfortunately, I'm only human, and while sex is nice—stellar, if I'm lucky—I need rest and time to heal. That is, if I was sick or injured, which I'm not."

He brushed his lips over hers, which left a pleasant buzzing sensation on her skin.

"You're wrong, Seer. Healing doesn't follow human rules here. And you're still injured from the energy blast. Trust me."

She stepped back.

"I don't trust anyone." She surprised herself by blurting out something she had said only to herself countless times before.

Grayson only smiled. "I know, my beautiful Seer. Then let

me show you instead." Before she could argue the point, he pulled her tight against him. He plunged his fingers into her hair while he captured her mouth with his.

Her hands found his chest, and her frantic mind sent her arms a signal to push him away, but her body betrayed her, and her fingers fisted in the soft cloth of his T-shirt. Heat sizzled between them, and she felt as if she would drown in the overwhelming sensations. Finally, his lips gentled against hers, and she was able to step away from him. She swayed slightly, but locked her knees and stared him down. "What are you doing to me?"

Grayson didn't state the obvious, but seemed to instinctively understand her real question. "Every Klatch has a special gift, and mine is to cause arousal in others. I can control it, but it comes very naturally, and most of the time I don't even realize I'm doing it."

"It's bad enough you're a walking wet dream, but now you think you can magickally cause arousal?" She slapped her hand over her mouth as she realized she'd said the words out loud.

Arousal? Hell, so far he's some sort of truth serum!

A pleased expression lit Grayson's already too-handsome features. "Not only have you shown more resistance to my inherent gift than any Klatch woman ever has, but you seem to have the same effect on me. *No* woman has ever affected me like this. Until you."

Inside her mind, Katelyn laughed at the ridiculousness of his statement. He thought she'd shown resistance? Hell, if Ethel hadn't interrupted, Katelyn might've backed him up against her display case and taken advantage of him right there.

Besides, he was delusional. He had to be. She'd never encountered any type of magick or energy that would do what he described. It sounded more like a case of male ego and less like an "inherent gift." Katelyn held up her hand stop-sign fashion. "On-demand arousal. Right. I don't buy it." She fisted her hands on her hips and glared at him. "Hit me with your best shot, Mr. Goddess's Gift to Womankind. Show me this 'inherent gift.' "

Grayson sighed as though disappointed in her lack of belief. "You're a very stubborn woman, Seer. Please remember that you specifically asked for this demonstration." He shrugged. "Although, it *will* help you heal, so I suppose it can't hurt."

Katelyn snorted. "You have no idea how stubborn I can be." She held out her arms wide, making herself a bigger target. "Bring it on, stud."

Grayson never moved, but a wave of his energy surrounded her, and her entire body burned with desire.

Her breasts ached almost painfully.

Her pussy throbbed with need.

Even her skin felt as if it might explode if she didn't have Grayson inside her.

Katelyn wanted hot, kinky, explosive sex, and she wanted it now.

She gritted her teeth and closed her eyes, drawing in lungfuls of air as she battled against her urges and desires.

Katelyn pictured a shield made of pure white light that surrounded her body and blocked his energy.

Immediately, the assault lessened but didn't stop. Apparently, even her strongest shields couldn't totally protect her. He hadn't been kidding about his "gift."

"Enough." The word slipped from her lips with effort, and she hoped Grayson heard it over the pounding of blood inside her head.

Just as quickly as the desire began, it stopped, as if Grayson had flipped a switch.

Katelyn locked her knees, fisted her hands, and screwed her eyes shut tight. She refused to crumple to the ground with relief like she wanted to.

When her heart had slowed enough so she was sure it wouldn't pound right out of her chest, she opened her eyes. She expected his expression to be smug. Instead, it was apologetic. He stood stock-still as though afraid to come closer.

"Okay." Katelyn sucked in a shaky breath. "Remind me not to ask for any future demonstrations from you."

Grayson winced. "I'm sorry. I did try to tell you."

"Don't be sorry. I asked, and you obliged." She swallowed hard as her body gradually returned to normal. Vision or not, she might as well figure this out—even though she'd never had a vision quite this . . . interactive.

Katelyn glanced up at him. "Is that why I've been fascinated by you since you stepped into my shop? I thought my hormones had gone haywire."

His closeness seemed to short-circuit the neural pathway that connected her mind to her mouth, because she could only stand and stare into those mesmerizing amethyst eyes.

"You have my word that I will keep my gift firmly in check with you, as much as I'm able." He carefully raised his hand as though giving her the chance to step away.

As if I could move even if I wanted to. Her entire body felt like it had turned into a giant pile of Jell-O in danger of wobbling to the floor.

"Let me show you what's between us—just us." His fingers skimmed along her jaw, sending tendrils of heat racing toward her nipples and straight to her core.

Now that she'd survived the full demonstration, she could discern her innate—normal—reaction to Grayson. The only energy that emanated from him was pure male arousal, which was more intoxicating than any "gift." Her body continued to respond in kind.

There wasn't any sudden switch that would give her relief from this—only good, old-fashioned sex. She hoped they got to that part of the demonstration soon.

Those sensuous lips curved, and Grayson threaded his long fingers into her hair until he cupped the nape of her neck. Then, so slowly Katelyn thought she'd go insane, he lowered his face toward hers until his warm breath feathered over her lips.

A shudder ran throughout her body.

She drowned inside his searching gaze. Using all her will-power, Katelyn opened her mouth to try to speak.

Or, more accurately, to beg him to get on with the kiss and put her out of her misery.

Grayson must have taken her parted lips as an assent, because he yanked Katelyn against him as he fused his mouth with hers. He traced her bottom lip with his tongue before delving inside to explore and possess.

Her blood fired in her veins, and Katelyn returned his fevered kiss. She twined her arms around his neck and pulled him closer before molding herself against the hard line of his body. A sigh escaped, and she ground her hips against his growing erection.

Grayson winced, and she tried to pull back. His splayed hand on the small of her back kept her in place. He rained open-mouthed kisses over her face and down the side of her neck. "My shoulder is still healing from the battle with the Cunts. But the sustenance you provide me should speed my recovery."

A thousand very logical questions rose to the forefront of Katelyn's mind, but she firmly pushed them all away. Vision or reality . . . she didn't care at the moment. Since she'd first laid eyes on Grayson, she'd wanted him, and she was determined to enjoy this.

He nibbled a path along the side of her throat, sending arousal arrowing through her, and ripping a long moan from her throat.

"Oh, Goddess . . ." Katelyn's head fell back, and her hips bucked against him as if they had a mind of their own.

All she could do was hold on to him as a storm of sensations assaulted her and threatened to tear her apart. "Swear to me you'll never stop whatever it is you're doing." Katelyn's husky voice hung in the thick air around them.

Grayson chuckled, and Katelyn discovered how right she'd been earlier. The bass vibrations echoed through her body, caressing her everywhere at once. Every inch of her ached to be touched and possessed.

Once Katelyn had gotten her fill of him, she wondered if he would be willing just to lie next to her naked and read the phone book—or read anything—just so those wonderful, low vibrations could skitter through her body, scattering all her thoughts and sizzling against her nerve endings.

"Patience, Katelyn. We have a lifetime to explore each other."

The word *lifetime* threatened to bring her out of the wonderful sexual frenzy, but then his large hand closed over her bare breast, and any protest died away on her lips.

How did I suddenly get naked?

Then she noticed his clothes were gone as well.

Thank the Goddess for balance in the universe—even inside a vision, She provides!

Grayson pinched her nipple, then gently pulled it, causing a rush of moisture between her thighs, as Katelyn's clit swelled and ached for attention.

"Grayson, please . . ." Katelyn's mind refused to cooperate or form the words that would demand he fuck her senseless before she exploded from frustration. She reached between them, her hand closing over the silky skin on the most impressive cock she'd ever wrapped her fingers around.

Thick and long, Grayson's cock overflowed her hand, and Katelyn stroked him from the base all the way to the swollen head. She grazed her thumb over the tip and groaned as her skin met the creamy wetness of his pre-come.

Grayson gasped and jumped back as if she'd scalded him.

"Before your coming of age, my essence may be dangerous to you, Katelyn. I'm not sure how it affects humans."

Katelyn's blood roared through her veins, and her pussy ached to have Grayson fill her. She'd gone too long without a man inside her to have him pull back now. "I have no fucking idea what you're talking about, and I don't care. All I can say is this vision better not end before we're finished."

She dropped to her knees in front of Grayson, surprised to find the grassy ground soft and giving beneath her. Katelyn closed her mouth over the swollen head of his cock, caressing him with her tongue and lips.

He stiffened, and she thought he might push her away, but he let her take him deep inside her throat while she gently massaged his balls between her fingers.

When a long, strangled moan ripped from Grayson, Katelyn made an "mmm" sound deep in her throat and slid his long shaft from between her lips until she could tease the underside of the head with her tongue. She glanced up at him and smiled to herself as he closed his eyes, seemingly lost in the sensations she provided. Grayson threaded his fingers through her hair, his large hand cupping the back of her head.

Katelyn wrapped her free hand around the base of his shaft and stroked him in time with the movements of her mouth. She increased her speed, and each time the tip of his cock bumped the back of her throat, Katelyn's own arousal spiraled tighter.

The salty-sweet taste of his pre-come burst over her tongue, and she groaned at the erotic sensation. Her pussy clenched, begging for attention, but an overwhelming need to feel Grayson come inside her mouth flowed through her.

His breath chuffed out in choppy pants, and his cock hardened further between her lips as his balls tightened against his body.

"Katelyn!" he roared as hot come spurted against the back of her throat.

A surge of energy flowed through her, making her skin tingle and every hair on her body stand on end.

She milked Grayson with her hand and lips until his spasms eased and then finally stopped.

Katelyn ran her tongue along his softening length and then sat back on her haunches to look up into his face.

Her body still ached with desire, and her skin was tight and sensitive.

Grayson smiled down at her, his eyes dark with passion. "If I didn't know better, I'd say you were a Klatch. But at this point, I'm glad you're human, and that my essence didn't harm you."

Katelyn filed that information away for later study. "Yeah, I think not. I can only provide arousal the good, old-fashioned way."

"I think you have more power than you know." Grayson dropped to his knees in front of her and then tumbled her backward onto the soft grass, capturing her arms over her head.

Katelyn squealed in surprise and then gasped as she found her hands magickally bound. She couldn't see or feel the bindings, which only served to heighten her arousal. But a slow trickle of fear tripped down her spine. Visions had shown her situations she had no control over before, but this entire experience felt almost real, although she knew, like Grayson had said, her body was either asleep or unconscious.

Just what the fuck was going on here? "Let me up!"

"You've tormented me enough, witch." Grayson smiled at her, a mischievous glint sparking inside his eyes. "It's now my turn."

Even though Katelyn had been a Seer her entire life, and many of her customers were practicing witches, she wasn't a witch herself. However, she'd picked up enough of a working knowledge to understand and respect their path. "I'm not a witch, and I've never before run into whatever type of witch you think you are."

He rubbed his stubbled jaw along the inside of her thigh like a cat marking his territory, scattering her thoughts. Goose bumps marched over her body, and her nipples tightened into hard buds.

When Grayson's face neared her labia, he spoke. "A Klatch witch, Seer. Not a human practicing a set of beliefs, but a being who needs sexual energy to thrive."

The meaning of his words scrambled inside her brain as his hot breath caressed her swollen clit. She arched her hips, offering herself, silently begging him to take her.

Using just the tip of his tongue, he gently traced a line from her clit down to dip inside her slick slit, and then back up to her clit. A surge of liquid fire flashed along Katelyn's nerve endings with every swipe of his talented tongue, and she thrashed against her invisible bonds as the sensations seared through her body.

Katelyn gulped in a breath as Grayson sucked her clit between his lips. He continued to suck, even as his tongue teased the sensitive tip.

A vortex of tension curled inside her, tighter and tighter with each pull of his lips. The sensations roiling through her reached a fever pitch, and she knew her body couldn't contain the sensations much longer.

Without thought, she struggled against her bonds and tried to twist away from his insistent mouth, but he palmed her ass inside his large hands and feasted on her—sucking, licking, and nipping until she thought she would explode.

A low keening filled her ears as a fine sheen of sweat broke out over her skin as he continued the relentless sensual assault.

Her orgasm slammed into her, stealing her breath and threatening to shred her reality. She rode the sensations as her body convulsed and Grayson continued to lick and suck.

She yanked against her bonds, expecting resistance, but they moved easily.

What the hell?

Katelyn gradually became aware of her sore body. Not the good ache after a steamy romp on the grass, but sore as if she'd been run over by an entire brigade of fire trucks.

Wisps of the "vision" floated inside her mind. The edges were fuzzy in the manner of a dream, but she knew without a doubt, that somehow, those events had actually occurred.

She resisted the urge to open her eyes because even the thought of opening them sent pounding pain along every nerve ending she owned—not to mention a few she was sure had been created purely to torture her.

Katelyn took a deep breath and then winced when the pounding increased.

Damn! I haven't woken feeling this bad since that unfortunate night with an entire bottle of vanilla rum.

The thought of rum and all the long ago diet soda she'd drank with it kicked her bladder into high gear, and she mentally sighed.

Put on your big-girl panties and deal with it. You need to figure out what's going on with the weird vision.

One of the unfortunate parts of being a Seer was having to interpret the visions she received. Sometimes they were very straightforward, but when there were subtle messages or misinterpreted symbols or events, life could really suck for a while. Katelyn knew she would have to make sense of the vision sooner or later, but first, she really had to pee.

With a silent plea to the universe to be merciful, she forced open her heavy eyelids. Light seared straight through her retinas and back inside her brain like a blowtorch. Katelyn groaned and pulled her forearm over her face until the pain receded to a tolerable level.

Memories of her shop in shambles flitted through her brain,

waking her body better than any "hair of the dog" would have. Rita would freak when she saw the shop like that, no matter how good her evening had been with her spooky new boyfriend.

Good thing her friend was used to opening the store. Days in which Katelyn had visions were often days she didn't make it into the shop at all because of the draining effects. Today she wasn't sure she could even move.

A quick flash of guilt for leaving Rita alone to clean up the mess and to worry about her whereabouts caused Katelyn to frown, but when pain from even that small movement ping-ponged inside her head, she winced.

She rolled onto her stomach and allowed the world to stop spinning before she gingerly lifted her head and cracked her eyelids open again.

When only minimal pain branded her brain, she rubbed her eyes to clear the haze from her sight.

Shit—definitely not in Kansas anymore, Toto.

The white walls with pink crystal veins running through them and the deep-colored, real-wood furniture made her think of a high-class hotel, only more homey somehow. Katelyn blinked, sure that this was an alcohol-induced illusion, and then bit back a yelp as she realized someone had installed sandpaper on the backs of her eyelids while she'd slept.

She curled into a protective ball, her forearm covering her face, her eyes firmly closed as she resolved never to open them again. "Someone just please shoot me. It would be more merciful."

"Seer?"

The soft, musical voice startled Katelyn, and her brain kicked into high gear. She gritted her teeth and forced her eyelids open again.

"Are you all right, Seer? Is there something I can get you?" A pixie of a woman stood at the foot of the bed, her large eyes the same liquid amethyst color as Grayson's.

As Katelyn tried to nod, a wave of nausea rocked her, and her stomach roiled and bucked.

The pixie woman rushed forward and grabbed a basin off the nightstand. She handed it to Katelyn just in time for her to embarrass herself and barf all over what appeared to be a very classy ceramic basin.

When Katelyn finished, a cool, wet cloth was pressed against her brow, and she accepted it gratefully, bracketing her hand over it to hold it in place. Another cloth wiped her lips and then retreated as the basin was lifted out of her hands and she was pushed back onto the soft pillow-top mattress. Downy covers settled over her, and Katelyn huddled under them, her eyes shut tight against the light.

The *whoosh* of drapes closing, and then the resulting blessed darkness, made Katelyn sigh with relief.

She wondered briefly if she had been drugged, but then the vivid memory of the blue bolt hitting her squarely in the torso returned with force. She lifted her hand to touch her chest, wondering if the area was sore as it had been inside her vision. When her fingers brushed her skin, pain flared as though she was healing from a sunburn, and she winced again.

"Lie back and relax, Seer. It will take a while for the effects of the draining spell to diminish. In the meantime, I've brought you food and drink to help you recover."

"Draining spell?" Katelyn asked from between cracked lips. "Was that the blue bolt?"

"Yes. Prince Grayson said one of the Cunts hit you with a draining spell last night. And from the nasty bruise on your chest, I'd say it was a powerful one."

"Prince Grayson?"

"Yes, my lady. Prince Grayson is the Seventh Prince of Klatch."

Katelyn's foggy memories supplied her with the meaning of

Klatch—some type of witch who supposedly thrived on sexual energy.

Right now, sex is the furthest thing from my mind—for once!

Katelyn didn't dare move the cool cloth but settled it more firmly over her eyes, and she dropped her arms beside her on the bed, only now realizing she was completely nude. She couldn't muster resentment at whoever had undressed her, because the cool sheets against her body were actually the only thing not painful about her current situation.

Questions sped through her mind, and she took a deep breath to slow them, shoving the pain aside so she could concentrate on the here and now. "Where am I?"

"You're on Tador, my lady. Prince Grayson was afraid the Cunts would come back for you if he took you to your home."

Because her home was actually upstairs above the shop, she had to agree with that.

Katelyn let the "cunts" comment go by . . . for now.

She wasn't a big fan of that word—except for the few instances in which it was warranted—but she had more pressing questions to worry about. "*On* Tador? Is it a boat or a ship or something? And who are you?"

"I'm Holly, your lady's maid. And Tador is a planet. The home planet of the Klatch."

Katelyn sighed. *I had to ask, didn't I?*

"Okay, Holly. I think I need that food and drink and a Volkswagen full of aspirin before I can even process any of that. But first, I *really* have to pee."

4

Sela, the queen of the Cunts, paced away from Aedan and back.

Familiar anger surfaced, and she shook her head as she glanced around the living room of the two-story Earth home in which she'd been forced to exist since her banishment from Tador. She'd been cheated out of living in the palace on her home planet, where, as the rightful queen, she should reside. If the Klatch thought she would meekly give up and live out her days here, they were mistaken.

After several deep breaths, she thought she could listen to Aedan's excuses for more than five minutes without killing him. She turned a deadly glare toward him.

Aedan, the leader of the team of five who had failed to capture the bastard prince and the Seer, stood proud and unflinching.

Unsure whether she should be irritated that he showed no fear or feel pride that he was brave enough to stand up to her, Sela crossed her arms in front of her. "Tell me why I shouldn't rip out your heart?"

Aedan's white-blond hair fell to the middle of his back, accentuating his broad shoulders and his clear blue eyes. It really would be a shame if she was forced to kill him. Aedan had been quite adept at amusing her lately—at least sexually. The man had a high tolerance for pain and could be quite inventive in his sexual play.

However, she would never let a good piece of ass get in the way of revenge.

It just wasn't good policy.

Aedan smiled, his features turning devastating and gorgeous instead of just handsome. "My informant was correct, Sela. The Seer and the prince were there, just as I was told."

"Which doesn't help us now. What about your pet human?"

"I missed our dinner plans last night, but she forgave me easily when I told her I'd been mugged. She accepted me back and now thinks we are engaged." A look of disgust marred his handsome features.

"No doubt a night of sex is why I see very little evidence of the attack on you." Sela pointed her index finger at him. "Be careful to keep up appearances. If she sees you heal too quickly from your fake mugging, it will raise suspicions. Keep her close and content. If we are to use the Seer to our advantage, we need a human who cares for her to sacrifice. Your little Rita will do nicely."

"Yes, Sela." Aedan's eyes darkened, and he raked his gaze over her body in a possessive gesture. "As you can see, all isn't lost, and you and I are compatible in so many other ways."

Sela's nipples hardened against her silk tank top, and she resisted the urge to lick her lips. A rush of hot arousal flowed over her skin as she remembered vividly just how compatible they'd been the other night when she'd let him fuck her while several other human women sucked on her breasts and fondled Aedan's balls.

Business before pleasure . . .

Aedan should never forget his place—even if he did make her scream his name as his hot come spilled inside her.

Sela smiled and took a deep breath as she allowed her magic to build like lava about to erupt. Then she relaxed and let the power flow through her arm, out her fingers, and across the room. Before Aedan knew she was displeased, her power slammed into him like a tidal wave.

He flew across the room, and his head made a loud *crack* against the far wall. He groaned, and then slumped to the floor, leaving a large round hole in the drywall.

An almost sexual thrill raced through Sela, and a laugh bubbled up from her throat to fill the small room.

When Aedan's eyes fluttered open, smug pleasure curled deep in Sela's belly.

It would have been extremely inconvenient to train a new operative, not to mention a new lover, if he died. But maintaining discipline was always worth the risk.

She stalked forward to tower over his dazed form. "Don't mistake me enjoying your body for anything more than my right. And you providing me with information about the Klatch is your duty." She prodded Aedan with the toe of her sandal. "I'm queen. I'm free to enjoy anyone and anything I wish. As I quite often do."

The blood drained from Aedan's face, and understanding shone in his eyes. He pushed up on his elbows and shook his head, trying to throw off the effects of his impact against the wall. He dipped his chin to his chest. "Understood . . . my queen. What do you wish me to do next?"

Satisfied Aedan once again knew his place, Sela turned and walked to the built-in bar along the far wall to pour herself a vodka on the rocks. "I want you to find the Seer and bring her to me. Also, we must find a way to make sure Queen—" she could hardly say the word without choking—"Alyssa, miscarries that half-breed fetus that grows inside her. Do those things and I'll reward you handsomely. Fail me again . . ." She let her words trail off, leaving the details to Aedan's imagination. However, because Sela had quite a reputation for enjoying her torture sessions immensely, he should get the idea.

Aedan paled and then nodded.

"Guards, take him out of my sight."

Two muscular Cunt warriors stepped forward and literally dragged Aedan from the room.

Sela sloshed more vodka into the crystal glass and narrowed her eyes. She'd worked hard to kidnap Alyssa all those years ago after it was clear the Cunt rebellion would never succeed. She'd raised the little bitch as part of her family for twenty-three long years. All so Sela could derail the ascension ceremony and punish the past queen and king—Annalecia and Darius—for daring to banish all the Cunts and anyone who fought with them during the civil war.

Sela flipped her white-blond hair over her shoulder and looked down at her hands, which still looked like they did when she'd been banished—smooth and unblemished. She prided herself on appearing much younger than her forty-four years. Thanks to all the sexual energy freely available on this backward planet, Cunts could regenerate and minimize the effects of aging. Although, if Sela were on Tador, there would be no need to constantly resupply herself for that purpose—anyone living on Tador enjoyed a significantly slowed aging process.

A low growl escaped from her throat. All her efforts so far to overthrow the Klatch and rule the planet that was rightfully hers had been thwarted. Alyssa had escaped Sela's carefully laid trap and had ascended the throne on Tador, restoring the planet—for now. And Sela's old nemeses, the past king and queen of the Klatch, had gone off to a comfortable retirement, while Sela and her people had been relegated to live on Earth with common humans.

The Klatch were nothing but breeding stock who should

serve as a sexual food supply for the Cunts. Even though, due to their inherent magic, the Klatch offered more sexual sustenance to their partners than humans. However, that just made the Klatch more high-powered food for the Cunts. No more, no less.

Tador was rightfully Sela's, and she intended to have it—no matter what.

She raised the vodka to her lips, anger flowing through her like a swarm of angry bees. "The Cunts will rule Tador, as it was meant to be. Very soon . . ." She took a sip and then tightened her fingers around the glass until it shattered in her palm.

Grayson lowered himself into a cushioned chair inside the council meeting chamber, wincing a bit as his back met with the chair. His shoulder had healed considerably after the dream he'd shared with the Seer this morning, but it would take either time or more sexual energy to heal it completely.

He had taken a seat near the raised dais—where the king and queen would sit once they entered—mainly because the stadium-type seating around the gallery wasn't as comfortable as the overstuffed chairs here on the main floor.

Until he'd injured his shoulder, Grayson had never realized how much he used those specific muscles. Now, nearly every movement speared shooting pains down his back and side.

The sharp clack of a *balda* gavel echoed through the chamber, distracting him from his discomfort as the crowd around him quieted.

King Stone and Queen Alyssandra entered through the same doorway Grayson had, and both cast him a smile as they stepped past him and onto the raised dais.

"Thank you, council head." Alyssandra nodded to the woman who had been in the job less than a month. After the last council head had attempted to kill the queen right after the ascension, the entire council had been interviewed and eventually replaced with those who were loyal to the ruling family. Of course, seeing your predecessor turned into a burned husk before your eyes could really inspire a desire to do your best.

Stone sat in one of the large thrones gracing the dais while Alyssandra remained standing and faced the crowd. She brushed her palms over the front of the gauzy white skirt she wore—an action Grayson had learned showed how nervous she was.

"As many of you know, the Seer has been found and is recuperating here on Tador from the Cunt attack."

Murmurs flowed through the crowd and then died away as the queen held up her hands for silence. "She was hit with a beam of Cunt energy during the attack, but otherwise appears unharmed."

Gasps of outrage erupted from the crowd until Alyssandra waved for silence and tucked her hair behind her ear—another nervous gesture. "We have not yet spoken to her about the triangle, and have decided not to mention it until she becomes comfortable with the Klatch and Tador. I would like to ask cooperation from everyone on this matter. It's no easy task to ask someone to give up their entire life."

Alyssandra's gaze roamed the room as she made eye contact with several Klatch. "Now I'll open the floor for questions, but please remember, the decision to move forward with the triangle has already been made, and I won't waste time rehashing those discussions. The time for everyone to band together and support the decision of your chosen ruler is at hand."

Here it comes . . . The decision to move forward with the triangle had basically split the populace, and only because Alyssandra was queen did the people not openly rebel.

Valen, the head royal chef, stood. Alyssandra recognized him and motioned for him to speak. "My queen, I and many other citizens have obvious concerns with introducing humans, even gifted humans, into the Klatch bloodlines. After all, the Cunts are a result of too many generations of dilution of our line. Might we not, with this decision, be breeding a new race who will seek to destroy us down the road?"

Grayson shook his head. He would never understand which part of "I won't waste time rehashing those discussions" these people didn't understand. He glanced up at Alyssa, whose jaw was clenched.

"Valen, as I've stated before on many occasions, the triangle has been used at least three times in our history that we know of." Despite Alyssandra's obvious displeasure, her voice was calm and commanding as it rang out across the chamber. "We are talking about taking human women with special gifts—human women who most likely have some Klatch blood in their distant pasts—and mating them with pureblood Klatch princes. The worry about diluting our bloodline will be moot if we no longer have a planet to live on."

"We understand the dire nature of our circumstances, my lady, but we respectfully disagree with the methods of repair. Surely—"

"Damnit, Valen!" Grayson's patience snapped like a brittle twig in a windstorm. He pushed to his feet, ignoring the lances of pain that shot down his back and shoulder. "We have talked this subject to death, and many of you don't seem to be listening to the answers." He stepped onto the dais, and Alyssandra squeezed his hand before taking a seat on the throne chair next to Stone, and yielding him the floor.

"There is no other way to save Tador." Grayson tried to stare Valen down, but the man refused to look away. "Our best researchers have searched for a solution since soon after the Cunt revolt, and only through uncovering the treachery of the past Klatch council and breaking the spells placed on the journals in the queen's archives did we find out how our ancestors handled this situation. They persevered, and so shall we, but we must maintain a united front."

Several members of the crowd nodded in support of his

words, but several more, including Valen, only glared or shook their heads.

"Everyone here was happy to leave the planet in Alyssandra's hands when Queen Annalecia was deteriorating and nearly at death's door. However, now that Alyssandra has ascended, you wish to second-guess her at every turn." Grayson made a sharp, chopping motion with his good arm. "Enough. Are there any questions about the Seer or the triangle itself? If not, there is no more business to be discussed today."

He turned and walked off the dais, his anger and frustration burning with each step. A sea of voices followed him out into the hall until he slammed the door behind him.

"It's a good thing I won't ever have to rule—diplomacy is definitely not my strong suit."

"Well, if I have to be abducted to another planet, this isn't a bad place to be taken." Katelyn took a drink of the strange tea and let the odd citrus-almond flavor flow over her tongue. She placed the cup on the table in front of her, leaned back in her chair, and closed her eyes as the distant thump of her previous headache slowly faded.

A light breeze played across the second-story balcony and brought the lush scents of gardenias and roses that spoke of a garden nearby. The sounds of running water, the soft chirrup of birds, and the gentle *whoosh* of the wind through the trees all lulled her, sending a tendril of peace deep inside her as though she'd suddenly come home.

The thought startled her.

She was certainly comfortable with her life in Phoenix, but she had never experienced this deep, intuitive *knowing* of a place like she did with this one, as though she was created specifically to exist here. All her internal alarms told her this place was as real as Earth, and not only that—she knew she'd been here before, as improbable as it sounded.

The thought irritated her. She had worked her ass off to carve out a life for herself in Phoenix. She co-owned her own business, she had friends—well, Rita, at least. She also had several steady customers and money in the bank, which offered her freedom to make her own choices. After all, that's what true freedom was.

She looked around, bringing herself back to the present and her circumstances here, not that she had a clue in hell where "here" happened to be, other than a planet called Tador. She didn't even know why she'd been brought here. Holly insisted Grayson had brought her here to save her from the "Cunts"—whoever happened to be unlucky enough to have that moniker.

All questions to Holly, the lady's maid, had only gotten Katelyn strange answers. Katelyn had given up finding out more until she recovered from her "energy hangover," as she had termed it. This morning she had gladly followed Holly through the winding halls of what the maid kept referring to as the "castle," and out to this beautiful balcony for breakfast.

Katelyn's only worries had been her shop and Rita. Her meticulously organized partner would freak when she saw the destruction of the shop. But, even worse, she would worry when she found Katelyn's purse, but no sign of Katelyn.

Hopefully Rita wouldn't panic. For someone who didn't believe in magic, crystals, Seers or anything "woo-woo," as Rita called it, the woman had helped Katelyn make her new-age shop a success. After all, what better place for a Seer to open?

Besides, Holly had insisted that Grayson would be able to get word to Rita that Katelyn was alive and well and . . . hmmm, maybe Katelyn was better off just sticking to "alive and well" for now. She didn't think telling Rita she was on another planet hiding from killer Cunts would go over real well.

She opened her eyes and looked out at the panoramic view visible over the short balcony wall. Thanks to the food and drink Holly had provided, Katelyn felt almost human again.

Which meant her questions had returned, along with her energy.

She sat in one of the two surprisingly comfortable wooden chairs that almost seemed to contour to her body. The chairs sat around a small round table covered with a bright blue tablecloth. More food and drink than Katelyn could ever eat was spread before her, including tea, several fruits she recognized (and several she didn't), pastries, eggs, sausages, and some type of blue pudding that smelled like a vanilla milkshake. Everything was neatly arranged on what Katelyn's untrained eye took to be fine china edged in gold.

She had sampled almost everything, rationalizing that someone recovering from any type of hangover needed something in their stomach. Besides, maybe the calories wouldn't count on Tador, or wherever the hell she was.

A soft knock sounded against the frame of the open balcony door.

Katelyn glanced over to see a stunning woman with dark hair that flowed nearly to her ass. Thin braids were scattered throughout her hair, and small lavender beads peppered the braids. Skimpy cotton boy shorts clung to shapely hips, and a half top of the same material allowed the bottom curves of the woman's full breasts to peek out from the underside of the top. Lavender eyes a few shades lighter than Grayson's studied Katelyn with warm curiosity.

Hard, hot arousal hit Katelyn like a sucker punch to the stomach. Slick moisture rushed to dampen her slit, and her nipples hardened into tight points, surprising her.

She had never been attracted to a woman before, and she wasn't sure how to feel about these foreign sensations. Thoughts of how those full lips would feel against hers spilled through her mind. Her heart galloped with a combination of shock and forbidden desire.

The woman's bewitching energy buzzed against Katelyn's, causing Katelyn's lips to curve into a smile.

"Hi, Katelyn. I'm Queen Alyssandra."

Queen? "I guess, because Holly called Grayson 'Prince,' that makes him your brother or something?"

The woman laughed. "No—actually, he's from a different royal family that's no relation."

Katelyn stood, glad the action no longer caused the room to tilt. "It's nice to meet you . . . uh . . . Queen."

Alyssandra laughed and waved Katelyn back to her seat. "Please, call me Alyssa. I've only been on Tador for a few months. I'm not used to the full formalities of my office yet." Alyssa eyed some sticky pastries on the table in front of Katelyn. "Do you mind if I share some of your breakfast?"

"Help yourself." Katelyn watched as Alyssa gently bit her lower lip, the pink flesh pillowed around even white teeth. A sudden urge to soothe the skin with her tongue stabbed through Katelyn, and she bit back a gasp as her body reacted.

Oh, my Goddess! I'm losing my mind.

Katelyn wrestled her mind back to the conversation at hand. "If you're the queen, I should be thanking you for all your hospitality."

Alyssa plopped into the chair across from Katelyn and snatched a baked pastry with blue filling and powdered sugar scattered over the top. She broke off a piece and slipped it between her lips and then leaned back in the chair and closed her eyes. As she chewed, she moaned in almost orgasmic ecstasy.

A vivid flash of bringing this woman to orgasm strobed inside Katelyn's mind. Her nipples hardened into tight, painful buds, and she winced against the intense sensation.

Not a vision—just her own overactive imagination.

Katelyn swallowed hard and forced herself to speak. "They're pretty good."

Alyssa opened her eyes. "You have no idea. Now that I'm

pregnant with the future queen, my lady's maid and my husband watch every morsel of sweets I eat."

Great, I'm having sexual fantasies not only about a woman, but about a pregnant queen.

Katelyn shoved aside her reactions and focused on the woman before her, who was not exactly what she would expect a queen to be like. Yet, Katelyn couldn't help but like this easygoing woman instantly. And talk about a relaxed dress code for royalty!

"So, you're a queen. Is there a king hiding around here, too?" Katelyn chose what looked like a tart and took a bite. Some type of green fruit oozed from the top. Flavor burst across her tongue, and she gave her own sigh of ecstatic bliss. She waited for another bout of physical reactions, but none came, so she relaxed.

If everyone ate like this here, why weren't they all three hundred pounds–plus?

"If he's smart, King Stone will stay out of my way until I finish this pastry and maybe several others." Alyssa took another healthy bite and chewed. When she swallowed, she fixed Katelyn with an expectant gaze. "Are you going to ask me if this is all real? I'm not sure if I'd handle waking up on a new planet as well as you have."

Katelyn sighed and sat back against her wooden chair. "I've tried to avoid thinking too much about it until I could ensure the room wouldn't spin every time I move. I remember the attack at my shop, and I'm not sure what to make of that. Either I'm insane, this is an extremely vivid vision, complete with breakfast, or I'm truly on another planet talking to a queen." She shook her head at the absurdity of the situation. "At this point, I'm not even sure which to hope for."

Katelyn thought the queen would laugh, but instead, she steepled her fingers against her full lips. "Let me put it this way. My reality growing up on Earth was much different from my current reality as queen on Tador. But I would gladly hand over my sanity or anything else to stay here." Alyssa laughed, a short, humorless sound. "You're welcome here as long as you like, Katelyn."

Something told her the queen had left something unsaid, but she wasn't exactly in a position to ask outright. Unsure how to respond, Katelyn reverted to her comfortable, sarcastic humor. "Not a bad offer if all the men look anything remotely like Grayson."

Alyssa laughed again—a genuine sound of mirth this time— and her eyes danced with mischief. "Let's just say you'll be pleasantly surprised in that regard. Although I have a feeling Grayson won't like your appreciation of any of the other men's good looks, or even the women, for that matter."

Katelyn bristled at any discussion of Grayson becoming possessive or proprietary over her. Katelyn had always prided herself on being independent and her own woman. If Grayson had a problem with that, they needed to resolve that misconception first thing.

Her brain suddenly caught up with her indignation, and she processed the last half of Alyssa's sentence.

Katelyn's cheeks burned, and a lead ball of mortification settled inside her stomach. Was Alyssa psychic? Had she picked up on Katelyn's strong attraction to her?

A crease formed between Alyssa's dark brows, and she leaned forward and rested her elbows on the table. "Oh, I didn't mean to embarrass you. I guess I thought, because you are partly human, Tador wouldn't affect you the same way it does the natives." She reached out for the pitcher of tea and poured it into a tall glass. "I assume from your reaction that you're experiencing strong sexual urges. Don't be embarrassed—sexual energy here on Tador is just as important as food or water. It most likely means you need sexual sustenance to fully recover."

Katelyn's temples throbbed. Grayson had said as much in

their dream vision, but he hadn't mentioned that she would suddenly be attracted to women, too. "I'm not sure what's happening to me. I've always had a healthy libido, but oh, my Goddess. Does the planet also make you attracted to people you weren't attracted to before?"

Alyssa took a drink and set her glass on the table. "You can rest easy on that subject—you're not crazy. Tador is a world of sexual energy, and there are very few things forbidden here. The planet will pull you strongly toward what you need to ensure you retain enough energy." She brushed a braid over her shoulder. "When you see Grayson you should have him give you a tour so you can see for yourself." The queen leaned back in her chair and studied Katelyn. "I like you already. If Grayson had to bring someone back through the *between*, I'm glad he found someone with a sense of humor."

Confusion flitted through Katelyn's brain. She set the pastry on the plate in front of her and wiped her fingers on a pillowy soft napkin. "*Between?*"

The queen nodded and then swallowed. "I'm sorry, let me back up. The *between* is a portal between our world and Earth. It's a dark void, and I've never met anyone who likes using it, but it's an easy way to travel, once you learn how to open the portal."

"Is it hard to learn?" It would be a relief to know Katelyn didn't have to rely on the Klatch to decide to let her leave.

"It took me a while. However, I think only Klatch or Cunts are able to open one." Alyssa's brow furrowed, and she seemed about to say something more when she stopped and shook her head. "Anyway, I haven't had much of a chance to talk to Grayson yet this morning, and he's been busy recovering from the injuries he received the other night. But he should be down in a few minutes."

Katelyn's palms grew clammy as unease trickled along her spine. "*Other* night? How long was I out?"

"Two days." Alyssa bit her bottom lip, choosing her words. "Well, I assume you mean in Earth terms. When it's night there, it's day here. So, when Grayson brought you back through the *between*, it was two nights ago, Earth time, or two days ago, Tador time."

Sick dread pooled inside Katelyn's stomach. Rita had probably reported her missing by now. *Crap!* "I have to get back. Rita will be freaking out."

Alyssa placed a hand over Katelyn's. The queen's hand was soft and warm, and Katelyn had a sudden urge to graze her thumb over the back of it the way Grayson had done to Katelyn's after her vision at her store.

Unaware of Katelyn's thoughts, or maybe in spite of them, Alyssa continued. "I figured you'd be worried about your store, so I had one of the guards write a note to your co-owner. They also cleaned up as best they could and brought your purse—it's in the bottom drawer of the nightstand in the room where you woke. Rita will think you and Grayson have run off for a week-long cruise." Alyssa cocked her head to the side to study Katelyn's reaction. "We've also left discreet guards in place around the neighborhood, and some inside the shop, to ensure the Cunts don't harm Rita to try to get to you."

Katelyn caught her breath. She'd been so busy coming to terms with her own situation, she hadn't stopped to consider Rita might be in danger. Hell, she still wasn't sure why *she* was in danger. "Thanks. I wouldn't want anything to happen to her." The comforting balm of relief slid through Katelyn, and she sighed. At least Rita wouldn't worry about her.

She took a breath to ask Alyssa why either she or Rita were in danger, but then Alyssa squeezed Katelyn's hand and let go to relax against her chair.

The breath backed up in Katelyn's lungs, and she swallowed hard as another thick surge of arousal surged through her. Her labia throbbed, and her nipples were suddenly sensitive, her breasts heavy and aching.

A gentle breeze teased the queen's hair, and the beads in her braids tinkled against each other like fairy song.

Katelyn dropped her hands into her lap to keep from reaching back out for Alyssa's hand. Whether this planet affected her or not, she found it disconcerting to react to a woman almost as much as she'd reacted to Grayson.

"It amazes me that men don't think of these things." Alyssa continued, hopefully unaware of Katelyn's discomfiting reaction. "But, then, they're men. They think we'll just blindly follow whatever they dictate without question."

Katelyn nodded. A subject change would be good—anything to get away from this sudden sexual attraction to the queen. She cleared her throat, hoping her voice would work. "So, do you know what this is all about? Why those pale guys showed up at my store?"

Pain, followed quickly by anger, etched across Alyssa's face, surprising Katelyn. "Yes, I know only too well who they are and what they want." Alyssa dropped the remains of her pastry onto the plate in front of her.

"About twenty-four years ago, there was a civil war here on Tador. The Klatch all look pretty much like Grayson and myself—dark hair, lavender eyes, the men muscular, the women curvy. The other race we warred with are called the Cunts."

Katelyn cringed at the term. "Yikes. What a horrible name for a race."

Alyssa laughed. "You have no idea." She topped off her glass of tea from the pitcher. "Most of the Cunts are products of a mating between two half-Klatch, half-human parents. Once the Klatch blood is diluted to that degree, their physical characteristics change, and their children are pale blond, with tight, athletic bodies and clear blue eyes. Over time, the Cunts decided they were superior to the Klatch and tried to overthrow the king and queen—my parents."

Katelyn sipped at her own tea, still trying to breathe through the physical reactions surging through her. "You said 'tried'—I assume the . . . the Cunts were unsuccessful?"

The queen nodded, but her lips thinned, and her eyes narrowed. "They may not have been entirely successful, but they did a lot of damage. When they lost, they fled to Earth to hide, but not before they kidnapped me and my nanny."

Alyssa's energy snapped and sizzled in the air around them and caused Katelyn to gasp. The queen was a powerful practitioner and wielded more energy than Katelyn had ever seen in one person. Because Alyssa concealed it so effortlessly, Katelyn assumed that, like most people, the energy bled through only when strong emotions threatened.

I wouldn't want to be one of the Cunts if she gets ahold of them.

Alyssa blew out a slow breath and smiled at Katelyn. "Sorry, there's a lot of history there, and it still makes me want to tear a few of them limb from limb." Her smile was self-deprecating. "Not a very queenlike attitude, I'm afraid."

The queen pulled off another small piece of the pastry on her plate and popped it into her mouth. "Anyway, they raised me but never let me know my true heritage. They planned to use me to overthrow the planet when I came of age. Luckily, Stone found me just before my twenty-fourth birthday, and last month I ascended the throne."

"Wow." Katelyn couldn't imagine everything Alyssa had gone through. She didn't want to. "I'm glad it all worked out. But I don't see what that has to do with me and my shop."

A flicker of a shadow crossed Alyssa's face and then disappeared, giving Katelyn the impression the queen still held something back. "We know they were looking for a Seer, but we weren't sure what they were going to do once they found one. Luckily, Grayson happened to be there and was able to keep them from taking you."

"Is that why Grayson was hanging around my shop?"

"Yes." The queen leaned forward, resting her forearms on the table. "The Cunts are extremely dangerous. They view humans as cattle, purely existing to feed them sexual energy." Alyssa's suddenly intense gaze rooted Katelyn to her chair. "They are also a very sexual society, but they don't have the same moral code as the Klatch. They think nothing of rape, necrophilia, bestiality, pedophilia, torture, and several other things the Klatch would never dream of doing."

A shudder ran through Alyssa, and she closed her eyes as though trying to chase away dark memories. Finally, her eyes opened, and she glanced over at Katelyn again. "It might be best for you to stay here a while. In the meantime, we will continue to search for more information on what the Cunts are up to."

Holy hell. What have I fallen into?

"Is Rita safe?" Katelyn blurted out the words. "Should I bring her here with me until whatever danger this is passes?"

Alyssa pursed her lips, considering. "We can, but do you think she'll come?"

Katelyn studied her hands for a long moment. "No. For a woman who owns half a new-age shop, she doesn't believe in anything supernatural or new-agey."

The queen nodded. "As I said, we have Klatch guards watching over Rita and your shop. No one will harm her."

Reluctantly, Katelyn agreed. Her first instinct was to tell them to thump Rita on the head and drag her cynical, skinny ass back here and out of danger. But how much did Katelyn really know about "here" yet? She didn't sense any immediate threat, and her internal alarms were blissfully silent, but what if Tador wasn't the right place for Rita right now? Katelyn knew better than most that everyone's individual path had a purpose in the greater scheme of things.

Besides, Rita was one tough lady. She would be all right, especially with some hunky Klatch hanging around. Maybe Rita would even drop that loser boyfriend after seeing some hot Klatch guys.

One could only hope.

"So, now that we've gotten through that, what exactly do you have to do as queen? Is it all state dinners and paperwork?" Katelyn sat forward, excited to learn more. Her imaginary playmates as children had included a prince, but never a queen. She smiled as the warm memories trickled just below the surface of her thoughts.

Alyssa's sudden bark of laughter surprised Katelyn.

"We are a very sexual society, remember? So my biggest duty as queen is to maintain a symbiotic relationship with the planet. And I'm glad because I think I would hate paperwork."

"Symbiotic?" Katelyn sipped her tea as she puzzled over the word. "It sounds very . . . Sci Fi Channel."

Alyssa cocked her head to the side. "Yes, I guess it does. But once you understand it, it makes a lot of sense. I get energy from the king through sexual interaction, and then I use that energy to heal myself and the planet."

"Wow, talk about pressure. So what happens if you don't create enough energy?"

The queen slumped back in her chair and sighed. "We are actually facing that problem right now."

As a Seer, Katelyn wasn't often shocked by the metaphysical, but other than sex magick, she'd never heard of using sex like a human battery to power a planet. She wondered what had caused a sudden shortage of energy if the entire society was as sexual as Alyssa had said.

Alyssa smiled as if she'd heard Katelyn's thoughts. "Usually, as the future queen grows into a woman, she begins to take some of the burden for the health of the planet from her mother. Think of it as on-the-job training."

Sudden understanding hit Katelyn. "And because you had been kidnapped and only came here a few months ago, your mother was on her own."

Alyssa nodded. "You catch on quickly."

"Surely there is something that can be done to fix the situation."

"We're working on it and hope to have a solution in place soon. But, like any world, the citizens are split about the right course to take."

Katelyn glanced out at the view from the balcony. A lush landscape that could rival the Garden of Eden spread before her. "So what happens when there isn't enough energy?"

Alyssa picked up her tea, and a drop of condensation caught Katelyn's attention.

Katelyn's sight grayed.

The familiar disorientation that accompanied her visions rocked her already weakened system. Her world tilted, and she gripped the edge of the table as a moan escaped her lips.

Suddenly everything righted itself, and she stood inside a large bedchamber with white walls, seams of pink crystals woven through them.

In her vision, a sense of urgency drove her gaze to the small round table next to the bed. The table held only a steaming ceramic mug and a book, laying facedown and open.

With silent steps, she crept forward and glanced around to make sure no one had seen her, but everything seemed calm and quiet. She squared her shoulders for courage and then tilted a dark vial of liquid into the mug, watching it disappear into the depths of the beverage.

The scene jumped forward, and Katelyn's stomach lurched.

She swallowed hard against the tang of bile in the back of her throat and then almost lost her breakfast when Alyssa, happy and smiling, took another healthy sip from the mug.

Panic clawed up the insides of Katelyn's throat as if trying to escape. Her mouth opened in a wordless scream as she tried to warn Alyssa—although she wasn't sure about what.

A tight band closed around her chest and made it difficult to draw breath as the queen crumpled to the ground.

Alyssa lay on the floor like a rag doll tossed aside, forgotten, her face pale, her lavender eyes open and staring.

"Oh, my Goddess! I killed her."

5

"Katelyn."

Grayson's deep voice made Katelyn's entire body tingle. She resisted the urge to shiver as his comforting presence chased away the last tendrils of terror that still gripped her from the vision.

Her eyes fluttered open, and she found herself looking into both Alyssa's and Grayson's concerned faces. Still trembling, she pried her fingers off the edge of the table and clasped them in her lap as she gulped in air.

Alyssa still sat across from her at the table—very alive—her dark brows knitted with worry. Grayson knelt beside Katelyn, his long, dark hair loose over his shoulders.

Even with the horrible vision still fresh in her mind, Katelyn had a strong urge to plunge her hands through that wavy mass and drag Grayson against her.

She did a quick double take as she realized he'd replaced his jeans and tight T-shirt with a deep blue tunic and trousers—something that looked more at home in a Renaissance festival than in the real world she was used to.

Then the remnants of her vision retuned in full force.

She blew out a shaky breath as she reminded herself that her visions didn't always mean what she thought.

This did nothing to calm her frayed nerves, but it kept her from full-blown panic. "I'm okay." Her stomach felt as if she'd swallowed a large stone, and her temples throbbed—normal after-vision reactions, but in her already weakened state, Katelyn was surprised she didn't feel worse. However, the fact that her body continued to ache with arousal concerned her.

"What happened?" Alyssa passed Katelyn a glass of ice water, and Katelyn pressed the cold glass against her forehead, which seemed to chase away some of the clammy dread that filled her.

A picture of Alyssa's sightless eyes flashed into Katelyn's mind, and she took a large gulp of the water. She let the frigid liquid cool her burning throat. "I . . . I may not be as recovered as I thought." *Or maybe I'm just losing my freaking mind!*

Grayson stood, his expression a calm mask. "I'm sure that's it. Alyssandra, I'll look after her and see to any needs she may have." A look of understanding passed between him and the queen, and Alyssa nodded. "The council meeting resumes soon, and you mustn't be late. I'm sorry I disturbed the last one."

The queen smiled. "Don't be. We needed a break."

Alyssa had told Katelyn about Grayson's need for sexual energy to fully heal—maybe that could account for what was happening to Katelyn. Did this mean that every time she had a vision here she would need to have sex to recover?

The possibility both excited and scared her.

A vivid flash of her earlier, almost-too-real dream vision with Grayson flowed through her mind. Heat seared her cheeks and spread out to her entire body like wildfire as she imagined him seeing to her "needs."

A small, knowing smile curved Alyssa's lips, and the breeze

tousled her dark hair, and she pushed it back from her face. As she stood, her chair scraped against the white stone of the balcony. "In that case, I'll leave you two alone, and we can talk later." The queen's beaded braids clinked together lightly when she rose. "Katelyn, it was nice to meet you. I hope you enjoy the hospitality of Tador. My door is always open if you need anything at all."

A hard slap of lust hit Katelyn and zinged hot need to her throbbing pussy and aching breasts. She swallowed back the sudden sensations.

Her mind told her that "anything at all" were simply three innocent words—appropriate and polite in this situation. Apparently, her body didn't buy into the whole logic scenario since vague images of Alyssa's naked body flitted through Katelyn's mind.

She shook her head to try to clear her thoughts but only succeeded in making herself dizzy.

One minute she had a vision about killing the queen, and the next she fantasized about her. Either Katelyn had suddenly turned into a spontaneous nymphomaniac, or Alyssa was right and this planet triggered all these strange reactions.

That had to be it. Since when had she ever fantasized about women before? Katelyn rubbed her hands over her arms and tried to reassure herself that this was actually reality.

Alyssa started toward the door to the balcony, and Grayson pulled her into a quick hug before he dropped a very brotherly kiss on her cheek.

After Katelyn's strong attraction to both of them, she expected jealousy to surge through her at seeing them so close. However, she hadn't expected the fleeting wish that she could have both Alyssa and Grayson at the same time. That Alyssa's bare breasts could press against hers while Grayson fucked her hard from behind.

Oh, my Goddess! I've finally snapped.

She furrowed her brow and buried her face in her hands. She didn't have an issue with women being attracted to women, or even threesomes—she'd just never been part of either of those arrangements, and she wasn't quite sure how to feel about these new inclinations.

Not to mention, she preferred taking dominant sexual positions. Since when had she ever wanted any man to fuck her from behind?

Just one of the many things she had to worry about right now.

Katelyn slowly raised her head and then picked up the glass of ice water and again held it against her forehead. The condensation cooled her skin, and she sighed, letting a small trickle of calm worm through all the other conflicting emotions roiling inside her.

Grayson's attention returned to Katelyn, and all the oxygen suddenly seemed very thin. Her gaze locked with his amethyst one as he stepped forward and took her hand in his.

His touch burned through her and ignited her senses as if she were kerosene just waiting for his spark to turn her into flames. She bit back a gasp and swallowed hard, then she hastily lowered the glass to the table before she dropped it.

Grayson raised her hand to his lips. His intense perusal pinned her in place before he brushed a light kiss across her knuckles and caused her to tremble.

Get a freaking grip, Katelyn!

This man aroused her much too easily—and, apparently, so did the queen, which irritated her and scared her for some reason she couldn't name.

What if she was hot and bothered for the whole planet? Talk about a new reason not to attend social events!

Grayson slid into the seat across from her with the grace of a predatory cat.

No wonder I always feel like prey when I'm around him.

"You didn't need to lie about your vision. Did something about the queen strike you as untrustworthy?" His steady gaze held only open curiosity.

Damn! He was too astute for his own good.

She barely knew this man. How would he react to a vision of her killing the queen? Probably not well.

She couldn't deny she'd had a vision. Grayson knew, just like he'd known the night at her shop.

Grayson smiled. "Forgive me. Trust is earned, not demanded. I know you'll tell me when you're ready, and I'll be available when you are." He poured himself a generous glass of tea and then grinned as though no response from her was required, which caused a surge of guilt to flood through her.

"So, how are you feeling this morning, Katelyn?" As usual, her name sounded erotic and forbidden as it flowed from his lips. "Did Holly treat you well?"

She rubbed at the fading sore spot on her chest where the blue blast of energy had hit her. "I feel better, now that my energy hangover is gone, or whatever you call that. But I'm still not very steady yet, thanks to the new vision." Her voice wavered as a sudden urge to straddle Grayson where he sat flashed through her mind. She growled low inside her throat and let all her frustration show as she grabbed a muffin and broke off a piece. She had to get some carbs to counteract the vision. "Your arousal gift really pisses me off. Is it a planetwide thing?" She chewed and glared across the table at him.

The realization that Grayson had told her about his gift inside her vivid vision this morning and not in "waking" reality slapped at her, and she stiffened in her seat. What would his reaction be?

Shock seemed to travel across Grayson's handsome features, and then he threw back his head and laughed. The amber highlights in his dark hair glinted in the sunlight.

Katelyn's throat constricted as a sensation of dread made its way through her anger. Maybe she really had imagined or dreamed that vision. Maybe, even now, she was firmly locked in some room with rubber walls, and only her mind was here in this beautiful place with a sexy, smiling man sitting across from her. Her irritation and unease caused her to lash out at Grayson. "What the fuck is so funny?"

It took several moments for Grayson's laughter to subside, and by the time it did, Katelyn's temper had neared boiling point.

"I'm sorry." The mischief still glinted in his eyes and belied his words. "But I hadn't expected you to admit that our interlude this morning was real. I thought you would deny it and attempt to rationalize it away."

He took a drink of his tea, and she became fascinated by the way his Adam's apple bobbed up and down with the motion. She wondered what the skin of his neck would taste like under her tongue. "You continue to surprise me in every way, Seer. I enjoy your surprises, and I enjoy you."

Katelyn started again as she realized she had just admitted to being hot for him—no "gift" or magick of any kind involved. Just . . . *him*. She was afraid to ask if this pertained to her reaction to Alyssa as well.

Mortification of openly admitting her vulnerable feelings roiled inside her stomach, and her breakfast threatened to inch its way up her throat. She dropped the muffin on the table and sank back against her chair, suddenly weak and spent.

Katelyn gathered her tattered pride around her and raised her chin. "How did you get inside my vision this morning? I know that's what it was, but I also know it was real. But Seer's visions just don't work that way." She took a deep breath in hope that the oxygen would revive some of her quickly waning energy.

It didn't.

Where's a freaking Starbucks when you need a quick caffeine fix?

He pinned her in place with a knowing look—the same look he'd had in his eye when he'd made her scream his name inside her morning vision.

Katelyn shuddered as goose bumps marched over her skin in a burning rush.

"This is a world where partners can communicate on psychic wavelengths. You and I are compatible enough for that communication to work. You let me in, or I wouldn't have been able to enter your thoughts or our 'shared' vision." Grayson's voice slid over her like liquid sex, and she had to admit that, "gift" or no, this man could singe women's panties at a thousand paces. "And you did enjoy it as much as I did, didn't you?"

Irritation sparked her temper. Just because she had enjoyed it didn't mean he could be so fucking smug about it! "I'm no one's partner, Grayson. Let me make that very clear up front." She pinned him with the most serious stare she could muster. "I'll admit I'm very attracted to you, and we'd probably be very good together in bed, but I'm not looking for more than that. Understood?"

The corners of Grayson's lips curved, and he seemed unconcerned about her warning. "My apologies for the poor word choice, Seer. I agree that we would be quite compatible sexually, and, here on Tador, that would also help us heal and recover faster—even from your lone visions." His smile widened, and amusement danced in his eyes. "Besides, I don't recall making overtures of love and marriage, unless you misunderstood something I said?"

Katelyn gritted her teeth. She knew he was teasing her, and she hated it that he had neatly turned the tables on her. The men Katelyn dated, or even slept with, were always the ones receiving the "no commitment" lecture, not her.

Somehow, Grayson made it seem like Katelyn had assumed too much, instead of the other way around.

Fricking infuriating man!

Her brow furrowed as she reminded herself that no commitment was exactly what she wanted. He was offering exactly that, so why was she pissed?

"As long as we understand each other," she finally said grudgingly.

Her limbs seemed almost too heavy to move, as though every bit of her energy was being slowly drained from her. She leaned her forearms on the table, half tempted to rest her head on the surface and close her eyes. "I can't believe I'm buying all this." When he reached out and captured her hand in his, Katelyn didn't resist.

Grayson's roughened thumb stroked slowly over the back of her hand, causing a flood of blazing energy from the point of contact to every erogenous zone she possessed. Katelyn's breasts ached with need—especially when a vivid image of his mouth closing over her hard nipple flashed through her mind.

Maybe he and Alyssa were correct about this whole sexual-energy thing. The carbs didn't seem to be helping at all.

"I know you have lots of questions, and Holly said you've not had a chance to visit the baths yet. Why don't I give you a tour, and then I can leave you at the baths for your morning ablutions?" Grayson's thumb continued to feather over the sensitive skin on the back of her hand and scattered her thoughts.

What normal person says "ablutions"?

Katelyn pushed away her arousal as best she could. "I'm not sure I can stand, let alone take a tour. My—" She snapped her mouth shut as soon as she realized she'd been about to say her vision about killing the queen had wiped her out.

"No problem. I'll send the maid up with a bath for you and prescribe the rest of the day for rest and recovery. There's time enough tomorrow to give you that tour." He didn't seem to notice her silence. He stood and started around the table toward her. "I think we can give you enough of an energy boost to recover more fully, if you'll trust me."

Her eyes widened, and she stiffened, suddenly unsure of herself and what to expect.

"Shhh." He walked behind her chair and laid his large hands on her shoulders. "Just relax, Katelyn. Our world may need sexual energy to thrive, but no one is forced to do anything they don't want to do."

His words caused her independent streak to bristle. "Don't worry about me. I'm a big girl, and I can tell you if I don't want something." Then she bit down hard on her bottom lip to keep from telling him that what she was afraid of was finding out just how much she *did* want.

His strong hands kneaded her shoulders, and she nearly moaned. The heat from his hands burned through her thin cotton top as his talented fingers chased away the knots of tension coiled inside her tight muscles.

Her eyes drifted closed as pure pleasure seeped into her and dissolved her resistance. His thumbs massaged her shoulder blades, and she arched into his touch as soft sounds of approval spilled from her lips. Relaxed more than she'd been in a long time, her head fell back to lean against his muscled stomach.

Her blood heated from the intimate contact, as Grayson's touch moved to her neck. Just the right amount of pressure chased away any discomfort or soreness and left in its place a growing awareness of the man who stood so close behind her.

Afraid to break the spell, Katelyn kept her eyes closed and allowed the sensations to wash over her.

Strong fingers moved to her scalp and spread tingling heat everywhere they touched. If he would only continue this for eternity, she'd sign over her soul and several other people's. "Mmm. I could definitely get used to this."

Grayson's soft laughter vibrated through her head, which

still rested against his stomach. His hands left her scalp. She opened her mouth to beg him not to stop, when he feathered rough fingertips over her cheeks and jaw, which drew a long sigh from her instead.

He thoroughly explored her face as though memorizing her in minute detail. The exquisite soft friction over her temples, forehead, and lips remained tender and gentle. When he caressed her lower lip with his thumb, she sighed and couldn't resist pursing her lips to place a kiss against his skin.

Her hands lay limp in her lap as her entire body turned into a noodle. She was surprised she didn't slither out of the chair and onto the balcony floor. Somehow, she knew Grayson wouldn't let her fall, so she didn't fight the languor stealing over her.

The breeze brought the soft, gurgling sound from the fountain and the scents of gardenias and other flowers, which only added to her lethargy.

"How do you feel?"

"Mmm" was all she could manage, although she thought the corners of her lips might have curved. She took stock of herself, surprised to find that no discomfort or disorientation remained. Her energy level remained low, but apparently, her impromptu massage had worked wonders.

Thoroughly relaxed, she wished Grayson's wonderful hands would continue their magic down her torso to her breasts.

Her nipples tightened as she imagined his strong fingers plucking them. The languorous heat turned to a slow, molten burn, and she reached up to cover Grayson's hands with her own.

As though he had read her mind, his fingers trailed down to trace the opening of her top. His finger left a fiery trail of awareness, and she arched against his hand, offering herself.

He pressed his lips to the side of her neck, and she realized he had knelt behind her chair. His hands traced and teased her aching breasts, and it seemed more erotic somehow that her bra and shirt remained a barrier between them.

Her eyes slid closed, and she let her head fall to the side to give him better access to her neck.

Grayson didn't disappoint her. While his fingertips teased her areolas, he trailed openmouthed kisses slowly down her neck until he reached her shoulder. Then he feathered his tongue along the neckline of her top, ripping a gasp from her as cascades of sensual shivers marched through her.

Katelyn fisted her hands so hard she was surprised they didn't go numb from lack of blood. She wanted to demand more, but her brain didn't seem ready to do anything besides absorb every sensation Grayson caused inside her.

Finally, he cupped her breasts in his hands and gently pinched her already taut nipples through the cloth.

A whimper escaped before she could stop it, and his warm breath feathered against her ear. "Relax, Katelyn. Let yourself enjoy."

He stood, and the warmth of him at her back immediately disappeared, leaving her cold and shivering. Her eyes fluttered open, and she realized he'd moved around her and now stood in front of her. She had sank down in the chair under his sensuous massage, and she now hung limply on its frame, her feet stretched out in front of her, her skirt riding up her calves.

Grayson knelt again and skimmed his hand up one ankle to her calf.

Katelyn's bottom lip trembled as his gaze locked with hers. She struggled to breathe normally, as if the air had suddenly become the consistency of molasses.

The warmth of his hand continued its leisurely path up her leg, pushing up the skirt as it went. When he reached her knee, his hand settled possessively at the start of her thigh, and his other hand went to work, giving her left leg the same treatment.

The normally silky cotton of her skirt scraped against her

sensitive skin until her entire body began to tremble from the overload of sensations. When his second hand finished its path to her knee, he edged closer until her inner thighs brushed against his waist. He hooked his hands behind her knees and pulled her down farther in the chair until her head gently bumped against the back of the chair and he could press himself tight between her splayed thighs.

Her skirt bunched in her lap, and his breeches scraped exquisitely across her bare flesh. Heat from Grayson's body seared into her, and a new rush of moisture rushed to her slit. She knew if he dipped his fingers inside her folds, she would be slick and ready for him.

A gentle breeze ruffled her hair, reminding her they were out in the open, and anyone could walk in on them. That knowledge only seemed to make this more erotic.

Grayson leaned forward, his stomach rubbing her swollen clit even through the layers of his clothes and hers. His large hands wrapped around her sides, his thumbs caressing the bottom curve of her breasts as he closed his mouth over one swollen cloth-covered nipple.

The sudden heat and wetness sizzled pure energy from her nipple straight to her clit, and she cried out as she buried her fingers in Grayson's hair. The silky strands were warm and soft and only added to the sea of sensations her body was trying to process simultaneously.

Grayson sucked hard, and the exquisite friction of her shirt and bra between her breast and his mouth nearly drove her insane.

"Please, Grayson. Stop teasing me." Her voice sounded hoarse and unused.

Grayson only chuckled and switched his attention to the other breast until Katelyn squirmed in the chair and bucked against him, trying to find enough friction to come.

He laughed and arched away from her, staying just out of

reach of her aching clit. "Patience, Seer." He traced his fingers under the hem of her top, gently pushing up the cloth and following the path with kisses that threatened to shatter her sanity.

When he finally dragged the top off over her head, leaving her sitting in her bra and bunched up skirt, the cooler air against her heated body raised goose bumps all over her exposed skin.

"Red lace." His voice held a reverent note as he stared down at her as if she were a priceless piece of art. "Beautiful cloth, but you would look much better bare."

He slipped his index finger under the front hook of her bra, and with one simple movement, popped the clasp open and spread the cloth away from her as though opening a long-awaited present.

"I didn't think the women here wore bras." Her voice was husky and low. "How did you get so good at that?"

His smile was predatory. "A man must learn all manner of useful skills so he is prepared for any situation."

Grayson's eyes darkened until the amethyst appeared nearly black.

He cupped her breasts in his large palms, and all her thoughts scattered. Her entire body had become an erogenous zone, and Grayson's firm caresses tightened the vortex of need swirling inside her and she bit her lip to keep from crying out.

He gently pinched her nipples, and her clit throbbed and pulsed as her breath backed up in her lungs. Her head thrashed back and forth as she silently begged him for more, unable to make her body work enough to ask.

He pressed his body against hers, bringing his waist snug against her aching clit. Then his mouth closed over her right breast while he pulled and kneaded the nipple of the other.

The storm inside her howled its fury, and her insides tightened until she thought she would snap from the pressure.

Grayson gently scraped his teeth over her sensitive peak, and she exploded.

A surge of energy flooded through her, snaking along every nerve ending.

Almost as if she were outside herself, she was still aware of Grayson sucking and licking her breasts and grinding himself against her aching slit. She rode the wave of sensations until her awareness merged with her body once more.

She found herself close to another orgasm, and tried to suck air into her lungs to slow the rapidly swirling sensations. Her fingers were still buried in his hair, and she gently pulled his face away from her, the loss of friction making her cry out.

His gaze again locked with hers, his expression dark and dangerous—but with passion, not with anger.

Her chest rose and fell as she sucked in breath after breath, trying to get her body to equalize. And yet every inch of her wanted Grayson to continue pleasuring her and never stop.

His hand still rested on her thigh over her skirt, and she reached down to grab his fingers in hers. She guided his hand under her skirt and laid it against the crotch of her panties.

"I'll give you as much as you let me, Seer." He slipped one finger under the cloth to gently trace her opening. He groaned and clenched his jaw as though fighting for restraint. "You are so slick and wet for me, Katelyn." He traced her some more, and then a feral smile curved his lips. "You still have your curls. In our shared vision I had imagined you bare."

She opened her mouth to deny that she was slick and wet for him, but she couldn't bring herself to say the words.

Grayson traced her swollen folds and dipped inside her slick slit to probe and explore.

Katelyn couldn't look away, her gaze was locked with Grayson's.

Without breaking eye contact, Grayson pulled the lacy

panties downward, and Katelyn lifted her hips to let him slide them over her legs.

When she sat back against the chair with only her skirt between her and the chair, she felt wicked and erotic. In invitation, she opened her thighs as far as they would go.

His gaze seared into hers as he dipped one long finger inside her.

Her internal muscles gripped him, and she tried to arch her hips to take more of him, but his other hand anchored her to the chair.

Grayson slid another thick finger into her.

Katelyn whimpered as he finger-fucked her in long, sure strokes. She fisted her hands into the folds of her skirt that bunched beside her in the chair as she drowned in Grayson's intense gaze. The vortex inside her tightened again, and she panted as she neared the brink.

Grayson withdrew his fingers, pulling a near sob from Katelyn's lips. Before she could object, he traced her slit, evenly distributing her moisture from her ass to her clit. He teased her swollen nub only enough to keep her drowning in arousal, but not enough to push her over the edge.

His gaze seared into her, and her logical mind wanted to rebel and wrest away control, but her body seemed to enjoyed the suspense of letting him do whatever he wanted. He pushed her skirt up to her waist and then dropped his gaze to look at her naked pussy.

Katelyn was astonished to feel exposed and vulnerable. She usually wasn't shy in this type of situation, but Grayson's hungry gaze nearly incinerated her on the spot.

He held her thighs wide with his hands and looked his fill. "Beautiful . . . ." The words were a rumbled whisper, and when he threaded his hands through closely trimmed curls on her mons, she gasped at the feathery light sensation—so different from the earlier pressure he had applied inside her and along her slit. "Klatch women stay shaved, as do most of the Earth women I have seen." He grinned up at her. "I love your beautiful red curls, Katelyn."

Heat burned into her chest and neck, and she was horrified to realize he'd made her blush. She tried to close her legs and push down her skirt, but he was still between her legs, his fingers feathering over her.

He leaned forward, trapping her body against the chair and his hand against her slit. "Don't be embarrassed, my enchanting Seer. You've nothing to be ashamed of at all." He captured her lips as if they were his to possess and control.

Katelyn tried to take control of the kiss, but he refused to relinquish to her. Instead, he slipped his tongue between her lips and brazenly explored her mouth.

He traced her slit and then simultaneously teased both her anus and her clit with the tips of his thick fingers.

Katelyn gasped, and Grayson swallowed the sound. No one had ever played with her ass before, and she was shocked to find it erotic and pleasurable.

He began a teasing stroke, dipping just inside her and then pulling back. She arched her hips, begging for more, and he obliged her, entering her farther each time until the flat of his hand slapped against her at the apex of each thrust.

The intensity of their kiss and Grayson's attentions burned through Katelyn. Her hands fisted in the shoulders of his tunic, keeping him pressed close to her as their tongues explored each other's mouths and his fingers continued to penetrate her.

The soft *whooshing* of wind through the trees and birds singing only increased her pleasure.

Grayson's breathing turned as choppy as her own, and his hips began a thrusting rhythm in time with his probing fingers and her arching hips.

His free hand gripped the hair at Katelyn's nape, capturing her against him and assaulting her with sensations.

The air around them prickled with energy, and Katelyn's entire awareness spiraled tighter and tighter until she knew her body could take no more.

The soft scrape of Grayson's tunic against her engorged nipples, and his rough hand pounding against her swollen labia, fed into the pool of sensations flowing through her until she shattered.

Pleasure and raw energy pulsed through her, singeing along every nerve ending and making her cry out. Distantly she was aware that Grayson had stiffened against her, the vibrations of his low groan rumbling through her to join with the other sensations washing over her.

The scrape of a shoe made them both stiffen, and Katelyn's eyes flew open to see a man with Grayson's coloring and height staring at them—his expression showing both surprise and hunger.

"My apologies. I was looking for Alyssandra. I'll leave you two alone." He turned and disappeared through the doorway.

Mortification threatened to swallow Katelyn whole. She closed her eyes, refusing to look at Grayson. "I just met the king, didn't I?"

6

Aedan sipped his bitter coffee as he scanned the dingy diner. It seemed almost a cliché place to wait for his informant, but cliché meant it had been used before—successfully.

The wallpaper was aged and yellowed, giving no clue as to the original color. Booths with cracked vinyl tops sat in neat rows, while a bored-looking waitress popped her gum and took orders at snail speed. The smell of old, burned grease permeated everything, and Aedan knew his clothes would reek of it.

Six other diners had chosen to overlook the ragged appearance of the place and gamble with their health to order food.

Aedan shook his head at the stupidity of humans.

He had arrived an hour earlier to ensure there were no non-humans here—especially the Klatch royal guards. If they found out the identify of his informant, months of careful work and planning would be ruined in an instant. Apparently, the man had a network of spies in place back on Klatch, and Aedan planned to use them all to the fullest.

Failure wasn't an option.

Sela had made that abundantly clear, and he was still healing from that "discussion." He reached to touch the goose egg on the back of his head where he'd hit the wall, and winced when pain lanced through him like lightning.

Hot anger flowed through his veins, and he ground his teeth. Sela was a beautiful and very dangerous woman—one he had hoped to tame. Her rebuke had been a cold awakening of just how far he still had to go toward that goal.

There had never been a king of the Cunts, but Aedan planned to change that. Sela had kept a figurehead "husband" in place only to help keep an eye on Alyssa until the time for her coming of age was near. When the false ascension plan failed, Sela had wasted no time killing the man.

Aedan planned on being much more than a figurehead.

He was Sela's match in every way—and she would soon realize it when he thwarted the Klatch's plans for the triangle. Then he would rule, at Sela's side, and both Tador and Earth would be his.

The bells over the door jingled, signaling the arrival of Aedan's informant—he hadn't bothered to learn his name, which had seemed to give the man a false sense of security.

The man had the same dark hair and lavender eyes as most of the Klatch, but several hundred years of living had thinned his muscles and streaked his hair with gray. Even the slower aging experienced on Tador eventually took its toll on its inhabitants.

The man nodded to the bored waitress as he said a few words to her Aedan couldn't hear. She popped her gum in answer and ambled off behind the ancient counter.

Impatience made Aedan's heart beat faster and his throat constrict. He might need this man for now, but soon his usefulness would be at an end, and Aedan would enjoy watching him die.

"Sorry I'm late." The man slid into the booth across from Aedan. "I had to avoid the royal guards. They're everywhere on both sides of the *between* since your failed attempt to capture the Seer." His still rugged features scowled as he looked at Aedan.

"Don't worry, we have a plan to take care of the Seer." Aedan clenched his coffee cup, denying the quick urge to smash it over the man's head for the condescending tone and the audacity of questioning a Cunt warrior.

"You'd better." He rested his arms on the tabletop and leaned toward Aedan, keeping his voice low. "The only reason I agreed to help you was to keep this triangle from happening. The new queen is foolish to relinquish part of her power to two mere humans to complete the triangle."

Aedan forced his fingers to relax, and remembered that charm and cunning worked better when dealing with Klatch arrogance. "I totally agree, which is why I'm helping you, remember?"

The waitress approached, and Aedan fell silent, not wanting her to hear his words. Her blond ponytail swung as she slapped an empty cup down in front of the informant and then sloshed steaming coffee into it from a pot she carried in her other hand. She topped off Aedan's without asking, leaning over far enough to give him an unimpeded view down her impressive cleavage. She winked at him—the effect ruined by a loud smack of her gum—and then walked away to flirt with some college boys a few booths away.

When Aedan was sure she wasn't paying attention to him and his booth companion, he continued. "There is still time to stop the triangle, we just have to change our plan now that she's already on Tador."

The informant sipped his coffee and winced, although from the heat or the overbrewed bitterness, Aedan wasn't sure. "You assured me she would never make it to Tador, remember?" He set down his cup and glared across the table at Aedan. "And not only did she make it to Tador, but Prince Grayson was injured in the process. You also assured me no harm would come to the prince!"

"I regret that," Aedan smoothly lied. "However, Grayson charged us when he foolishly tried to save the Seer, and he injured himself. It wasn't anything done by my men."

The informant looked unconvinced, his lips thinned into a hard line. "Maybe we should just concentrate on finding the Healer before the royal family does."

"Waiting until half the triangle is in place—with the queen and the Seer—still weakens the queen's hold on her power and leaves Tador unstable." Aedan picked up his coffee cup and took a drink, ignoring the bitter liquid that slid over his tongue and giving his words a chance to make an impression on the informant. He could tell the minute they hit their mark—the man stiffened in his seat, a deep crease furrowing his brows.

Finally, the man nodded his reluctant agreement. "The royal family has asked that no one mention the triangle to the Seer. They want her to become comfortable on Tador before they tell her what they want of her. We may be able to use that to our advantage when the time is right."

Aedan resisted the urge to smile as satisfaction curled inside his belly. Klatch were almost as easy as humans to manipulate if you understood them. "That's perfect. Let the Seer find out that they want her to give up her entire life and tie herself to a man she's just met, and she'll most likely run straight back to Phoenix."

The informant nodded. "True. She'll need help getting through the portal, but I'll let you know when I have any further information."

Maybe this situation would reverse itself more easily than Aedan thought. He needed quick results if he hoped to achieve his aims with Sela and remain alive.

* * *

The next day, Grayson guided Katelyn outside onto the front steps of the castle and into the midday sunshine. Her fiery hair glinted a thousand hues of molten fire, and her green eyes sparkled with curiosity. All his willpower couldn't keep his gaze from tracing over her luscious body.

She still wore the same green vee-necked shirt that matched her eyes, and Alyssandra had loaned her a pair of blue jeans and some worn riding boots.

Grayson was convinced that each piece of clothing had been specially made for her because each lovingly hugged her generous curves.

Either that or they'd been fashioned to torment *him*. And they were definitely doing their job on that count.

The breeze gently tousled Katelyn's unruly mane of hair, bringing the scent of lavender that always clung to her to infuse his senses. He leaned closer and inhaled.

"Whoa, stalker boy." She flattened a palm against his chest and kept her arm straight to put distance between them. "Hasn't anyone ever told you sniffing a woman is a little out there?" Katelyn's lips curved into a sensual smile, and she seemed more amused than irritated.

"I'm sorry." Chagrin flooded through him, and he stepped back until her arm dropped back to her side. What was it about this woman that made him act like a stag in heat whenever she was close? "You smell of warmed lavender. I couldn't resist." He shrugged and adopted what he hoped was a harmless expression.

She pursed her lips and perched her fists on her hips as she considered him. "The only reason I'm going to let that slide is that I happen to like scents, too. In fact . . ." Katelyn stepped close and leaned in until her nose almost touched the side of his neck. She inhaled, and the motion brought her breasts so close to his chest he could feel her body heat radiating between them.

The majority of the blood in his system rushed due south.

His cock swelled almost painfully inside his breeches, and he internally winced.

Katelyn stepped back, closed her eyes, and exhaled slowly, savoring his scent. "Mmm, you smell like chai and man, which I don't understand, because you didn't have any chai upstairs."

He laughed, easing some of the sharp arousal swimming inside his veins. "Chai? I've never had a woman tell me that before." He couldn't help the self-conscious grin. "I have a supply of chai I keep in my rooms. It's something of a vice, I suppose. One of those Earth drinks we can't seem to make here."

Katelyn's smile widened. "As vices go, that's not a bad one. It's a sexy smell." Her eyes glinted with mischief, and she grabbed his hand, threading her fingers through his. "Are you going to show me around, or are we going to stand here sniffing each other all day?"

This woman amazed him. He thought after Stone had caught them upstairs that she would be embarrassed and hesitant. Granted, the mood had been spoiled, and they had each gone their separate ways to change. But after he'd found some nonsoiled breeches, he'd met her at her chambers, and he had sensed no hesitancy in her at all.

She tugged on his arm, breaking him from his thoughts. "I'm dying to see the fountains I heard from the balcony."

Apparently, Katelyn had come to grips with her stay on another planet and was ready to explore. Grayson loved her infectious energy and optimism and the way she quickly adapted. He couldn't help but laugh. "All right, Seer. I must remind you that this is a sexual society, and public places are utilized differently here than they are on Earth."

Katelyn squeezed his hand and cocked an eyebrow while she mock glared at him. "I'm a big girl, *Prince* Grayson. I won't faint dead away at the sight of people having sex."

He shook his head even as he realized he enjoyed their

friendly banter. "Fair enough. I just didn't want you to be surprised."

She stepped close and pressed a quick kiss to his lips before moving away so quickly he thought he might have imagined it—except for the warmth still burning his lips. "It takes a lot to surprise me. Although I could have used that warning yesterday before 'meeting' the king like I did."

On Tador it wasn't uncommon to come upon couples or even groups engaged in sex several times throughout the day. Thankfully, Stone must have realized that Katelyn was embarrassed by his sudden entrance, and he had left quickly.

"I apologize," Grayson said. "We often forget that the humans we interact with aren't used to the same degree of openness our society displays."

"No worries. I'll be prepared next time."

Grayson's cock surged to life at the mention of "next time," and Katelyn smiled as though she'd read his mind. Most likely she'd just seen the immediately larger bulge in his breeches.

"Down, boy." Katelyn glanced at Grayson's crotch and tsked. "Right now I want that tour. But I'm not done with you." She glanced up at Grayson as if she hadn't just carried on a dialogue with his aching erection. "Are you ready?" Her voice was all innocence and curiosity, catching him off guard yet again.

He cleared his throat, hoping his voice wouldn't crack and betray his struggle with his hormones. "This way, Seer."

Katelyn smiled to herself as she allowed Grayson to lead her down the stairs and toward the main fountain. She gasped when they rounded the side wall of the castle and the fountain came into view.

The fountain was three levels high, the top two tiers respectively smaller than the tier below it. The footprint of the fountain seemed to be as big as a single family home back in Phoenix.

The entire structure was made of the same snowy white *balda* stone as nearly everything else on the planet. Water geysered out of the top and then frothed over, forming two waterfalls on the lower levels, which created seemingly private rendezvous places. Places the natives were taking full advantage of.

Several Klatch splashed and played in the sparkling blue water, some naked and some dressed, the cloth on those who wore clothing nearly transparent from the water. Off to the right were the baths, where Grayson had promised to bring Katelyn after her tour, and off to the left were the gardens.

"Wow, this is beautiful. Look at that water." Katelyn rushed forward, dragging him impatiently. She dropped his hand and then leaned over the waist-high white stone rim of the fountain and dipped her arms into the water.

Crisp, cool water surrounded the skin of her arms, and she sighed blissfully as she wiggled her fingers, enjoying the resistance and ripples she caused. She glanced up to see some of the closer Klatch watching her, open curiosity plain in their expressions.

Katelyn smiled and received several smiles in return, but a few moved away from her or toward the other side of the pool. Her smile died on her lips as she watched them, and she wondered if they were just shy of strangers or if there was some other reason they kept their distance.

Grayson stepped up beside her and dipped his hands into the water also. "As the lone redhead here, you do tend to stand out." His voice held a teasing note.

Her brow furrowed as something about Grayson's words seemed off—as though he was holding something back. Very similar to the impression she'd gotten from the queen this morning. She thought about asking him straight out, but realized she had nothing to go on but a few vague impressions.

"Some of them don't seem too happy to see me." A thought lodged in Katelyn's mind and wouldn't let go. "You aren't married or engaged or anything, are you?" She instantly chided herself for such a thought. Most likely Grayson had slept with quite a few of these women and would do so again. It wasn't any of her business, and, really, she didn't care. After all, she didn't want anything more from him than a good time herself.

Her words stopped, but her mind continued to churn. Both Grayson and Alyssa had said that social rules here weren't like those on Earth. However, as much as Katelyn steered clear of Earth relationships, that didn't mean she wanted to break someone else's apart. Her gut tightened as she imagined one of the scantily clad women before them in Grayson's bed.

Grayson's eyes lit with amusement as he studied her before speaking, which only seemed to spiral the conspiracy theory building inside her head. "No, my curious Seer. I am neither married nor betrothed. Yet." He splashed a few droplets of water at her with the back of his hand.

The cool drops hit her neck and chin, stopping the out-of-control spiral of her thoughts, and she chuckled at herself. Then she instantly sobered when the slight pause he had put before the word *yet* registered. Why should that one word arrow straight through her? It wasn't as though she would still be here when he entered into either of those states.

"Were you ready to fight for me, Katelyn?"

A snort of laughter escaped before she could stop it, even though the exotic way he had said her name made her want to sigh like a teenager. "You're pretty cocky, you know that?" She pulled her arms from the water and rubbed her wet hand over her chest and over the back of her neck. The wet slide of her hand felt wonderful against her heated skin, and she momentarily wondered how it would feel to pick up where she and Grayson had left off yesterday—this time inside the large fountain with dozens of other people watching.

Her nipples tightened into hard buds, and her clit throbbed in support of her sudden fantasy.

Katelyn swallowed hard against her own thoughts.

"I've been told many times that I tend to be cocky, but that's one of the things you like about me." He grinned like an unrepentant child, making her laugh.

She pretended to study him critically for a long moment. "Nope, that's not it."

Grayson's lips quirked up at the edges, but he didn't comment.

Splashing sounds from inside the bottom waterfall caught Katelyn's attention, and she turned to see a Klatch woman sandwiched between two well-endowed Klatch men. All three were gloriously naked, water streaming from their bodies, and even through the thin veil of the waterfall Katelyn could make out the ripe curves of the woman and the hardened muscles of both men.

The woman's legs wrapped around the waist of the first man, his large hands cupping her ass as he thrust his impressive cock inside her. The second man stood behind her, pumping his erection deep inside her ass, his hands wrapped around her to pinch and pull her nipples as she moaned out her pleasure.

Katelyn stood, transfixed, unable to break her gaze away from the intimate threesome in front of her. Around her the other Klatch continued to splash and play in the water, and there were even a few others having sex inside the fountain, but for some reason, the three just beyond the waterfall captured her attention.

Her lips parted as her breathing deepened and liquid heat rushed to her labia and breasts, leaving her aching with need.

Grayson stepped close behind her, gently trapping her against the outer wall of the fountain. Heat from his body burned through their clothes and seared into her. He moved her hair aside and rested his chin on her shoulder, just next to her ear. "Do you like watching them, Katelyn?"

She licked her dry lips and nodded.

"If you wished to participate, they would most likely welcome you with open arms. As I said, we are a very open society." The words hung in the air between them for a long moment before he continued. "Or we could enter the pool and continue what we began upstairs yesterday."

Katelyn jumped as both ideas flashed inside her imagination and she forcefully shoved them aside. "I don't think I'm quite ready to have public group sex with total strangers, and Stone's entrance yesterday showed me I wouldn't be ready for the latter either." Her pussy throbbed in direct contradiction to her words, and she squeezed her thighs together to try to relieve the ache.

She turned in Grayson's arms to face him. This position grazed her sensitive nipples against his chest, and she remembered how his hands and mouth had felt on her body this morning. Warm, thick arousal curled inside her, and she glanced up to find Grayson watching her.

This man affected her like no one ever had—except for the queen—but she would examine that later. Right now she needed him inside her. A good sexual release would leave her clearheaded enough to think. After all, it was just like drinking caffeine when you were tired; match the symptom to the treatment. In this case, the treatment happened to be several pleasurable hours with a very naked and willing prince. "I think I'd rather have you show me somewhere more . . . secluded."

Grayson's eyes darkened with passion, and the muscles in his arms tightened on either side of her as he gripped the stone wall of the fountain. He leaned close, his warm breath tickling her lips. His energy vibrated around her—contained violence as though he was having trouble keeping himself in check.

Her gaze dropped to his lips briefly before returning to those intense eyes.

"Do you . . . ride?"

His words slowly registered, and Katelyn's brows furrowed

as she tried to make sense of them in the context of the current topic of discussion. "Ride?" Her voice came out breathless as her already overactive imagination kicked into high gear, providing a very vivid picture of her riding Grayson's thick cock.

His smile was strained as if he knew exactly where her mind had gone. "A horse."

"Oh." *Damn.* Why did that have to come out sounding so disappointed?

Grayson only smiled. "Never fear, Katelyn. I am perfectly willing to accommodate any other type of ride you wish."

7

Rita turned the deadbolt and hooked the chain on her front door before hanging up her keys and placing her purse inside the top drawer of the side table.

The familiar citrus scent of her house surrounded her in its comforting embrace. She toed off her shoes just inside the coat closet as she imagined Katelyn teasing her for being such a creature of habit and order. It was a familiar argument between them, but Rita thrived on organization, even if Katelyn didn't.

Thoughts of Katelyn made her smile as she padded barefoot through the darkened hallway to the kitchen. She already missed her boisterous friend, even though it had been only a few days since she'd run off on a spur-of-the-moment cruise with the hunk who had been haunting the shop last week.

Three days in a row of double shifts at the shop were definitely taking their toll. Exhaustion weighted Rita's limbs and slowed her steps. She knew Katelyn would happily return the favor at the end of the year when Aedan took her on their honeymoon. "It's about time Katelyn spends more than one night with someone," she mused aloud as she poured herself a glass of Pinot Gris.

Katelyn was a terrific woman, one Rita would love to see happy and in a relationship instead of married to her work. Too many years of being seen as different because of her gifts as a Seer had jaded Katelyn and made her friend cynical. Not that Rita really bought into the whole supernatural angle, but even she had to admit that some of the things Katelyn "knew" out of the blue were just plain eerie.

She shuddered as she remembered the night Katelyn had warned Rita that her mother had died—hours before the event. Rita shook her head as the hairs at the back of her neck prickled and stood on end. She still couldn't explain it and preferred not to think about it at all, if she could help it.

Her eyes slid closed as she raised the wineglass to her lips.

A large hand clamped over her shoulder.

Rita jumped, her yelp echoing through her kitchen.

The glass slipped from her fingers and shattered in the bottom of the sink.

She whirled around, her breath catching in her throat until she recognized the pale features and the blond hair that flopped over one brow.

"Aedan! You scared the hell out of me." Her heart still hammered, and a throbbing headache began just behind her eyes as her fight-or-flight response stalled, and she slumped back against the counter.

Aedan stood with his hands held out at his sides, a sheepish expression on his face. "I didn't mean to scare you. I let myself in, and you left the chain off the front door, so I figured you were expecting me."

Rita's brow furrowed, and a stab of unease churned her stomach. "I know I set the chain. I always set the chain." She played back the events inside her head and admitted to herself

that in her exhausted state, she could've forgotten. Even something as second nature to a woman living alone might have fallen
by the wayside when her mind had been on something else.
"You were supposed to come by the shop earlier, weren't you?"

"I got held up, so I figured I'd just drop by here." Aedan
stepped forward and pulled her into his embrace. He kissed the
top of her head and then tucked her head just under his chin,
while his strong arms wrapped around her, enveloping her in
his musky scent.

After a moment, her adrenaline finally thinned, and she relaxed against him. "Well, even though you nearly gave me a
coronary, I'm glad to see you." She punched him lightly in the
shoulder. "It's been a long day."

"Have you heard from your partner yet?"

Something in Aedan's voice stopped her, but the words were
innocent, and she detected nothing in his voice she could put
her finger on to explain her discomfort.

I really need to get some sleep! I'm jumping at shadows.

She mentally shrugged off the uneasy sensation. "No, I
haven't heard one word from her, and I'm assuming that's a
good thing." His body melded against hers, and Rita wished
she could close her eyes and fall asleep where she stood.
"Hopefully, she's having a great time, eating too much, having
lots of sex, and maybe even getting a nice tan."

"I still think it's dangerous for her to disappear with a man
she doesn't know anything about."

Rita leaned back so she could look into Aedan's face.
"You're kidding, right? You've never even met Katelyn. She's a
grown woman and can take care of herself." Her tone edged
into frustration, and Aedan's brow furrowed.

"These double shifts are taking their toll on you, love. I didn't
mean anything by that." He chucked her chin, and she felt foolish for her reaction to his innocent statement. "I'm sure your
friend is protective of you, isn't she?"

Rita laughed as she remembered Katelyn's reaction to her relationship with Aedan—a man she hadn't even met yet. "You're right. I'm sorry." She glanced up at him again. "I'm just hungry and tired . . . and apparently grumpy."

He ran a hand over her hair and grinned. "Don't worry about it, love. Why don't I make you some dinner and then tuck you in—as soon as I clean up the broken glass?"

Rita sighed. "I wish I knew what I did to deserve you so I could do it all over again."

Aedan brushed a gentle kiss over her lips. "I can honestly say I'm with you purely because of who you are, love."

Several hours later, Aedan slipped inside Sela's personal rooms and bowed his head as he waited for Sela to acknowledge him. The guards openly glared at him, their displeasure obvious because he had Sela's favor.

Aedan risked a quick glance toward Sela's large four-poster bed, which would easily sleep ten full-grown men. The imposing, solid-oak frame and double-pillow-top mattresses commanded the center of the room, and, in fact, there were four steps leading up to the bed.

Both the headboard and footboard of Sela's bed had been outfitted with padding as well as various restraints for different types of sex play. Even as often as Aedan had visited this chamber, he had yet to see all the restraints in use. Then again, he had always been the one restrained while groups of humans and Cunts had used him however they wished—no one found themselves inside Sela's inner circle without showing devout obedience. Not that he minded, though he did prefer being dominant.

Only the last three times here had he and Sela been totally alone. Apparently, she had sensed his willingness to indulge her other more private wishes.

"Has your human plaything heard from the Seer?"

Aedan raised his chin to look at Sela, who had just emerged from the bathroom.

She wore a filmy, zebra-striped wrapper and nothing else, her pale pink nipples poking against the cloth, taunting him. Her hair spilled over her shoulders in a straight, glossy flow of white-gold, and her pale blue eyes blazed with intensity.

"No, my queen. She's buying the cover story the Klatch left about Grayson taking the Seer on a cruise." He stepped forward, invading Sela's personal space, deliberately testing his boundaries after his previous punishment. He fisted his hands at his sides to keep from touching her before he was invited—if he acted before invitation, it would only earn him more penance. "However, I think she's becoming suspicious. It hasn't been easy to make her doubt her own reactions. Also, she came home early and nearly caught me searching her office."

Aedan leaned closer and caught the faint hint of jasmine that always clung to Sela. "There was nothing to find we didn't already know. From what I saw on their business operating agreement, the Seer has no family or other business associates except for Rita. I was unable to get close enough to the store to search the Seer's apartment."

Sela leaned forward and nipped Aedan's bottom lip hard enough to draw blood. The sting at his lip and the unexpected violence of the action caused his cock to surge to life. He gently licked at the wound, enjoying the way Sela's eyes darkened with lust.

"What did you tell the human when she caught you?"

The heat of Sela's body taunted him, and he had to force himself to concentrate on answering her. "I convinced her she left the chain off the door and I let myself in." He ground his teeth as he thought of all the time and energy he had wasted on this human. His only consolation was that if he stayed in Sela's favor, he would get to fuck the Seer while Sela plunged the knife into Rita's throat during the ceremonial sacrifice. His cock hardened further at the thought. "Those damned Klatch are everywhere, and at least four shadow Rita at all times. It took me all day to find a hole in their defenses to sneak into her house. There was absolutely no chance to go into the shop—it's guarded like a fortress. It's been very difficult to keep my team from killing the Klatch guard."

Sela's eyes hardened. "No one is to touch those Klatch, do you understand? We need them to think Rita is of no consequence to us. We need them to think our plan lies elsewhere." She stepped closer and brought her face next to Aedan's so she could whisper in his ear. "Can you manage that, Aedan, or should I find someone else who can?"

The sharp pain of Sela's teeth against the tender skin of his ear pulled a groan from him as pre-come pooled at the tip of his cock inside his tight jeans. "Well, Aedan?" Sela literally purred against his ear as she brushed her hard nipples over his chest. "Are you man enough for this task and any others I might have for you?"

He swallowed hard, reminding himself she hadn't given permission to touch her yet. To touch her before that would be a grave and painful error, one that Sela enjoyed taunting him to make. "I can keep my team in check, my queen. I can do anything you ask."

Sela stepped back and traced her red-tipped index finger down Aedan's stomach and over his engorged cock. "Have your informant keep an eye out for any opportunity to get the Seer to return to Earth on her own. Otherwise we will have to take her by force, and that could prove very messy." She cupped him and squeezed hard, her sharp nails digging into his sensitive shaft through the denim.

Aedan gasped. His blood heated, and his balls drew up tight against his body in anticipation of whatever Sela might do next.

"Did you save some of this for me, or did fucking that mousy bitch tonight wear you out?" Sela's voice came out low and dangerous. Aedan hid a smile as he detected what he thought was a note of jealousy.

"Everything I have is for you, my queen." He deliberately used the title, playing to Sela's vanity. "Will you allow me to fulfill your every desire?"

An angry grimace marred her pale features even as her blue eyes darkened with lust. "Everyone out!" Her voice echoed across the room, and the guards who had accompanied Aedan or who routinely stayed inside Sela's chambers left and closed the door behind them. Sela's gaze never wavered from Aedan's.

Aedan resisted a smug smile. He knew Sela would never risk her most secret desires becoming public knowledge. She would not only lose the respect of the male Cunts, but the fear that kept the entire race in line.

"You know what I want," she whispered urgently as though afraid someone would hear even that small admission. "You have until dawn to make me forget all about your failure the other night."

Triumph surged through Aedan's veins. Sela trusted very few with her occasional fantasy. The fact that she wanted this now was a good sign for all his plans. Besides, this was a personal favorite of his as well.

It wasn't often that Sela liked to be dominated in *any* arena. "I promise you, Sela, you won't be disappointed. And you know what I want before dawn."

"I'll never ask you for that—you'll have to take it by force or go without." Her voice had a low, desperate edge to it. He knew Sela hoped he would lose control and take—which had become a contest between them.

"We shall see," he said, finally allowing himself the smug smile. He reached out and grabbed her thin wrap in both hands and yanked hard. The sound of ripping cloth filled the room.

Sela stumbled to her knees as he stripped her bare, but she stubbornly remained silent.

The musky scent of Sela's arousal filled the air around Aedan, and he laughed as he grabbed her by the hair and dragged her toward the bed. "Your body betrays you already, Sela. It knows you like to be treated like the slut you are."

She kicked and fought, but per the rules of her own game, she used no magic, and his physical strength was much greater than hers.

He, on the other hand, was allowed to use any means necessary to achieve his objective—although they both preferred physical force.

Aedan dragged her toward the four short stairs to the bed before he loosened his grip on her hair. Unable to adjust from his sudden release, her head thunked against the carpet as her shoulder hit the wooden bed frame.

Sela growled and lunged forward to bite him.

Aedan sidestepped quickly and backhanded her across the cheek, using all his strength. The sound of flesh hitting flesh filled his ears, and his blood pumped faster. The impact reverberated down his arm, and he nearly came in his pants from the resulting adrenaline rush.

Sela flew backward to land hard against the footboard. She sat slumped, but her eyes fluttered open, which told Aedan she was only stunned.

He took advantage of her disorientation to bend down and grab Sela around the middle, her soft skin a definite temptation.

He knew better than to trust her before she was restrained. He had never dared before—had never braved her wrath and fury but rather enjoyed the illusion of forcing her to submit to him by restraint. In fact, he still had a scar from the first time alone with her. She had bitten his inner thigh—only because he had moved at the last minute so that she missed one of his balls. Other than the fact that Sela agreed not to use magic, there were absolutely no rules in this competition—other than those Aedan had added in their battle of wills.

Aedan draped her over the raised footboard, the one-inch-thick frame hitting right at the top of her thighs where her torso would bend forward. While he held her down with an open palm against the small of her back, he snugged one restraint over her right ankle. A quick tug pulled it tight against the bottom of the bed frame, which locked her foot in place on the floor.

Sela began to stir, finally recovering from the blow. The second she realized he had captured one leg, she began to curse and squirm under him, kicking back with her free leg and bucking against the footboard like an angry bronco. "I'll rip your puny dick off with my teeth, you bastard!"

Aedan waited for her to break her own rule and use magic, but when that blow never came, he smiled grimly. Sela wanted this, but her pride would never allow her to admit it.

Still pressing his palm against the small of her back, Aedan smacked his open palm across her luscious ass, which stopped her cursing and earned him a low moan from Sela.

"You didn't threaten to rip off my cock when I was fucking you senseless a few nights ago, Sela. If I remember correctly, you begged me to come inside you." A perfect red handprint marred her creamy skin, and he smacked the other ass cheek even harder, which made her gasp. The smell of her female musk hung heavy in the air around him.

Taking advantage of her momentary distraction, he leaned his elbow across her lower back, ignoring her thrashing even as she scored deep furrows down the back of his arms with her nails. With his free arm, he wrestled her other foot into the restraint and pulled it tight.

"Bastard!" Sela screamed as she struggled against her bonds, her movements becoming frantic.

Aedan leaned over her, still using the weight of his body to hold her down so he could capture her flailing arms. He pulled them over her head and held both wrists in one of his hands, leaving his other hand free to roam over the soft skin of her back and the sides of her breasts.

Sela continued to struggle underneath him, her breath coming in short gasps, her voice becoming scratchy and hoarse as she continued to scream and curse at him.

Aedan used magic to bind her hands to the bed over her head, and then he grabbed a handful of her golden hair in his fist, yanking hard.

Only a small squeak escaped through Sela's lips as he pulled her head back at an awkward angle. "You know you want this, Sela. You want to beg me. Why don't you push past your pride and just admit it."

Sela spit in his face, which made him laugh at her spunk. "You haven't won yet," she whispered through gritted teeth.

Aedan ran the tip of his tongue down her cheek and then jumped away when she snapped her teeth at him. "I love it when you play rough, Sela. One of these days you'll freely admit that you love being my personal whore."

Sela bucked against her restraints like a wild animal caught in a trap, and Aedan let go of her hair and ignored her struggles.

He calmly walked around the bed to pick up two restraint cuffs, fastened into the headboard, attached to nylon rope that could be winched tighter or looser to meet the needs of any occasion. "I've been looking forward to using these on you ever since they were installed. I can't wait."

Sela collapsed against the bed, gasping for air and staring at him with blatant hatred. "Fuck you, Aedan. You've gone too far this time. At dawn I'll kill you and scatter the body parts around the city."

Aedan shook his head. Sela was a powerful woman, and this was the only way she could allow herself to let go of her control—role-playing and losing herself inside the rules of their agreement. He hoped to use that particular weakness against her and addict her to her secret life as his personal plaything. What a terrific way to keep his queen in check.

"Make no mistake, Sela, you'll scream my name before morning. You always do. And this time you'll beg me to fuck that beautiful ass. You know that's what I want, and you also know you want to give it to me." He snugged the restraints around each of her wrists and then, using a tendril of energy, tightened the winch at the end of the headboard until Sela's body formed an *L*, her torso parallel with the top of the bed but suspended at least six inches above it.

Sela cried out as the tension reached just beyond what was comfortable—her lower body was captured tight against the footboard.

This left her at the perfect height for fucking or anything else Aedan might have in mind. Her breasts hung down invitingly, her tight, pink nipples suspended above the comforter, which would allow him to slide underneath her on the bed, or just to reach around and torture those luscious peaks.

He stepped back to admire his handiwork. Sela's legs were spread in a wide vee, which showed him a tantalizing glimpse of her glistening pink slit and the tight pucker of her ass that begged for his attention.

The two previous times he had played this game with Sela, she had screamed his name on numerous occasions, but he had yet to enter her ass. In fact, when he had first suggested it, she had kicked him in the crotch, leaving him writhing on the floor.

However, because she hadn't killed him, it wasn't too difficult to figure out her secret desires. Sela didn't often let anyone else play dominant, so she had probably never had a cock fill her tight hole. He planned on not only being the first but having her beg him for the honor.

She was an extremely stubborn woman and had so far held out on that count. But he had used their past encounters well and knew her body craved it even if her pride was loathe to admit it. He planned to use her dark desire against her, and tonight he would win.

Aedan unbuttoned and unzipped his jeans, freeing his hard cock with a sigh of relief. He enjoyed the way Sela's entire body tensed as he stepped behind her and rubbed the swollen head of his cock up and down her silky slit.

Sela groaned, and her hands fisted inside her restraints.

Aedan continued his slow, sensual assault, careful not to rub his cock against either her ass or down toward her clit. "Why don't you let yourself fully enjoy tonight, Sela. Tell me what I want to hear right now and I'll spend the entire night fucking you hard in every way you've secretly dreamed of."

As soon as his last words died away, he rubbed himself over her tight ass and smiled as she jerked in response. He pulled away, and Sela's body shuddered, but she remained quiet.

"All right, you leave me no choice but to take what I want. Not your body, but your begging."

He grabbed a handful of Sela's hair as he positioned himself at the entrance to her pussy. A quick, hard thrust fully seated him inside her tight channel while he yanked back on her hair. Her internal muscles milked him, begging him to move, but he gritted his teeth and remained perfectly still. "You like me filling you, don't you? Imagine how it would feel with me moving inside that sweet ass, stretching you wide. After you get used to it, we could even find another man with a big cock so we could both fuck you at once—front and rear."

She squirmed against him, and a soft whimper escaped from her.

Aedan leaned over her and captured her small breasts in his hands as he slowly withdrew and then plunged back inside her. "Say it, Sela." His voice sounded strained, and he nipped the side of her neck with his teeth. "Give us what we both want, or it's going to be a long and frustrating night." He pinched her nipples between his thumbs and fingers, enjoying the way the nubs hardened under his touch. He pulled her petite nipples as he began a punishing rhythm, plunging inside her, his balls slapping against her labia.

Her silky sheath welcomed him with each thrust, her breathing becoming harsh and fast as her internal muscles massaged him seductively, tempting him toward release.

He growled as he pulled out of her with a wet, sucking sound, accompanied by an outraged gasp from Sela.

"What's wrong?" he asked, not really expecting an answer. "Do you want more?" He smacked her ass hard, leaving another full handprint overlapping the last one. The sound of flesh hitting flesh sounded loud in the quiet of the room, as Sela shook her head in denial.

Two fingers traced over her slit and dipped inside her sweet pussy. He carried her juices up to the pink ring of muscle that guarded her tight ass. The tips of his fingers slowly circled the sensitive rim, gently probing the enticing opening.

Sela arched toward him—as much as her position allowed—and he smiled as triumph flowed through him. He slid his cock back inside her pussy as he pushed his index finger inside her ass, slowly stretching her.

A long, low moan broke from Sela, and he pulled out his finger and his cock before sliding them both inside her welcoming channels again.

Aedan set a slow, steady rhythm, stretching her ass wider with each slow thrust.

Small sounds of need spilled from Sela's lips as every movement ratcheted energy through his body, which sizzled between them everywhere their skin touched.

Her tight internal muscles clamped around him, and he forced himself to pull out of her and step away.

"Aedan!" Her head thrashed from side to side, and she renewed her struggles against the restraints. "Damn you!"

"Tell me you want my cock inside your ass, Sela." He teased her anal opening with his fingertip. "Tell me you want me to dominate you, mind and body, and I'll make you come for the rest of the night in ways you've never imagined."

"Fuck you, Aedan. Make me come. Now." Her voice held the imperious note of command it held outside of their game. "I'm calling this off, Aedan. Make me come right now, or you'll wish for death."

"If this is truly over, break our truce and use your magic." He continued to tease her tight pink pucker with his finger and slid just the aching head of his cock inside her pussy.

"Make me stop, Sela. Make me do as you ask, or be honest with yourself and with me and tell me what you truly want."

Soft mewling sounds were spilling from Sela's throat as he teased her mercilessly for several minutes.

"You like anything that rides that fine edge of pleasure. Just think how exquisite it would feel." He slid his finger inside her ass to the knuckle and enjoyed her gasp and groan as her muscles clamped around him. He plunged his cock back inside her pussy, but kept the rhythm slow and his penetration shallow.

"You've ordered me to fuck humans in the ass while you watched. I've seen your reactions and how horny it made you." He continued to tease her body but pulled out any time she neared release. "Tell me what you want, my beautiful little whore. Tell me honestly, and I'll give it to you immediately."

"Shut up! Just make me come, Aedan. I swear you'll pay for this." She bucked as much as she was able inside the restraints, her torso twisting from side to side and both her tight sheaths squeezing him hard from her efforts.

He reached inside his pocket and pulled out something he had brought for just this occasion—nipple clamps. Pulling out of her body, he leaned over her and let her see the shiny metal clips attached by a chain.

"You had better not fucking touch me with those, or I'll

clamp them on your balls, you slimy son of a bitch!" Sela renewed her struggles.

Aedan grabbed another handful of her hair, which slowed her struggles enough for him to close each tight clamp over her erect nipples.

Sela moaned and then stilled as she absorbed the new sensations.

He slid his cock inside her again and teased her ass with his finger while he reached around her to pull gently on the chain attached to the nipple clamps. As her tender flesh pulled and tugged, Sela cried out, and a new rush of moisture coated his cock, making her channel even more slick.

Minutes slid by as he continued his slow assault on her senses, withdrawing if she got too close to release. He remained relentless in his sensual torture until she could barely speak, her voice hoarse and scratchy from screaming and moaning. Both her ass cheeks were bright red from his open palm, and her entire body quivered with suppressed need.

Aedan's cock felt as if it would split open at any moment from the immense pressure of his need. But he had sworn that when he pumped his come inside her tonight, it would be in victory or not at all. She wasn't the only one who could be stubborn.

"Finish this, Sela. You're the strongest woman I know, which is why I want you." He reached around to slowly massage her clit—the first time he had touched the sensitive bud since they had begun.

She jumped from the contact, and her body continued to quiver underneath him as a small whimper sounded deep inside her throat.

"Accept this, ask me for this, and only behind closed doors will I be your dominant. Everywhere else, I will be loyal and obedient to you. It's everything you want. You need only ask for it. Right now."

Tense silence hung between them until, finally, Sela relaxed against her restraints, her head sagging into the vee created by her bound arms. "I want your cock in my ass, Aedan."

The words were so soft, he barely heard them. Elation flowed through his body, and he wasn't about to push his luck by asking her to repeat those words.

Aedan pulled his cock from her pussy and repositioned it at her ass. Her sheath had been so wet he was still coated with her juices. He pushed inside her tight ass in one steady thrust as she stretched to accommodate his girth—until his stomach was flush with her ass.

Sela cried out, the sound scratchy and desperate and ending on a long, low moan. "Fuck me, Aedan."

Her hoarse whisper was all the encouragement he needed. He grabbed her hips in his hands and began to thrust inside her in a steady rhythm, changing the angle as her body relaxed to accept him.

Sela's body was so primed that after only a few more thrusts, she cried out her release, her entire body shuddering, her ass tightening around his cock as internal spasms rocked her.

The pressure inside his own body built to the breaking point until finally he exploded, his come shooting deep inside her sweet ass. He continued to thrust deep, wanting to extend his victory for as long as he could.

Finally, he collapsed against her back, panting, his body still joined with hers.

"Three hours till sunrise." Sela's voice was nothing but a croak, but the words made him smile.

"Don't worry, my queen. I plan to use every minute."

8

Katelyn rode her glossy black mare a few lengths back from Grayson as they traversed some of the most verdant countryside she had ever seen.

After a rocky first few minutes at the stables, during which Grayson had had to remind Katelyn which side of the horse to mount from, she'd picked it back up almost as if she'd never stopped riding. Granted, her ass and thighs would be so sore in the morning she wouldn't be able to get out of bed, but for now, she was in pure heaven!

Several years ago, she remembered driving through Tennessee and thinking there was no more beautiful location in the world.

That was before she came to *this* world.

Vibrant colors in every hue imaginable dotted the landscape in the form of flowers, shrubs, bushes, birds, small animals, lizards, and even fish. The scent of fertile earth and all manner of blooming plants filled Katelyn's senses and lifted her spirits. With every turn of her head, some new sight filled her with delight and wonder.

Paradise. . . .

Home. . . .

She stiffened in her saddle, and wondered where that last thought had come from. This was most definitely not home.

Sure, she enjoyed Grayson's company—and, all public nudity aside, the people here had been kind and generous. However, that didn't mean she could just pick up and leave the life she'd worked so hard to make for herself. Her store, Rita, her apartment . . .

Katelyn racked her brain for a few more minutes for things to add to the list of what she would be leaving behind, but none seemed to come readily to mind.

"Damnit!" Just because she couldn't think of any didn't mean they didn't exist. She was sure there were dozens of other things she could add to her list if she really thought about it.

The sound of her horse's hooves hitting the ground in a steady staccato made a rhythmic counterpoint with Grayson's. He rode only a few feet away, his dark hair brushed back by the wind.

As she looked over, Grayson waved and began to slow his horse. Curious, Katelyn did the same. She followed Grayson, reining her mount until they faced back toward the castle.

She patted her horse's glossy black neck and then glanced up.

Katelyn's breath caught in her throat, and her lips parted in shock.

This castle—she'd seen it before.

More than seen it—she'd created it inside her imagination when she was a child.

The neighborhood parents were reluctant to let their little darlings play with the strange girl down the street (who seemed to know when their pets would die or when their parents were getting divorced), so Katelyn had created her own playmates.

Her parents had supplied her with dolls and toys, and her fertile imagination had filled in the rest.

Several Barbies, Lego people, handsome princes, fun monster sidekicks—and, of course, herself, cast as the heroine, played in literally every room, pantry, and dungeon of the castle before her.

The handsome prince never saved her—she had usually saved him, or they had partnered together to beat an evil wizard or whatever villain her imagination could conjure. No, Katelyn had never allowed herself to be cast as the wimpy girl who needed a boy to save her.

She nearly smiled as she remembered the arguments she'd had over just that issue with her imaginary prince. Her hungry gaze raked over every inch of the castle, allowing the happy, long-gone memories to seep into her like a balm. How many years had it been since she'd even thought about those happy afternoons?

A flag fluttered in the breeze atop the highest tower of the castle, and when the wind whipped it open to reveal the flag design, she gasped and buried her fingers in her horse's mane to keep from toppling from the saddle.

A curved sword crisscrossed a rose on a purple background.

Katelyn's hands grew damp, and she had to concentrate to pull air into her lungs. She remembered drawing that crest everywhere as a child. In fact, several of her teachers had scolded her for scribbling it in the margins of her assignments.

"That can't be. . . ." She said the words out loud, hoping that they would start to compute with her logic. A deep knowing rang inside her, but her analytical side still demanded satisfaction, and doubts began to crack the edges of her confidence.

Did this mean she really was locked in a rubber room somewhere, and this was just another fantasy? Suddenly weary, she allowed her eyes to slip closed.

"Katelyn?" Grayson's warm voice rolled over her, and she

had the urge to wrap herself inside the comfort it offered and stay there. He laid a gentle hand on her arm. "What is it? You look like you're about to pass out."

She opened her eyes and forced her gaze back to the castle to each familiar turret, brick, and window. A lump of emotion clogged her throat, and she swallowed hard before speaking. "You grew up here, living inside the castle, right?"

"Yes, I was born inside the castle. Why?" Grayson's voice held concern and something softer she couldn't pinpoint and didn't have the energy to decipher just now.

The gentle breeze toyed with the flag as if mocking her, and her gaze was drawn to the small white tower beside it: a squat, round room with two slitted windows and a cone-shaped roof.

That room had been her favorite. Whenever real life had made her cry or feel like an outcast, she had retreated to her bedroom and then let her imagination transport her to that room. The room where she would usually find her prince play-mate.

She studied Grayson and let out a small breath of relief as she decided he couldn't have been her imaginary playmate. His features were too different, even if she allowed for his growth into a man. Besides, it was the eyes of that young boy she would never forget. It surprised her to remember that his eyes were purple like nearly everyone she had met here. But whereas Grayson's eyes looked like melted amethyst, her young prince's eyes had been so dark purple they appeared nearly black.

A small laugh escaped her. Now she was chasing ghosts. She returned her gaze to the tower and pictured the interior in which she had spent so much time.

When she had looked out the windows, she could see for miles. There used to be a small cot inside that her prince play-mate had padded with goose-down comforters and pillows and silky, soft sheets. On the opposite side of the rounded room had sat a small table and two chairs where they would share snacks or just glance out the window and talk about their dreams.

They would talk for hours, and he would tell her that one day she would have to let him rescue her. Then she would laugh, and usually punch him in the shoulder, reminding him that women didn't need rescuing, that they only needed a good friend to be there for them when they were sad. Katelyn started as she realized her beliefs about men had begun even earlier than she'd thought.

The vivid memories burned through her, and thick emotion tightened her chest as if a giant hand were squeezing her heart.

"That room—the round one with the cone roof." Her voice sounded strained, and she swallowed hard to chase back the emotions that still assaulted her. "Does it have a large wooden door held together with black metal?"

Grayson's dark brows drew together, and he leaned forward in the saddle, the leather creaking softly with the effort. "Yes. How did you know that?"

Katelyn shook her head. She had expected the answer and could picture the room perfectly in her mind's eye. "Next to the cot, is there also a large chest of drawers with peeling paint, and if you shove it to one side, there is a passageway small enough for a child that leads into the nurse maid's room?"

Grayson looked as if she'd slapped him. "Only Ryan, Stone, and I—" His features clouded, and then he laughed, startling her. "Of course. I forgot for a minute that you are a Seer."

She opened her mouth to tell him she hadn't seen the room in a vision and then stopped before the words could escape. How did she really know her childhood fantasies hadn't been elaborate visions? She had already ruled out the possibility that Grayson was the prince she had met and played with, and she knew it wasn't King Stone. Once she ruled out Ryan, she would know her imagination was playing tricks on her.

After all, even as she'd closed her eyes and lived out stories and wonderful afternoons inside her mind, she had known that when she returned to the real world, she would be sitting inside her room in Phoenix.

She wasn't insane—she'd only been a lonely child who had invented a world as a way of coping. Is that what she had done now?

"Do you often see visions of the past?" Grayson's softly spoken words startled Katelyn and her body jerked in reaction, making her horse neigh and shift from foot to foot. "Or are most of yours from the future?"

It took her a minute for the meaning of Grayson's words to penetrate her consciousness before she could reply. "Either or both, depending on the energy I receive from those around me or messages of things I need to see to understand something."

She pulled up her childhood visions inside her mind and tried to remember how they felt—if the sensations reminded her of a possible happening or a true vision of something that had happened. However, time had gilded those cherished memories around the edges, and the only sensations associated with them were happiness, security, and warmth.

Grayson reached back into his saddlebags and pulled out a Milky Way bar and a water skin. "I came prepared, in case you had any visions on this trip." He smiled as he passed her the candy and the water. "The guards who cleaned up your shop after the attack found your stash." The fact that he had remembered touched her.

"Thank you." She raised her face to him. "I have something of an addiction when it comes to these things."

"I noticed." He chuckled. "And not to get anyone in trouble, but Rita tends to raid your candy drawer as well."

Katelyn clutched the candy bar to her chest and laughed. "I *thought* I was going through these pretty fast. I can't believe that Rita—anal, everything-in-its-place Rita—snags my chocolate." A smile bloomed over her face, lightening her mood along with it. "Wait till I get back!"

A quick flash of disappointment flowed across Grayson's face before he hid it. Katelyn's own smile faded as she watched him.

Disappointment flowed through her as well at the thought of leaving this place, but she shoved it aside, reminding herself that she had worked hard for her life and couldn't give it up so easily. "How about the rest of that tour?" She pasted a bright smile on her face.

"Of course." He grinned, turning his face from handsome to devastating.

No fair! That's cheating.

Grayson turned his horse and started back down the path.

Grayson rode for several minutes in silence, wondering how they would finally tell Katelyn about the triangle. He knew she would be angry that they'd hidden it from her, but he also knew if he told her up front or even now, she would run and never get a chance to know him or the planet.

He sighed and shook his head. All he could do now was enjoy his time with her and hope it was enough to influence her future decision. He smiled as Katelyn caught up and pulled her horse alongside his.

Her voice carried to him on the wind, but he couldn't quite make out what she said, so he slowed, and she easily matched his pace.

Her cheeks were flushed with color, and the sun glinted off her waterfall of red hair. He still remembered how soft her lips had been when he had kissed her that morning on the balcony, and he couldn't help but stare at her enticing mouth. When her lips quirked upward into a sardonic smile, he raised his gaze to her eyes as he realized she had been speaking to him and he hadn't heard a word.

"I asked what was down the other path." Katelyn pointed east toward a fork in the road that led to parts of the planet already dead or dying.

Grayson had spent the last several years marveling at how certain areas seemed untouched by the blight and how other areas were completely lifeless. Katelyn must have noticed the thinned foliage off to the east as they rode.

"There's not much left alive that way. It's a gruesome sight." It caused him nearly physical pain every time he went there, since he still remembered how lush and teeming with life it had been just ten years ago before the toll of the planet had weighed so heavily on Queen Annalecia.

"I'd like to see it." Katelyn's calm demeanor gave him no clue as to her mood, but he sensed an underlying resolve of steel in her words. "The queen mentioned this morning that parts of the planet weren't getting all the energy they needed."

Grayson hid his surprise that Alyssandra had revealed even that much. But he supposed as long as Alyssa hadn't mentioned the triangle, it wouldn't hurt to reveal other truths. Maybe the queen had the right idea, giving Katelyn as much information as possible without scaring her. "There really isn't much to see, believe me. The hot springs are up ahead, and I know you must be getting hungry."

"Is there anything dangerous there? In the nonhealthy areas, I mean?"

"No—"

Without waiting for him to finish, Katelyn flashed him a quick smile and then reined her horse around. She rode off toward the fork in the path before heading east.

"Damn stubborn woman." He startled at the note of respect and pride in his voice and then laughed. "Just the way I like it."

He followed but allowed her to set the pace. Not so much as a mosquito lived in the worst sections, so he wasn't worried about her safety. He had hoped to show her the best before introducing her to the worst, but the choice had just been taken out of his hands.

Sooner than he'd expected, the foliage thinned to nearly nothing and became brown and shriveled, as though its life force had literally been sucked out. In essence, it had.

Apparently, the deterioration was spreading faster than even the royal family had thought.

Grave news, indeed. If the triangle wasn't put in place soon, their entire world would die, along with their way of life. A cold fist squeezed Grayson's heart, and he clenched his jaw against a wave of pain.

He and his people were doing everything within their power—he just hoped it would be enough. Everything hinged on the woman before him and some still unnamed Healer to agree to help them and to give up their previous lives and everything they'd ever known.

His horse jumped over the remains of several fallen logs, easily clearing them and landing on the other side. He followed Katelyn as she wound through the increasing destruction.

Every time Grayson traveled here, he expected the stench of decay and rot, but that would have meant that bugs and microscopic organisms still lived here to break down plant and animal matter. No. What remained here were dusty husks that hadn't yet disintegrated and hard-packed earth that had been stripped of all nutrients.

Still, Katelyn continued forward. When the landscape became nothing but barren dust for as far as the eye could see, the Seer slowed and finally stopped.

Grayson brought his horse alongside. His mount pranced nervously, and even when he pulled tight on the reins and patted the glossy black neck, the horse's nostrils flared, and his eyes darted nervously from side to side.

Even the animals sensed the wrongness of this place.

"It's so silent here. It's eerie." Katelyn's voice seemed loud in the hushed quiet, as did the soft snuffling of the horses and the occasional creak of the leather from their saddles.

"As the plants died, the animals moved on to better hunting grounds, until nothing at all remained."

Silence hung between them, heavy and thick, and Grayson left Katelyn to her thoughts. A barren wind ruffled her hair around her shoulders but failed to remove the crease from between her brows. He fisted his hands against the urge to smooth away the line of worry. Somehow, here, in this place, such a caress didn't seem right.

"How long?"

Her quiet voice startled him. "Long?"

"Until the entire planet becomes . . ." she gestured around her, ". . . this." Her voice was edged with a deep pain that surprised him.

He shrugged, a short, choppy motion. "We don't know. The damage seems to be spreading quicker than we expected, but we don't have an exact time frame." Mental pictures of the castle grounds, deteriorated to a lifeless dust bowl, bubbled anger through his veins, and he closed his eyes against the onslaught of emotion.

He had been raised as a warrior, but there was no enemy to fight or evil to banish here, and it left Grayon feeling useless.

True, the Cunts had started this chain of events by kidnapping Princess Alyssandra a quarter of a century ago, but destroying the entire Cunt race—while satisfying in the short term—would not repair the damage to his home world.

"Alyssa said there were things that could be done to reverse this." Katelyn gestured around her. "How quickly before those remedies are in place?"

Grayson couldn't quite meet her open gaze. "We aren't sure. Plans are in progress, but these things take time, and even now the Klatch aren't all in agreement with the actions underway."

"Surely the Klatch would do whatever it took to keep this

place beautiful and pristine. It's their home. I couldn't imagine anyone letting it die, and I've only been here a few days." Katelyn's voice was filled with passion, and that gave Grayson hope.

He bit his tongue against telling her more. Now wasn't the right time. It was still too soon. But hopefully the seed had been planted, and she would come around to the idea soon enough. "Let me show you the areas that are still pristine, and you'll understand the full impact of what we are facing."

She nodded, her eyes still shadowed as she glanced around at the devastation. "I'm ready."

9

Stark images of the desolate countryside she had just left behind burned through Katelyn's thoughts until she shook her head to try to clear them. She was very glad she wasn't driving a car in her current state, or she'd end up driving right off a cliff. Horses definitely had an advantage as a mode of transportation in some cases.

She leaned over the horse's neck, urging the animal to run faster and to put as much distance as possible between her and the ruined paradise they had just left. The sensation of the devastation following her made the hair on the nape of her neck stand at attention. Most likely it was her own confused thoughts that followed her.

As the greenery and vibrant colors thickened around her and even encroached on the path, Katelyn slowly began to breathe easier. She could rationalize that this was because there was more oxygen here, due to all the plants, but she knew part of her reaction was due to the strange emotions roiling through her.

Even if this had only been her imaginary play land as a child,

Tador felt like an indelible part of her. The thought of it dying away tore at her emotions and made her chest tight and her eyes burn with unshed tears. Somehow, in just a short time, she felt a close bond with this place she had never experienced anywhere else.

She followed Grayson into a dense patch of foliage and the sight on the other side scattered all her thoughts.

Her horse took a few steps inside the large clearing and then stopped to crop grass as though he had visited this spot many times.

Katelyn looked around, trying to take in everything at once and wishing she had a camera, though she knew a picture could never capture the awe-inspiring beauty that surrounded her.

Thick strands of trees ringed the clearing on three sides, but it was the fourth side that captured her attention. A small mountain of sparkling white *balda* thrust out of the ground until it disappeared behind a covering of vines and clinging ivy liberally scattered with multicolored flowers. No wonder everything in this world was made of the snowy-white rock—it seemed to be the only type of rock on the planet.

A small path wound from the base of the mountain up to several steaming pools that appeared to be etched into the rock but still not manmade. Katelyn found herself standing on the ground but didn't remember dismounting. The sparkling waters drew and held all her attention.

"It's beautiful, isn't it?" Grayson's voice whispered against her ear, and she jumped, since she hadn't heard him approach. His low laugh warmed her, but her gaze remained fixed on the sight before her.

"Breathtaking." The word couldn't begin to do justice to the sight before her, but she was so awed her usually prolific mind couldn't seem to conjure any other words.

Grayson looped his arm around her waist, and she relaxed back against him, his chin resting on her shoulder, leaving the two of them cheek to cheek. A comfortable silence fell between them, and Katelyn just enjoyed his nearness.

Just a few moments earlier, her emotions had churned through her in an exhausting rush because of the deadened piece of the planet she'd seen, but now she felt safe, happy, and content. She wasn't usually a woman who experienced mood swings, but something about this planet and this man had really thrown off her rhythms.

Her gaze tracked around her, letting the pinelike scent of the trees and the clean, fresh scent of the grasses and flowers fill her senses. The seclusion of the clearing was intimate and special, like a hidden retreat. Grayson's strong presence radiated against her aura, leaving a gentle buzz of energy between them.

He pulled back, the short stubble on his jaws chafing against the sensitive skin of her face and neck and leaving her to remember how those rough cheeks felt against the insides of her thighs.

The thought made her smile with definite speculation, and a warm hum of arousal zinged through her body.

"This is one of my favorite places to come to think. I wanted to share it with you because it's also one of the most breathtaking places on the planet."

His unsaid words—*at least for now*—hung between them, and the tension she thought had left her flooded back, tightening her chest and shoulders—her apparent favorite place to hold stress. What was it about this place that made her feel she had to do something to save it? She was only a Seer, not a queen or even one of the natural residents.

She chewed her bottom lip and dropped her gaze to Grayson's chest. Her usual manner of easy confidence seemed to have escaped her all of a sudden, and she missed it. She felt exposed and vulnerable.

Grayson's roughened fingers raised her chin until he captured her gaze with his.

A flash of intensity sparked between them, and Katelyn knew she couldn't look away—and she didn't want to. For the first time, his gaze lost the teasing, sensual quality, and he looked at her with what she somehow knew was a rare glance at the real man beneath the easygoing facade.

She stood on tiptoes to brush her lips over his.

Grayson cupped her cheeks in his large palms and returned her kiss, unhurriedly exploring her mouth as if savoring a delicacy.

His lips were warm and firm, and he tasted male and spicy, a flavor she thought she would never tire of.

She pressed her breasts against his muscled chest, and she fisted her hands in his tunic, enjoying the slow assault on her senses. A slow burn started deep inside her belly and fanned out in every direction.

When Grayson gently pulled away, his hands still cupping her cheeks, their gazes locked. Katelyn was afraid to move—afraid she would break the spell they had somehow fallen into.

"Let me show you the springs before I lose all control and take you right here on the grass." He smiled down at her and brushed his lips over hers once more before dropping her hands and stepping back.

Katelyn blew out a long breath as she allowed her body to adjust to the loss of Grayson's assault on her senses. She sucked her bottom lip into her mouth, enjoying the lingering taste of him on her tongue. "Wow. Do they teach all the men on this planet to kiss like that, or are you just extra gifted?"

Grayson smiled, but it looked strained around the edges. "I haven't kissed any of the men, so I can't really say, but you could definitely give some of the Klatch women a run for their money." He unhooked the saddlebags from his horse and draped them over one of his shoulders.

She laughed and then remembered her intense attraction to the queen this morning. "Thanks. I think."

Grayson captured Katelyn's small hand in his, making her feel petite, and because she'd been five-foot-nine since the sixth grade, the feeling was something she had rarely experienced.

Grayson raised her fingers to his lips and brushed a gentle kiss over her knuckles. "Shall we begin?"

Katelyn only nodded and allowed herself to be led toward the path. As they neared the base of the mountain, she was surprised to find several couples or small groups, as well as a few lone Klatch, already utilitizing the pools. The people were still far enough away that Katelyn couldn't quite make out individual features or even see what they were doing—but she had a pretty good idea.

She held Grayson's hand, trusting his lead while she tried to look everywhere at once. The path beneath her feet was covered with thick green grass that had been trampled a bit by foot traffic. She glanced down; white rock was visible through the grass blades, which confirmed her initial assumption, that the mountain was made of solid *balda*. She wasn't sure how the grass grew out of solid stone, but she admitted she was no botanist.

Everything glittered white and pink on the mountain ahead of them. If she didn't take the texture of the sides of the mountain into account, it seemed as if the entire thing were made of pristine snow with pink jewels sprinkled in. Phoenix didn't get a lot of snow, but she had visited Flagstaff or Colorado enough times to see snow up close and personal—or at least as up close and personal as a desert dweller would want to get.

As Grayson and Katelyn neared the base of the mountain, the grass disappeared, leaving a path of only smooth, timeworn *balda*. It was easy to imagine several generations of Klatch walking between the pools, slowly wearing down the path into the mountain rather than chiseling it out.

Grayson led her silently, as though he sensed her need to steep herself in the beauty of this place after the desolate wasteland she had seen earlier. They followed the winding road for several minutes before they came even with the first of the steaming pools of water that dotted the mountain. Each pool looked just big enough for two to four people, but the pools were spaced far enough apart to offer a modicum of privacy.

"Is this natural, or did the Klatch dig these pools?"

"Entirely natural and surprisingly well designed for something that happened through eons of erosion from the hot springs below." He pointed up the path, and as her gaze followed his direction, her mouth dropped open. From this vantage she could see hundreds of similar pools.

"There are thousands of pools all over the mountain," he said, blowing her estimate out of the water, so to speak. "Some are outside, and the Klatch who don't mind, or who even encourage being watched, tend to prefer those."

He didn't need to spell out what these Klatch were doing while allowing themselves to be watched. Two days on the planet were enough to drive that point home to Katelyn. "Some of my favorites are the more concealed caves with their own private pools," he said, "where the pink crystals glow in the dark."

"Glow in the dark?" Katelyn wasn't a geologist, but she knew most crystals reflected and didn't emit light.

"The crystals are conductive, so the crystals outside the mountain collect the sunlight's energy and feed it to the inner crystals, which allows them to glow."

Katelyn wanted to see for herself, but mostly she wanted Grayson alone. The sensual intimacy that had blossomed between them just before their earlier kiss hadn't disappeared, and she found herself wanting to explore the limits of this strange new sensation. "Can you show me your favorite cave with the glowing crystals?"

He smiled and led her forward, deeper into the mountain, skirting dozens more pools. When they reached the end of the path, Grayson led her to the right, down a long tunnel that seemed to curl and twist into the bowels of the mountain. After a dozen steps or so, the path curved to the left, cutting them off from the bright sunshine outside.

The thickness of moisture in the air increased the farther they walked, and the slight tang of sulfur on the back of Katelyn's tongue told her these springs were probably the result of a long-dormant volcano. A faint, pink glow from the crystals in the rock around them allowed them to see the path, but not much beyond. However, Grayson's steps never slowed as he guided her.

A companionable silence fell between them, and neither seemed in any hurry to break it.

Grayson turned sharply right, and she was surprised to see him continue into what she would've sworn was a wall of solid rock.

She stepped behind him into the inky blackness and found herself inside a tight space with solid stone on either side—if the smooth, cool texture against her cheek was any indication. She hadn't ever seen *balda* without the rough deposits of pink crystals running through it—even the furniture had the crystals, though the *balda* furniture had been sanded so it was smooth to the touch.

Maybe this was some other type of rock?

Katelyn's breathing didn't echo around her as she expected it to, which told her that while the crevice was a tight fit for her, it probably opened quite a distance above her. After several minutes of following Grayson inside what appeared to be countless winding, S-shaped curves—like a huge, curly straw—the angles of the walls became gentler and finally widened.

A faint glow emanated from somewhere up ahead, and as she continued to follow Grayson's lead, the glow increased until it resembled soft, flickering candlelight.

Abruptly, they emerged into a large cavern tinged pink by millions of glittering crystals.

An intimate, steaming pool of water sat off to one side, surrounded by fine, white sand that covered every inch of the floor. Katelyn glanced up and then tipped her head back to get a better look. The glittering, pink glow rose so high she couldn't even estimate how tall the roof of this cavern was. Maybe even as tall as the mountain itself.

"Wow again." She turned in a circle, taking in the beautiful sight. The intense sensation that this place was her home thrummed through her, churning her emotions. She shoved them aside and spoke, trying to break this strange closeness that had formed between Grayson and herself. "You really know how to impress a girl. How many women have you charmed, with the help of this out-of-the-way cavern?" She grinned over at him, but her lips became a straight line when she saw the expression on his face.

He had once again dropped the facade he usually wore, and his emotions were raw and real and clearly etched in his eyes. "I've never come here with anyone except Ryan and Stone. It's our private getaway." He seemed almost embarrassed to admit it. "I'm not sure if Stone has even brought Alyssandra here yet."

Katelyn's throat felt tight as shock and confusion churned inside her stomach. She stepped close to him, and her brow furrowed as she studied his face. "Then why bring me here?" Her words sounded harsh and accusing, but Grayson didn't flinch, instead his gaze turned thoughtful, as though he hadn't yet figured out that answer either.

His gaze caught hers, and she found herself unable to move or look away. "I saw how you looked when you saw the devastated section of the planet. Even though this isn't your home world, you grieved for its ruined state." He paused, searching for the right words. "That's the same pain I feel every time I look at the destruction, or think about what's going to happen if our plans to heal the planet aren't successful. Somehow, this place calls to you as it does to us, whether or not you want to admit it."

He sighed and finally broke eye contact, glancing around the cavern. "And since we left, the memory of that awful sight has haunted you. It shows in your eyes, in your expressions, and in everything you say and don't say." He shrugged and looked back at her. "I wanted to show you something to remove the shadow of sadness from your eyes. Something beautiful and special." He gestured around him. "This."

A warm, liquid heat curled around Katelyn's heart along with a small trickle of fear. No man had ever done something for her purely to make her happy or to remove her pain. Not that she had allowed them to.

Leave it to Grayson to slip past her defenses and do something that touched her deeper than she wanted to admit. Men could be such a pain in the ass. "Thank you." Her voice was a mere whisper, but it was enough.

Grayson cupped her cheeks in his large palms as he had in the clearing outside. It was a tender, loving gesture.

Katelyn wanted to be angry at him for presuming that she would want this. But, more than that, she wanted to relax into the sensation and let it seep into her. Almost as if she were caught in a spell, she softened in his arms.

Their eyes locked, and Katelyn saw tenderness and understanding in Grayson's eyes—though she wasn't sure what exactly it was he understood.

He brushed his lips against hers, and her eyes slid closed as if she had no conscious control over them.

Grayson slipped his tongue inside her mouth—sucking, nipping, teasing, tempting. All the while, the roughened pads of his thumbs gently stroked her cheeks. Katelyn's skin heated, and her blood seemed to thicken inside her veins as her body softened against him.

"What do you do to me, Katelyn?" he whispered against her lips. "You're like a drug."

His energy buzzed against hers, and even as lost in the magic of the moment as she was, she gathered her own energy around her like a shield. She had never let another person inside her energy aura, and she honestly didn't know what impact it would have on her if she did. And yet she was tempted.

Grayson's long fingers caressed the nape of her neck, sending shivers of awareness down her spine. His scent, masculine and spicy, surrounded her, infusing her senses even as her heartbeat filled her ears, drowning out the gentle gurgling of the water behind them.

Fear niggled at the edges of Katelyn's awareness. Fear of how right this felt and of how easy it would be to lose herself and drop her emotional and energy shields and merge with this man who made her feel things she didn't want to name.

Her eyes flew open, and her body stiffened against him as she braced herself to pull away.

Grayson's heavy-lidded eyes searched hers, and then another kind of understanding lit his face. He dropped his hands to his sides and stepped back. "My apologies, Seer. I didn't mean to frighten you." His voice was gravelly and low.

Frighten wasn't exactly the word to describe what she had experienced, but his withdrawal would put some distance between them long enough for her to get her emotions under control.

She closed her eyes and took a fortifying breath, rebuilding her composure in quick layers. When her eyes blinked back open, Grayson stood watching her—the mask of his facade firmly in place. "Grayson, I—"

"Katie-Cat? Is that you?"

10

The husky voice sent a fission of recognition through Katelyn, and she turned toward the opening in the rock face through which she and Grayson had entered the cavern.

The man who stood before her was stockier than Grayson or King Stone and built more compactly. He reminded her of a boxer. He stood only a few inches taller than her own five-foot-nine, but he exuded enough confidence and sensuality that no one would ever describe him as "small"—even beside Grayson and Stone.

He shared the same olive skin and dark hair that spilled over his shoulders as the other Klatch, but while his eyes were purplish, they were so dark they almost appeared black, with rich, purple flecks. An angry red scar ran from his right temple down his cheek and to the corner of his lips—a scar he hadn't had when she'd met him as a child.

As soon as he noticed her studying the scar, he tilted his chin, using his waterfall of dark hair to cover the worst of it. That vulnerable gesture made her even more curious about how he'd gotten it.

"Oh, my Goddess. You can't be real." She searched his gaze, and the spark of recognition was unmistakable. "Prince?" she ventured, her voice uncertain as she faced an adult version of her imaginary playmate.

She'd never called him anything but "Prince," and now that he had said her nickname, she recalled he had only used her real name once before dubbing her "Katie-Cat" because of her green eyes.

Suddenly, her imaginary childhood world had become even more real, if that was possible.

Grayson's hand tightened around hers, and she barely noticed as Prince's handsome features lit with joy. The wide smile pulled at the angry scar where it connected with the side of his mouth, but it didn't seem to cause him any discomfort.

Prince rushed forward and pulled her into a hug, twirling her until her feet left the ground, and she had no choice but to join in with his joyous laughter. "I knew no one else could have that mop of red hair and that distinct voice," he said.

She hugged him back as snippets of thousands of happy childhood memories flooded through her mind. For a fleeting instance she braced herself, in case the hot stab of arousal occurred as it had with Grayson and Alyssa. But Prince was warm and solid, and she felt safe and comfortable within his arms—nothing more.

When he finally set her on her feet, he pulled back to look at her but kept his hands loosely at her waist. "Damn, but you've grown up to be a temptress." Prince glanced at Grayson, and Prince's grin widened even as a wave of surprise flowed across his features. He dropped his hands from her waist and pinned her with an affectionate gaze. "You're the Seer? I'll be damned."

Grayson stepped forward, slipping a proprietary arm around Katelyn's waist. He radiated so much jealousy she thought he might whip out his cock and mark his territory on Prince's shoes at any moment.

"Ryan, when did you meet the Seer?" Grayson's voice was stiff and formal, and he was irritating Katelyn with his possessive caveman routine.

Ryan—so he does have a name besides "Prince." Now that Katelyn thought about it, she had never asked his name; she had just dubbed him "Prince" since every imaginary castle had one. She wondered if he was even part of the royal family here.

She pulled away and glared at Grayson. "I'm not a toy to be yanked back and forth, gentlemen."

"Stand down, Gray." Ryan held his hands in front of him as though warding off an attack, but his amusement only seemed to increase at Grayson's protective attitude. "Do you remember when you and Stone began formal schooling before me, and I told you I had a playmate who would meet me in the castle turret?"

Grayson's brow furrowed, and he glanced between Katelyn and Ryan. "We thought you made her up because you weren't old enough to start spell training with us."

Ryan laughed and grabbed Katelyn's hand. "I didn't share her with either of you, because I was mad at you both for leaving and going off to training without me. After all, it wasn't my choice to be born a year later than you two, was it?"

"Wait a minute." Katelyn's head spun with unanswered questions that had no logical answers. "You were my imaginary friend, and I made up the entire castle. I don't understand any of this!" She rubbed her now throbbing temples with her fingertips and wished for a nice strong rum and Diet Coke.

Grayson huffed out a laugh, amused with himself. "That's how you knew what the nurse maid's room looked like." He shook his head, all trace of the Neanderthal protector gone. "Why didn't you tell me it wasn't from a vision?"

She threw up her hands in frustration. "I'm already half convinced I've lost my mind. I didn't want anyone else buying that theory, too." A wave of hair fell into her face, and she brushed it back with an impatient shove.

"Katie-Cat, you're a Seer—you know better than most humans that visions, magic, and everything else are just energy, which can take on any form." The calm matter-of-factness of Ryan's voice reminded her of how he had often spoken to her as a child, and she nearly smiled. "You had to live in a human world that wasn't very accepting of you, if my memory is correct, so you came to visit me and the castle when you needed somewhere that would accept you as you are."

Katelyn closed her eyes and tried to absorb Ryan's words. Her entire life would make much more sense if she could just stop comparing everything to Earth norms, but those norms had been ingrained into her over a lifetime. She sighed. "Great, so because I can't handle Earth intolerance as an adult, I've jetted off to imaginary lands, developed a sudden craving for women, and started having visions about bumping off the royal family." A bitter laugh escaped her lips, and she opened her eyes to see both Grayson and Ryan staring at her.

Grayson's eyes narrowed. "What do you mean, 'bumping off the royal family'? Was that the vision from this morning you didn't tell me about?"

Katelyn sighed and paced away, the scuff of the fine, white sand under her boots loud in the intimate cavern. "It was just a vision. It doesn't mean it *will* happen, just that it could." She paced back, using her arms to make wide hand gestures for emphasis. "And sometimes visions happen exactly the way I saw them, but they don't mean what I originally thought."

Grayson's hands settled over her shoulders, warming her and chasing away her fears that she would see revulsion in his eyes for both her gift and their content. "Tell us what you saw, Seer."

Katelyn turned, trying to ignore her frustration that he'd called her "Seer" in a cold, professional tone rather than as the term of endearment he usually used. She glanced between Grayson and Ryan before taking a deep breath and describing the vision about poisoning the queen.

When she was finished, they both nodded as though taking her words in stride.

Grayson stepped forward and cupped her cheek in his hand, the contact sending sizzling awareness over her skin despite the concern in his tone. "As for your attraction to women—I didn't realize the pull of the planet was affecting you so quickly."

Katelyn winced at Grayson's words. She had hoped they had forgotten about that part of her confession and would stay focused on the vision.

No such luck!

He dropped his hand from her face. "From your words, I assume you have previously never been attracted to women, but since coming here, you are?" Grayson's manner seemed interested and yet relaxed.

Not at all what Katelyn had expected, though heat did burn up her neck and into her cheeks. It wasn't every day she had a calm discussion with two hot men about her sudden bisexual tendencies. This was starting to remind her of the seedy online-dating chats advertised on late-night TV.

She huffed out a breath of frustration that also blew her bangs out of her face. "That's a little embarrassing, you know. Talk about intrusive, not to mention rude." She crossed her arms and glared up at Grayson, hoping he would take the hint.

A sound somewhere between a laugh and a cough came from Ryan, and he grinned when she sent her glare toward him. "Here on Tador, attraction is a perfectly natural thing. Grayson's question wasn't meant to be insensitive . . . for once." His last words, spoken under his breath, earned him a dirty look from Grayson. "That just helps ascertain how the planet is affecting you. Your cravings are actually a clue about what you need and what the planet needs to thrive."

As much as Katelyn hated to admit it, it made sense. Even Earth had an energy coexistence with its inhabitants, whether they realized it or not. Tador seemed to operate under that same principle but on an exponential scale.

She pursed her lips, screwing up her courage. "Just Alyssandra." She gazed around the room—everywhere but at the two men. "Nothing for the lady's maids, just the queen." She shrugged. "Those are the only other women I've met."

Ryan and Grayson exchanged a look that said there was something they weren't telling her.

Frustration and a flash of anger coursed through Katelyn and she gritted her teeth. "Okay." She poked her index fingers toward both of their chests and tilted her chin back to look up at them. "What exactly did that look mean? I have a right to know what's going on here because it pertains to me."

"You're just as bossy as you always were, Katie-Cat." Ryan grinned unapologetically, just like she remembered. "We don't know what it means yet. Usually an attraction to specific people—besides the obvious—means the planet needs something from the two of you, or the two of you need something from it."

"Anyone else?" Grayson's voice was calm and devoid of any emotion, which told Katelyn how much of his true feelings he was hiding behind that cool veneer. For some reason, her answer was important to him, but she wasn't sure why.

"Other than you, you mean?" she shot back.

When Grayson didn't react at all, her irritation mounted.

Ryan cleared his throat gently beside her. "I think what Grayson is so poorly fishing for is if you're attracted to me or the king."

Grayson's lips thinned into a hard line, confirming Ryan's words.

Ah, jealous, are we?

Katelyn mentally shook her head. Grayson was a six-foot-plus walking wet dream, and yet he still had insecurities? She guessed everyone had their own demons to fight. "Well, King Stone is extremely attractive, and I do seem to have a penchant for men with dark hair, olive skin, and purple eyes."

Grayson's eyes hardened, and Katelyn bit back a smile. She shouldn't enjoy baiting him, but after his possessive Neanderthal display earlier, he deserved it. She whirled her finger in the air toward Ryan. "Turn around so I can see the full package and judge your effect on me."

Ryan laughed and complied, posing and running his hands down over his tight ass for her inspection. However, when his profile would've shown her the side of his face marred with the scar he dropped his chin so his shoulder-length hair again slid over his cheek to hide the worst of it.

She wasn't sure why he bothered—even that angry scar didn't detract from his appeal. His compact body was truly a thing of beauty. She would love to see him entirely naked, but it would be more of an appreciation for male beauty than for lust. "I have to say, you grew up to be rather yummy, Prince . . . er . . . Ryan. Especially those biceps." She eyed the impressive forearms and resisted the urge to trace them with her fingers. "But, nope, sorry."

Ryan gave a dramatic sigh. "Lost to the old man, did I? Ah, well, may I say, Katie-Cat, that you have grown into an extremely stunning woman yourself. And if you ever realize what a total and utter ass Grayson is, I shall still be here waiting to save you."

Katelyn's lips quirked at Ryan's teasing tone, and then she glanced toward Grayson, who didn't seem amused. The male ego was a fragile and interesting thing to behold. "Stone and Ryan are perfect male specimens, and all three of you together are a group-sex fantasy waiting to happen, but that gut-deep lust reaction happens only with you and the queen. Does that answer your question?" She frowned and then said under her breath, "Even though it doesn't answer any of mine about why."

Grayson's expression didn't change, but she immediately sensed a change in his energy aura. Almost as though it relaxed with relief.

The two men again exchanged the look that spoke volumes, but this time she sensed confusion instead of an exchange of knowledge.

Good, maybe they aren't intentionally keeping things from me. Maybe they are just as confused as I am.

Grayson nodded toward Ryan, apparently done with their previous conversation. "Anyway, did you need something, Ryan? I hadn't expected anyone to be here today."

Katelyn resisted the urge to punch Grayson in the stomach. Instead, she bit her tongue and let them talk.

Ryan seemed oblivious to Katelyn's irritation. "I didn't realize you wouldn't be alone. I just returned from . . . my trip and wanted to talk with you. Alyssandra told me where you'd gone." He glanced at Katelyn and then back at Grayson. "But I can catch up with you later at the castle."

Katelyn wondered if the slight hesitation had been intentional. And, if so, why would he be reluctant to speak about it in front of her? But, she reminded herself, Ryan's trip was none of her business. "Why don't you two go ahead and catch up?" She smiled over her shoulder at Grayson to let him know she wasn't angry. "I can poke around outside and entertain myself. You can come find me when you're done, and then I can head back to the castle and grab a shower before lunch."

Grayson watched Katelyn disappear through the opening in the rock face and wished Ryan could have waited another hour or so before interrupting them. Katelyn hadn't been frightened by him but by what she was feeling.

"Well, that was interesting." Ryan's eyes tracked Katelyn's

retreating form, too, and Grayson fisted his hands to keep from forcefully changing his friend's line of sight. "I've thought about that feisty little redheaded playmate often over the years. But I never would've guessed she was our Seer."

"You could've told us about her at any point during the past fifteen years, you know."

Ryan shrugged. "She was my memory and mine alone." He grinned. "Or so I thought."

"Didn't you have something to tell me?"

"Yes, but before I do, I just want to make sure you are good to her."

Anger simmered in Grayson's veins, making his heart pound. "It's too late to ask me to switch to the Healer, Ryan." Grayson's tone was low and serious, and he was shocked at how much he meant those words. He couldn't imagine Ryan or any man with Katelyn, and he didn't want to.

Ryan held Grayson's gaze without flinching. "I'm not competing with you, Gray. It would be a bit like tumbling my sister. But I do care for her and would like a chance to know the woman she has become." Ryan broke eye contact to glance down before returning Grayson's gaze. "I still see a lot of that little girl within her. A little girl who was an outcast and set her own boundaries so no one would get too close. Just have a care with her, is all I ask."

At Ryan's sincere tone, Grayson's temper banked and receded. How could he fault Ryan for protecting her? In fact, he would probably think less of his friend if he hadn't. "You have my word. She's a very special woman."

Ryan studied Grayson for a long moment before nodding. "Good." His stance relaxed, and he glanced at the entrance to make sure no one had entered. "Listen, the reason I came looking for you . . . I've had no luck at all finding the Healer, but I did find something very interesting."

Foreboding prickled over Grayson's skin, and he knew whatever Ryan had found was significant. "Tell me."

"I stopped by Rita's shop to see how the guards were getting along and if they've sighted any of the Cunts nearby." Ryan paused dramatically, and Grayson considered wringing his friend's neck. This sense of drama was only entertaining when Grayson was already in the know and Ryan was practicing his timing on someone else.

"And?" Grayson prompted, trying to keep his voice even. If he showed irritation, Ryan would only drag the information out further.

"And the guards heard from an informant that Rita has been dating one of the Cunt warriors and is now thought to be engaged to the man—she showed up wearing a sizable diamond on her finger the next morning."

"Damn. I knew I wasn't going to like this." Grayson sighed. "I wonder if Katelyn knows him or has met him. Most likely Sela put him in place to stay close to Katelyn."

"That was my thought. He also slipped inside Rita's apartment last night and was seen leaving. The team let him go, hoping to find out what he's up to rather than take him out now."

Grayson turned over this new development in his mind. Not only was Rita in danger but also Katelyn. The Cunts were masters of using those you loved against you, and from what Grayson could tell, Katelyn was something of a loner, and Rita seemed to be her only close confidant. The Klatch had to speed up their timetable somehow and hope Katelyn didn't run from the triangle.

"I know what you're thinking, Gray. But she hasn't been here long enough not to bolt if you tell her about Rita or about the triangle. We have to trust the guards to keep Rita safe so we can let Katelyn settle in."

"We have only one more day until her twenty-fourth birthday. She needs to be ready for the coming-of-age ceremony by then." Grayson's cock hardened inside his breeches as he thought about sliding inside Katelyn. She wasn't the queen, so her coming-of-age would be a simple joining with the Klatch of her choice. Grayson planned to be that man and hoped he could tell her before then.

While it was a simple ceremony, Katelyn had already shown an affinity for the energy of Tador, so their lovemaking, combined with that milestone, might have some interesting side effects that couldn't be explained away except with the truth. He sighed and brushed his hair away from his face. "Let's just hope she's ready."

"For all our sakes."

11

Katelyn stepped out into the dark tunnel and turned right, trailing her fingers along the wall so she didn't stumble in the dim, pink glow.

She followed the curve of the wall rather than veering off toward the path she and Grayson had followed on the way in. This new path wound around several pools until it came to an outcropping of rock nearly as tall as Grayson. The rhythmic sounds of waves echoed around her and made her wonder if there was some type of waterfall farther down that was causing the wave effect. Muted swishing sounds she couldn't figure out rent the air, making the mountain sound like it was breathing in time with the waves.

Katelyn's curiosity peaked, and she peered around the side of the rocky outcropping. Her breath caught at the sight before her.

Five people glistened, wet and naked, inside a pool that seemed barely larger than the ones she had already seen—but none of the occupants seemed to mind.

One woman was sandwiched between two muscular men who were obviously having sex with her, even though the water hid everything below their chests. The remaining two men were just as nicely built as Grayson but several years younger, possibly in their early twenties. They were buried to their necks in the water and kissed each other with more passion than she had seen between some male/female couples. They threaded their fingers through each other's thick, dark hair, and the tenderness in their motions made her heart ache.

A slow throb began between her legs, and her nipples tightened.

Katelyn had never seen two men together, and she couldn't look away, now that she had. She assumed from a basic anatomy perspective that, because they were face-to-face, they hadn't had sex yet, and she was surprised to find that she wanted to stay and watch.

Now she understood why she had thought the wave sounds were echoing—each time the men thrust inside the woman from the front and rear, it made the water lap against the sides of the pool. Their labored breathing and low moans were what had sounded like the mountain breathing.

A soft scuff sounded behind her.

Katelyn jumped, a small squeak escaping from her throat as she whirled around.

Grayson stood, smiling down at her, and she had the strange sensation of being caught doing something forbidden. He motioned her to follow him, and he walked softly away from the pool and its five inhabitants. "I didn't mean to startle you. I figured you didn't want them to see you watching, because you stayed out of sight."

"Thanks." Her body still thrummed from even the quick glimpse of the activities in the pool. "I'm going to have to go toy shopping if I stay on this freaking planet much longer."

A crease of confusion and concern formed between Grayson's dark brows. "I've never met anyone who wants children's toys after a voyeuristic experience."

Katelyn allowed herself a huff of laughter. "I didn't mean those kinds of toys. Don't the Klatch have sex toys?"

Understanding lit Grayson's features, along with what Katelyn could only describe as a wolfish grin. "I have seen many such toys on Earth, and some do find their way here. However, because sex is so freely offered here, not many people have need of contenting themselves on their own."

"How's your shoulder?" Katelyn chastised herself for not asking earlier. He'd just been injured a few days ago, he should still be in pain.

Grayson rotated his shoulder and winced only a little. "The dream vision from yesterday gave me quite a bit of healing, as did our stint on the balcony, so it should be fine for a while yet. Maybe you'll give me another chance at setting up a romantic rendezvous a bit later? I'm sure we would both benefit." Grayson's gaze seared into hers, and she found she couldn't look away. His eyes darkened, and a wall of passion and attraction sizzled between them, stealing her breath and making her clit and nipples tingle with anticipation.

"Perhaps you would let me bring you back here this evening, and we can try for a more . . . private encounter?" He smiled, and his gaze slid toward the pool and its five occupants. "Unless you would prefer a more public outing?"

Her cheeks heated, but she only smiled. "I think private is good to start." The thought of having sex with a group or in the midst of a group sent another surge of molten arousal straight to her clit and nearly made her gasp. But for some reason, she didn't want to share Grayson just yet. She had been very glad to see Ryan, even though she was still wrapping her mind around finding her imaginary childhood playmate here. Yet she wanted time alone with Grayson.

Not at all like her to want time alone purely to *be* with a man, sex or no, but this feeling was something she wanted to explore.

Grayson raised her hand to his lips. "Tonight it is, then. Right after dinner. The ride out here is beautiful in the moonlight."

The skin of her forehead and neck grew clammy, and she swayed as her vision grayed around the edges. "Damn! Not now."

She heard Grayson call her name, but then the vision sucked her under, and she found herself inside a large chamber with a thousand flickering candles painting moving designs on the walls.

Her wrists hurt, and when she tried to move them, she found out why. She was tied to an altar on her back, her hands bound tightly over her head. Her knees were bent, and her feet were placed flat against the cold stone of the altar, her thighs spread—and she was entirely naked. Fear burned bright inside her, blossoming into full-blown panic. Her heart galloped, and her breathing grew frantic.

Voices sounded all around her, but they were garbled and made no sense. When she blinked, it took her eyes a minute to adjust—almost as though she had been drugged. When her eyes did focus, she noticed a large triangle painted on the far wall in red.

Her eyes riveted toward the design as something niggled at her memory. She couldn't place it, but she thought she had seen something similar at one time—but this drawing seemed wrong somehow.

The top point had a crude crown painted next to it; the lower right had an eye with a large blade sticking out of it and small drops of blood dripping from the bottom. The lower left had a crudely drawn symbol that resembled a fat teardrop, but where the top point usually ended, both lines continued outward for several inches. Between the two outward lines sat a single blood-red dot. She had no idea what the symbols meant, but when cold dread flowed through her veins, she knew it wasn't good.

The burst of fear and adrenaline had cleared her mind enough so she could look at the rest of her surroundings. She turned her head and, after several tries, lifted it enough to see over her arm and around the room. Dozens of pale blond men and women milled about the room. They were entirely naked, their tight, athletic bodies gleaming softly in the candlelight. Their expressions were hard, their eyes cold and . . . *evil* was the only way she could describe them.

Another altar sat about ten feet away from her with a naked woman strapped to it. Her dark hair seemed familiar somehow, but Katelyn's fuzzy thoughts refused to make sense of them. Then the woman turned her head, her dark eyes boring into Katelyn's.

Katelyn's breath caught inside her throat.

Rita . . .

The betrayal shining inside her friend's gaze cut through Katelyn's heart as if someone stabbed her.

Pain and panic clawed up her throat until they emerged in a strangled scream. She screwed her eyes shut as the strangled cry of pain echoed inside her ears.

"Katelyn? Katelyn!"

Strong arms encircled her and rocked her gently back and forth. Warm lips kissed the top of her head as reality slowly returned.

She blinked her eyes open to see a group of concerned Klatch faces. Most of them were nude or dripping wet—she even recognized a few of the five people she had seen in the pool earlier.

Grayson must have felt her stir because he loosened his grip and turned her chin to face him. "Are you all right?"

She nodded and burrowed against his chest, the dozen eyes of the bystanders making her feel exposed and vulnerable.

Grayson's deep voice rang out through the caverns as he said, "She just had a vision, and they weaken her. She'll be fine." He lifted her, and she kept her face buried against his tunic, one hand fisted into the soft cloth.

"Please, take me back to the castle." The words came out nearly a sob, and she realized that hot tears already coursed down her cheeks, and her throat felt raw.

Grayson cuddled her closer as if comforting a small child and again kissed her hair as he carried her out into the sunlight.

Grayson gently laid Katelyn on the bed inside the room she had woken in earlier that morning. She curled into a ball, cold from the loss of Grayson's body warmth. She sighed gratefully when someone settled a fluffy blanket over her, but she kept her eyes shut tight. Her eyes were puffy and red from the steady stream of tears that had flowed the entire ride back, and her throat was still scratchy and raw.

No vision had ever affected her the way this one had, but she was too worn out to question why.

"Holly, bring some light lunch and let Alyssandra know the Seer and I are back from our morning excursion." Grayson's voice flowed over Katelyn in a comforting cadence, and she wished he would lie beside her. The wish for comfort from a man should have shocked her, but she pushed it aside to think about when her energy returned.

"Yes, Prince Grayson. Right away."

The bed dipped beside her, and then Grayson's hard body settled next to her, and he pulled her tight against him. His large hand gently caressed her cheek and stroked her hair back from her forehead. "Katelyn." A gentle kiss was pressed to her forehead, and she curled into the comfort he offered. "What did you see in your vision?"

She let out a shaky breath and opened her eyes.

Grayson's handsome face filled her line of sight. Concern darkened his eyes, and the beginnings of dark growth shadowed his jaw. A tendril of dark hair had escaped from its tie and hung across his forehead. Her hands were wrapped tight around Grayson's body, or she would've reached out and brushed back the loose hair.

His gaze searched her face, and one roughened thumb traced over her bottom lip in a tender gesture that reminded her of what had happened between them in the cavern before Ryan had shown up.

She licked her dry lips before trying to speak. "I'm not sure why this vision has affected me so badly. I'm sorry."

"You can't help your visions, Katelyn. That's part and parcel of being a Seer, is it not?"

The way he said her name—almost reverently—startled her, but she chalked it up to the mood and her overactive imagination. "I suppose it is. But you carrying me in front of you on your horse the entire way back to the castle with an injured shoulder—all because I have a mental meltdown—*isn't* part of being a Seer."

He laughed, the sound nothing more than a low rumble she felt more than heard through their close contact. "That's because you aren't used to leaning on anyone or relying on anyone besides your friend, Rita. It's time you understood that there are others out there who could care about you if you let them."

At the mention of Rita's name, all the overwhelming emotions from the vision flooded back, but this time she was ready for them. She wasn't sure she totally agreed with Grayson's theory, but right now she didn't have much of a choice. Naked women tied to altars sounded much more of this world than of Earth. Maybe Grayson *could* help.

She took a deep breath for courage and then described the entire vision—the emotions, reactions, and all. When she was finished, her body felt like an empty shell, but the pain, the pressure, and the roiling emotions were also gone.

"What you're describing—at least the layout of the room— sounds like a Cunt version of one of our ascension rituals. However, the symbols you described sound like something mentioned in our queen's archives."

A heavy silence hung between them as Grayson seemed to debate his next words. When he finally spoke, his words were soft, as though he was unsure he should tell her. "In fact, it sounds like one of the options we had considered for regenerating the planet."

Katelyn's mind churned over his words as the picture of herself and Rita tied to altars formed clearly in her memory.

"Don't get me wrong, we don't force anyone to do anything, and the only time anyone is tied up here . . . it's very voluntary and very pleasurable."

Katelyn shivered as the possibilities of his words chased away the previous memory and replaced it with something that made her body ache and want. Too much had happened today, yesterday, and even the other day at her shop. Her emotions were stretched thin, and she only wanted to feel.

Without thinking, she rolled forward, pressing her lips against Grayson's.

His lips were warm and firm, and he threaded his fingers through her hair as he cupped the back of her head.

Her lips parted, and she met his seeking tongue with her own, deepening the kiss as she enjoyed the slow heat that spread through her. He tasted of sweat and spicy man—a taste uniquely Grayson.

She pushed at the comforter until he freed it from under him, also freeing her arms so she could pull him closer and trace the strong muscles of his shoulders and then his jaw.

Prickly stubble scraped her fingertips, and she sighed into Grayson's mouth at the erotic texture.

Her hands found their way under his tunic, tracing the taut muscles and threading through the coarse hairs on his chest that continued down in an enticing line to disappear inside his pants. She followed the line of hair with her fingertips until she traced the waist of his breeches and dipped her fingers inside to find the silky head of his erection already slick with pre-come.

Grayson groaned into her mouth and rolled her over until she lay flat on her back, with him straddling her hips. He pulled off his tunic, baring his golden chest and shoulders, and leaned forward to loom over her, braced on the best set of forearms she had ever seen.

She barely resisted the urge to run her tongue over a bulging vein that ran just next to the muscle all the way down to his wrists.

"You're driving me insane, my little Seer." He helped her up to a sitting position long enough to strip off her top and bra and then crushed her against him to nibble a path down her cheek and lower to her neck.

A wave of erotic shivers flowed through her from his lips all the way to the tips of her toes. Her skin grew sensitive and achy, and the familiar low throbbing began between her thighs.

"Mmmm, you smell of lavender, and you taste like heaven."

He leaned forward slowly until she fell back against the pillows as he continued his way nibbling down her collarbone and to the upper swells of her breasts.

Her head lolled against the pillow as the sensations of his hot mouth on her skin and his hard thighs pressed tight to hers flowed through her. She let her eyes drift closed as she threaded her fingers through his silky hair and his mouth found her breast.

He laved a hot line over one nipple, making her gasp, and then sucked the sensitive tip between his lips as he gently kneaded the round swell of her breast. Each pull of his mouth sent liquid arousal straight to her aching pussy, which was already slick in anticipation.

Grayson leaned back, and she groaned as cool air assaulted her wet breast, pebbling the nipple even further.

Katelyn's hands slipped from Grayson's hair down to his muscled shoulders. When Grayson's mouth closed over her other breast with the same intensity, her nails dug into his flesh. A smug sound deep in his throat reverberated through her breast and into her body, making her squirm with need.

Her hips began to buck but didn't have much room since he still straddled her.

There were too many clothes between them, and she wanted his hot skin against hers. She reached for his trousers, fumbling with the ties.

Grayson caught her hands in his and smiled down at her. "Not yet, my little Seer. Those talented hands of yours would most likely finish me off in a few minutes, and I think we both need more sustenance than that." His voice was full of dark promise, which made her shiver with anticipation.

He lifted her hands over her head, and when he sat back up, she found she couldn't move them.

She waited for panic or fear, but only a dark trickle of excitement rushed through her.

"Trust me, Katelyn." His hot breath feathered against her wet nipple, and she moaned. "I would never hurt you."

Those five words seemed to hold a world of meaning, but before she could study them, Grayson's mouth closed over her breast again, scattering her thoughts. As he laved, licked, and nipped at her, his hands traced and caressed and touched until she felt like he'd explored every exposed inch of her.

When she thrashed wildly against her bonds, words neither of them understood spilling from her lips, he flicked open the button of her jeans and then slowly unzipped them. The sound of metal releasing metal sounded loud in the room, and then he slowly stripped her jeans over her hips, taking her red lace panties with them.

He crawled onto the bed, kneeling between her open thighs. He sat on his haunches and studied her.

She lay totally bare before him, her arms bound over her head, Grayson's possessive gaze roaming over her.

He reached forward to thread his fingers through the close-trimmed, wiry red curls. "I love this." He glanced up again, his gaze tracing up her belly and over her breasts to her face. "You're breathtaking, Katelyn."

She couldn't think of a single thing to say, so she lay quietly and let him look. His gaze said he definitely liked what he saw.

One large finger traced her slit, sliding easily through all the moisture her arousal had created. His jaw tightened, and a small, round circle of moisture stained the front of his trousers where the head of his hard cock sat just behind the waistband.

Katelyn wished she could taste the small pearl of pre-come, but then one large finger caressed her slit again, and her thoughts scattered. Her eyes slid closed as he continued to slowly trace and tease. Her hips rose and fell with the rhythm he set.

He dipped one blunt finger inside her and then ran it forward all the way to the silky underside of her clit before reversing directions and drawing a firm line all the way down to her ass.

She jumped at the sensitive contact and gasped as her eyes flew open. "Goddess, Grayson. Please . . ."

Grayson only smiled and lowered his lips to her navel, where he laid a circle of openmouthed kisses around the small indent.

Katelyn hissed at the intense sensations against her sensitive skin and squirmed under him.

Grayson ignored her, and his mouth dipped lower, nibbling a line down the crease where her thigh met her body.

Katelyn's legs began to shake as he nipped and pleasured every bit of sensitive skin except her clit or her aching pussy. He was going to drive her insane, and she couldn't even concentrate enough to form the words to protest.

Small whimpers fell from her lips, and she thrust her hips up shamelessly into his face, begging for release.

Finally, Grayson lifted her, his large palms cupping each of her ass cheeks as he brought his mouth down on her. He nibbled against her swollen labia and then licked a slow line along the outer crease of her slit, teasing her.

Her hips arched as her stomach muscles bunched and clenched, and Grayson responded by blowing a puff of hot air against her aching flesh.

Katelyn fisted her hands inside her invisible bonds and thrashed against the bed—as much as she was able, with her ass held six inches off the bed and her thighs spread wide, her feet falling over his shoulders.

"I love your scent and your taste."

The dark, sensual words ratcheted her desire, and her entire body began to tremble.

Grayson finally took pity on her and began to feast on her sensitive flesh. His tongue probed between her swollen labia to lave over her aching clit, swirling over the tip and ripping a strangled cry from her throat.

He lapped at her center as if he were a cat licking cream from a bowl, and he sucked on the sensitive lips of her labia until she thought she would scream.

She lost all sense of time and place until her entire focus became Grayson's mouth on her body. He periodically made "mmm" noises or smug grunts of satisfaction when she would gasp, moan, or even scream his name. But as soon as her orgasm would near, he would lighten his touch or change his movements to keep it elusive.

She heard words chanted over and over and finally realized she was speaking them. "Please . . . please . . . please" echoed through her head as her mouth formed the barely whispered words.

Grayson sucked her clit between his lips and teased the slick underside of the sensitive bud with this tongue. He increased the pressure, each pull of his mouth causing an answering wave of lava through her body.

Katelyn's heart raced, and the pounding of her blood thundered through her ears as her climax hit her hard. Every muscle in her body, which had been clenched so tight she thought she might never relax, convulsed and contracted even more as pleasure spurted through her and she screamed her release.

Colors flashed around the room tinged with pink sparkles, and she thought she smelled something burning.

Dimly she was aware of Grayson settling between her thighs, the head of his cock teasing her sensitive opening. She didn't remember him undressing, but right now she didn't care. His hard length sliding inside her was all she wanted at this moment.

Grayson lowered himself over her, the stiff hairs on his chest rasping exquisitely against her sensitized nipples as he captured her lips with his.

His large hands cupped her cheeks in a gesture she was growing to look forward to. His thumbs feathered over her jaw and chin as he slowly explored her mouth.

Her hands traced over his back, and only then did she realize her bonds had been released. His taut muscles bunched and moved under her questing fingertips as he slowly inched inside her tight channel. He was thick—larger than she was used to—

but she was so slick from all the foreplay, there was no discomfort, only an easing of her body as it accommodated his invasion.

Katelyn wrapped her legs around him, arching up to allow him a deeper entry, but Grayson wouldn't be hurried.

He continued to slowly and thoroughly explore her mouth while he slid inside her a little farther with each gentle thrust. His sensuous movements were like nothing Katelyn had ever experienced, and she found they were more erotic than the hard, fast, and quick sex she usually had with her one-night stands. When Grayson's cock was fully seated inside her, he paused for a moment to savor their kiss as the tip of his swollen head bumped deep against her core.

He raised his face to look down at her, and the breath caught in Katelyn's throat at the wonder she saw reflected in Grayson's eyes.

In much the same way, Grayson nearly drowned in Katelyn's green eyes, which had darkened to a forest green, along with her passion. He continued to thrust slowly inside her, enjoying the way her tight channel milked and gripped him with each movement.

The only sounds in the room were the little gasps of needs that escaped from Katelyn every time he filled her, along with the *shush* of the sheets sliding with each movement.

Urgency built between them, their bodies heating with the deliberate pace. Katelyn pulled him down tight against her and captured his lips with hers. Her tongue delved inside his mouth, mimicking the purposeful movements of his hard cock claiming her body.

His balls tightened against his body, but, as if by mutual consent, he and Katelyn both kept the pace steady to draw out this first full joining of their bodies. Grayson pulled back as the familiar pressure built at the base of his cock, his body trembling from the effort expended to keep from pounding inside her.

Katelyn didn't protest, but her lithe body trembled underneath him as well. He stared down into the green depths of her eyes as she tightened impossibly around him. A small whimper spilled from her full lips as her climax caught her and her tight pussy convulsed around him in waves.

Her green gaze burned into his as the pressure at the base of his cock exploded, jetting his essence deep inside her.

12

Awareness returned slowly until Grayson realized he still lay on top of Katelyn, his cock still buried inside her. Not wanting to crush her with his weight, he rolled them both over until she was on top.

She sat up slowly and smiled, her eyes heavy lidded, her movements languid. "Mmmm." Her pink nipples were pebbled and inviting, and Grayson thought if he had any energy left at all, he would lean forward and capture one enticing tip in his mouth.

He laughed at both of them. "Mmmm, indeed. Are you feeling better, Seer?" He threaded his fingers behind his head.

"Almost." She rose up, sliding his cock out of her channel. Then she scooted back until she straddled his knees. Her long fingers closed around his cock, and he hardened again in her hand. His skin was still wet with her juices, and the air was thick with the smell of Katelyn's musky arousal and their lovemaking. "I've been dying to taste you, and I guess this way I get to taste us both."

Grayson's balls tightened at her sensual words, and he

thought he would explode when she lowered her lips over the head of his cock and made anther "mmm" sound deep inside her throat. He fisted the pillow to keep from thrusting inside her mouth.

She licked him as if his cock were covered with chocolate syrup instead of her own juices. "My Goddess, you taste amazing like this, and the whole room smells like sex."

"Katelyn, you're going to kill me."

She laughed with his cock inside her mouth as her tongue swirled over him, and she sucked him hard every time she neared the tip. When she lightly scraped her nails over his balls, he thought he would die.

Grayson couldn't stand it any longer, this woman would make an eunuch hard. He pulled her up, away from his aching cock, and rolled her under him, burying himself deep inside her in one punishing stroke.

She moaned and clamped her thighs around him. "Yes. Hard, Grayson."

He pistoned into her, dimly aware that her fingernails dug into his back as she urged him on. The sounds of flesh slapping against flesh filled the room as he drove himself inside her.

She cried out as she came, and as her internal muscles clenched around him, his essence once again spilled inside her.

Grayson watched Katelyn's retreating form until she disappeared from sight, following the queen.

He could still taste her lips, and the sensation of her soft skin against his burned into his memory. The wonder and the passion inside those enchanting green eyes surprised and humbled him. How many times had countless women looked at him like that and he hadn't noticed because he'd been too intent on his own pleasure?

With Katelyn, everything was different. But why?

Stone clapped him on the shoulder, breaking him out of his

thoughts. "It's only a few hours, and then you can have her back. Surely you can wait that long." The king smiled and glanced down the hallway, where Queen Alyssandra and Katelyn had just disappeared. "I'm surprised you're feeling this much of a pull toward her already. I'll have to check the archives to see if any of the previous princes who participated in the triangle were affected so quickly."

Grayson nearly laughed at his friend's assumption. Grayson and Ryan had practically had to hold Stone back when anyone had come within arm's length of Alyssandra before the ascension ceremony. The future queen always emitted strong hormones as she neared her twenty-fourth birthday. The nearly uncontrollable ardor between Alyssandra and her future king helped ensure a close bond between the future rulers of the planet. In addition to that, Stone had visited Alyssandra in her dreams every night since she was fourteen. The emotional connection they'd built had only strengthened the effect of the hormones.

However, Grayson knew the planet wasn't responsible for his own actions. "I think I'm in bigger trouble than that. It's the woman herself who has bewitched me."

Stone laughed. "I can see that for myself."

Grayson smiled but ignored his friend's jibe. "Did Ryan tell you what he found out on Earth?"

Stone nodded. "The guards will tighten their watch to keep Rita safe, but as soon as Katelyn learns her friend could be in danger, she'll want to leave."

"Which will put *her* in danger. We have to ensure she doesn't find out until she understands what she's up against and won't go alone."

"Good luck with that." Amusement danced in Stone's eyes. "From what Alyssandra tells me, your Katelyn is as much a fireball as my queen."

"My Katelyn. . . ." Grayson liked the way those two words

sounded and wished they were his to say. But the Seer wasn't ready yet to hear the truth, let alone commit to Grayson or any other man.

"I heard the Seer had a breakdown at the hot springs. Was she all right?"

Grayson's jaw tightened. He knew that some of those who had witnessed the aftermath of Katelyn's vision had been among the factions who didn't agree with the triangle. Therefore, it was no surprise that what had happened at the springs would be blown out of proportion and spread around the planet as gossip. "She had a vision. They normally drain her, but this one hit her hard emotionally as well."

Stone's expression clouded. "Did she tell you what it involved?"

"It sounded like a Cunt version of the ascension ceremony, except for the fact that it was Katelyn and her friend Rita tied to the altars naked." He held up his index finger. "Here's where it gets strange. Painted on the wall in the ceremony chamber was a triangle with a crown at the apex, and at the lower-right corner was an eye with a blade through it, dripping blood. But the one I didn't recognize was at the third point—a fat teardrop, the top lines where it would meet at a point continued outward." He demonstrated by crossing his two index fingers. "And there was a dot in between the top lines."

"I'll see if some of the researchers know of such a symbol, but because the crown obviously is for the queen, and the eye is for the Seer, we have to assume that third symbol is for the Healer."

"I thought the same thing. But that gets us no closer to knowing what the vision means." Grayson blew out a long breath. "Or how to protect Katelyn, for that matter."

"Gray, I remember the effects of the planet-induced ardor seemed very real at the time. My reactions subsided to normal levels after the ceremony, thankfully." Stone studied Grayson with concern. "Perhaps that's what you're experiencing with Katelyn."

Grayson paced to the balcony wall, turning his back on his friend and resting his hands on the cool, white *balda*. "This isn't hormones or Tador or even the triangle. It's her." He turned his head as Stone stepped forward to stand beside him. "She's different from anyone I've ever met. And it gets more and more difficult to lie to her, or, more accurately, to keep the truth from her. I'm not sure if I can bear her feelings of betrayal once she finds out."

Stone's dark brows furrowed, and he pursed his lips, deciding what to say. "We already discussed this, and we don't have any choice for now. She's a strong woman, and once she understands why we didn't tell her right off, she'll see reason." He crossed his arms and studied Grayson. "How can you be sure that what you're experiencing isn't Tador pulling the participants of the triangle together and nothing more?"

A gentle breeze ruffled Grayson's long hair as he remembered the righteous anger in Katelyn's expression when the Cunts had stormed into her shop. A smile curved his lips. "I know what you're getting at. There isn't a maid within the castle grounds who hasn't warmed my bed at one time or another, and, come to think of it, that probably goes for several of the outlying villages, too." A fast blur of faces and soft, rounded flesh raced through his mind. "But it was purely the moment of pleasure that drew me, and although I hope I've not done more than dash a few hopes, my attention never lasted for long."

Grayson turned and leaned his hips against the waist-high balcony wall, his hands resting lightly beside him. "Katelyn is different. From the moment I began watching her to see if she was the Seer we sought, she stirred my interest, and it has never waned." The faint scent of lavender that always clung to Katelyn's hair seemed to hang in the air as a welcome reminder of her in his arms.

"You were on the hunt. Your interest never wanes until after you've claimed them." Stone's words hit home, and Grayson didn't refute them. "And because the claiming here is for the triangle, you may not lose interest until after—"

Impatience snapped through Grayson, and he cut off the king in midsentence. "I can't explain why this is so different, but I know it is." He searched his emotions for a way to explain to Stone, to make him understand. "I watched her interact with customers, laugh at a child's knock-knock joke, slip an old man a piece of cake when his wife wasn't looking, and then fight like a warrior when the Cunts attacked us in her shop."

The scenes played over again in his mind as he listed them for Stone, and a tight band of warmth wrapped firmly around his chest.

When Stone remained silent, Grayson looked up, surprised to see a wide smile on the king's face. "What?"

Stone laughed out loud at the question. "Oh, you really are in trouble." He clapped Grayson on the shoulder while his laughter carried away on the breeze. "You respect her. You like her as an actual person. Have you ever gotten to that point with any woman besides your mother?"

Grayson ignored the jibe and thought back over his life. Maybe Stone had a point. All other relationships with women had started as flirtations and ended with sex. They'd never gone any deeper, and in a society where sexual energy was as necessary as food—it hadn't seemed important to find anything more.

After all, he was the Seventh Prince of Klatch. His entire life, he'd known that upon his coming of age, he would be betrothed to a full-blooded princess, and they would have heirs to continue the royal line. He had hoped that, over time, he and his wife would grow to care for one another, but he'd had no illusions about finding true love as Stone and Alyssandra had.

By the time Grayson had come of age, all the eligible

princesses remotely close to his age were either already married to other princes or had died trying to ascend the throne in Alyssandra's place before Alyssa had been recovered. So Grayson had continued as before, enjoying the pleasures offered and moving on.

"I can see it in your face." Stone's voice held an edge of amusement. "I'm right, aren't I?"

Grayson nodded as an unwelcome thought occurred to him. "What if she decides not to stay? To go back to Earth and leave us to find someone else to fulfill the triangle?" A twinge of disappointment and regret snaked through him at the thought. He glanced over in time to see Stone's face dark with recent memories. "You went through this with Alyssandra, didn't you." It wasn't a question.

The queen hadn't learned of her true heritage until just a few months before, and she could very well have refused to attempt the ascension because so many before her had tried and failed. Yet Stone had left the decision up to her, knowing that if she had walked away, he would have been forced to ascend with another woman while his heart stayed with Alyssandra.

Grayson hadn't realized at the time just how difficult the situation had been for his friend.

Stone turned to look out over the balcony as though he couldn't face Grayson for whatever he was about to say. "I don't think I ever told you, but if Alyssandra would've chosen to walk away, I would've gone with her."

Shock jolted Grayson, and he stared at Stone. "You would've doomed your entire home world for the love of one woman?

Stone's steady gaze told Grayson he had meant what he said. "Love has a way of complicating things." He cleared his throat. "Just be careful."

A lead weight settled over Grayson's chest. Stone had lived his life for honor and duty. For him to admit he would've betrayed everything he'd believed in for a woman told Grayson that Stone's warning was very real.

"Why doesn't that make me feel any better?"

Stone clapped Grayson on the back. "Because now you know you may have to make that same decision, and there are no guarantees of the outcome."

Grayson nodded grimly. "I really hate it when you're right."

Katelyn followed Alyssa off the balcony, out through the cavernous hallway, and down a massive spiral staircase. The entire building—walls, floors, ceilings, everything but the doors and the decorations—were made of the same pristine white stone with small lines of pink crystals she had been fascinated with since she'd arrived.

Katelyn had come this way earlier when Grayson had taken her out to the fountains, and again before they'd gone riding, but now that he wasn't there to distract her, she had a moment to appreciate her surroundings.

Her body still hummed from her interlude with Grayson, and now, as she followed the queen, Alyssa's full curves beckoned to Katelyn with every step. Katelyn swallowed hard, afraid her reaction might be visible to the naked eye, but she pushed it aside to concentrate on her surroundings.

"Is the *balda* everywhere on the planet? I've never seen anything like it." Katelyn stepped close to the wall to run her fingers over a seam, which reminded her of rich, pink sapphires. The crystals hummed under her fingertips, warm and alive.

"There's energy here. . . ." Her voice trailed off as she remembered Alyssa's comments about the queen providing the world with energy. This rock might funnel energy through it, like Grayson had said at the cavern, but how did the queen convert sexual energy into usable energy?

Katelyn traced another shiny line and shivered as the crystal's aura thrummed against hers.

"As far as I can tell, the *balda* runs throughout the entire planet. I haven't seen any other kind of rock here at all. It's very much a living part of the planet." Alyssa stepped close beside Katelyn and touched one long finger over the same seam Katelyn had touched. Power surged out in a nearly visible wave toward the queen as if it knew her. "The rock is native to Tador, and the pink crystals are very conductive—as you've already discovered." Alyssa dropped her hand away from the wall, a small smile playing over her lips. "Stone and I are used to our sexual episodes affecting the *balda*, but now we know how strange it is for everyone else to see."

Katelyn's fingers itched to reach out and capture one of Alyssa's beaded braids before delving into the dark, wavy mass of hair below. Instead, she pushed her own hair back from her face, wondering if Alyssa's hair would feel as soft against her palms. "How do your sexual episodes affect the *balda*?"

"Well, the energy we generate is picked up by the *balda*, so there are usually lots of pink sparks and a burning sulfur smell." She smiled. "It definitely keeps things interesting."

"I still don't understand how the rock picks up sexual energy. It's not like it's transmitted through the air or anything."

"Well, I'm not sure of the exact mechanics." Alyssa shrugged, sending her braids dancing. "All I know is that it works. It's one of the ways the planet exchanges energy with its inhabitants. As queen, when I build up sexual energy, I release it to the different parts of the planet that need healing. In return, the planet constantly regenerates all the Klatch people and enhances my natural powers."

"Powers?" Katelyn had seen the woman leak energy when she was angry, but she wondered what other gifts came with being queen.

"I'm still learning everything I can do, but I know I can cause arousal in others, I can manipulate energy, and I can break other's spells." Alyssa worried her bottom lip with her teeth. "I didn't grow up here, so I missed out on the day-to-day training that comes from being a Klatch witch. But I'm trying to catch up the best I can." Her tone held a wistful note.

Katelyn wondered what it was like to wake up one day and find out your entire life to this point had been a lie. Her own parents had died in a car crash when she was seventeen, so she'd been on her own for the last seven years. She found herself envying Alyssa the close-knit family she'd found. In fact, other than Rita, who she saw only at work, Katelyn didn't have any close friends.

She'd been too busy building her business and keeping distance from people who didn't understand her Seer's abilities.

Katelyn closed her eyes and trailed her fingers over the crystals again, letting her senses reach out and join with the throbbing energy they contained. The current readily met hers, merging a bit where their two spheres of power met. Katelyn had the impression it was tasting her—almost sampling her.

Power zinged up her arm like thousands of ants scurrying just under her skin.

She opened her mouth to scream, but the strong current raced to fill every cell in her body with white-hot arousal, which ripped a gasp from her throat instead.

An aching need so intense it was almost painful sliced through her as even each strand of hair had become an erogenous zone.

More and more electricity filled her until she thought her body would break apart into a million pieces.

Katelyn whimpered against the incredible onslaught of sensations, unsure how to make it stop, or even if she wanted it to. The power surging through her rode the thin line between pain and pleasure, and a buzzing awareness zinged along each nerve.

She heard her name, but it sounded strange, as if someone had said it underwater.

As suddenly as they'd come, the sensations stopped, and the

voltage drained out of her, leaving her shaky as her entire body throbbed from the aftereffects.

She opened her eyes to find herself on her back on the floor, with Alyssa staring down at her.

"Katelyn?"

She swallowed hard and licked her dry lips. "I'm all right. That was stupid of me. I just used my aura to brush the planet's, and I guess it liked me."

Alyssa helped Katelyn sit up, and Katelyn closed her eyes and took a moment to let the world and her stomach settle in the upright position before she opened her eyes again.

"I guess it did." The queen rubbed small circles over Katelyn's shoulders. The gesture was most likely meant to be comforting, but it only served to rekindle Katelyn's need. She bit down hard on the inside of her cheek, allowing the pain to chase back some of the ardor.

"Give me a second. . . ." Katelyn closed her eyes again and let out a slow breath. Energy buildups weren't new to her—except on this scale. Whenever she meditated or purposely tried to trigger a vision, she manipulated chi and aura energy. The concepts should remain the same in this situation, as should the solution.

Katelyn pictured a large tube running from her crown chakra, located in the top of her skull, all the way down her spine and deep into the Earth—er, Tador—to ground herself and equalize the energy inside her.

A powerful blast of current slammed into her, knocking her flat on her back again.

Her head hit something soft. After her ears stopped buzzing, she realized she'd fallen into Alyssa's lap.

The flow of power continued, and she felt like a balloon stretching and adjusting to take more and more air. She wondered what would happen when she reached her breaking point.

Icy tendrils of fear crawled down her spine, nearly paralyzing her.

"Katelyn, listen to me." Alyssa's voice sounded far away, and yet the vibrations feathered through Katelyn's body like a sensual caress. "Don't fight the energy. Relax, and I'll help you release it."

The loud buzzing in her ears increased to an almost deafening level, and she thrashed her head from side to side, since that seemed to be the only part of her body she could still control.

"Relax!"

The sharp command pulled her mind back to the surface, and she concentrated on her breathing. One breath in. One breath slowly out.

Her eyes stung as moisture gathered and terror clawed up her throat in thick, raw scrapes.

Too much! I can't . . .

"You have to trust me, Katelyn. I know what's happening, and I know how to relieve it. Let it flow." Alyssa's voice rolled over her like a calming wave, though the vibrations seemed to dance over her skin, making her shiver.

Strong fingers massaged Katelyn's scalp as she relaxed back against Alyssa. The energy curling inside her surged toward the sensation like a cat wanting attention.

Something soft and warm feathered over Katelyn's clit, and she cried out as the power howled for more. She opened her eyes, surprised to find no one in front of her and both Alyssa's hands still massaging her scalp.

Someone touched me. But who?

She expected fear or even outrage, but instead, anticipation burned through her. Another firm stroke against her clit startled her, and her hips arched upward, begging for more.

The phantom strokes became more insistent, and she whimpered as her pussy clenched in frustration, begging to be filled.

Invisible hands plucked her sensitive nipples, sending fresh surges of liquid heat straight to her aching clit, magnifying each stroke against the swollen nub and spiraling her closer to orgasm. She raised her legs, planted both feet against the floor, and let her knees fall open in surrender. Her hips bucked in a timeless rhythm as her vaginal walls clenched in frustration.

"More ... Please ..." Katelyn wasn't sure who or what she begged for, but if she didn't have more, she might die here on the floor with Alyssa's fingers buried in her hair.

All the sensations continued to sear through her—her scalp, her nipples, her clit—and then something slipped between her slick labia, slowly seeking entrance.

Her muscles clamped around the invasion—milking it, capturing it. It didn't fill her like Grayson did, but her muscles tightened around it anyway.

The sensation pressed forward, just under her navel, and all the power gathering inside her exploded outward.

Lights flashed inside her mind, and heat and pleasure scorched through her, branding her.

Someone cried out, and she thought Alyssa's strangled cry joined the first. Energy spiraled through Katelyn, escaping through every pore, and she gasped at the continued assault against her sensitive flesh.

The air around them sizzled and popped, sending an electric tingling across the surface of her skin.

What seemed like several hours later, the world returned to normal. Or, at least, what passed for normal since she'd met Grayson.

Katelyn sighed and took stock. Her body hummed with just the right amount of energy as well as the languorous afterglow of a great orgasm.

The faint smell of burning scented the air, but silence reigned heavy around them. Alyssa's fingers were tangled in Katelyn's hair, but they were still, as though Alyssa was recovering, too.

"How do you feel?" The queen's voice was husky and low,

confirming Katelyn's suspicions that she hadn't been the only one affected.

Katelyn opened her eyes, glad to find that the light didn't make her wince as when she'd woken this morning. Damn— had she only been aware of this strange new existence the last few days? "Good, I think." She swallowed hard, her throat dry. "What the hell happened?" But she was afraid she already knew—especially because of the light show and the burning smell that filled her lungs.

Alyssa cleared her throat as though nervous about how Katelyn would react to her next words. "I should've warned you that traditional techniques to rid yourself of excess energy don't work here." Alyssa brushed a strand of hair out of Katelyn's eyes. "Anytime anyone opens a conduit to the planet— except for myself—the planet thinks you need energy and gives it to you. The Klatch are taught how to regulate the flow from infancy, but those of us who are latecomers have to learn the hard way."

Katelyn sat up carefully. She felt surprisingly good for such an eventful day. "Something . . . touched me." She glanced over her shoulder at Alyssa. "Did you feel anything?"

The queen blushed and chewed her bottom lip before raising her lavender gaze to meet Katelyn's. "Remember how I told you about my gifts? I mentioned that I can control energy, but I didn't get into details."

Katelyn wasn't sure what the queen was trying to tell her. What did controlling energy have to do with the sensation of something or someone touching her?

Unless . . .

Katelyn shook her head. It couldn't be. Even the most accomplished practitioners couldn't use their energy that specifically.

"I'm sorry if I made you uncomfortable." Alyssa suddenly looked very young and unsure of herself. Nothing like the confident queen Katelyn had met this morning. "The quickest way to release the energy was to make you come. And because I hadn't explained everything to you yet . . ."

Understanding flowed through Katelyn, along with warm tendrils of excitement. The beautiful woman in front of her, the one she'd been attracted to since the first moment they'd met, had been the one caressing her clit, her nipples—and delving inside her. It may not have been Alyssa physically touching her, but it only served to make Katelyn curious how Alyssa's actual mouth and hands would feel against her body.

A low throb started deep inside Katelyn's belly that had nothing to do with excess energy from the planet. Her body wanted the queen, and if the flurry of excitement snaking through her was any indication, so did Katelyn herself.

Am I a lesbian? Or bisexual?

She swallowed hard and studied Alyssa. The queen was a beautiful woman, there was no question about it. She had long, dark hair that flowed over her shoulders and accentuated the generous curves and the smooth olive skin. Katelyn's gaze skimmed over Alyssa's heart-shaped face, full lips, and liquid lavender eyes, a few shades lighter than Grayson's. The queen resembled an exotic ancient goddess come to life.

Katelyn couldn't deny the almost magnetic pull she felt toward this woman. But she still wasn't sure what it meant.

Regardless, Alyssa had saved Katelyn from her own folly with the energy, and Katelyn wasn't about to quibble over the method. "I appreciate your help. I'm just . . . coming to terms with everything that's happened since I've been here."

Alyssa nodded, still chewing her bottom lip. "Katelyn, the attraction you feel for me is most likely a result of the planet. Tador recognizes you as . . . a powerful Seer—one who knows how to use energy." She paused, searching for the right words. "You have to remember that this isn't Earth, and sexuality is viewed very differently here. While there are matings for life, and even marriages, there is no real distinction as far as homosexuality—in fact, there is no stigma associated with same-sex liaisons as there are on Earth. Everyone is free to gain sexual sustenance with anyone they wish. And almost anything between consenting adults—even mated or married adults, with the approval of both—is fair game."

The ramifications of Alyssa's words seeped into Katelyn's mind, and she allowed them to churn while she examined them from every angle. She'd never thought of herself as being stifled by Earth's societal sexual mores, but maybe she just hadn't been exposed to the possibilities before. A small knot of societal guilt loosened inside Katelyn's chest and was replaced with the thrill of the forbidden.

She wasn't on Earth right now, and Katelyn had never been one to hide from her true feelings. It was rather liberating to know no one would judge her for following her desires—whatever they might be. Not to mention, she might never get another chance to indulge in them since she didn't see Earth changing to the Klatch system of sex anytime soon. "Thanks, Alyssa. That actually helps."

Alyssa smiled, her face lighting with relief. "I know it's difficult to get used to. In fact, I'm still getting used to my new life. Every now and then I'll wake up expecting to be back in my dingy apartment, whacking off with my showerhead being the high point of my day. I was lucky enough to have Stone visit me in my dreams, but I thought he was just that—a dream."

Katelyn laughed at the showerhead comment, glad she wasn't the only woman who considered the hardware store a great place to shop for sex toys. "I keep forgetting you've been here for only a few months. Even though a lot has happened to me just today, I can't imagine all you went through."

Alyssa shrugged. "We do what we have to do. Oh, I almost forgot. Grayson mentioned you'd had a vision that he thought was a Cunt version of the ascension."

Katelyn shivered as the memories of her vision came back to her in vivid detail. She took a deep breath and described everything to Alyssa as she had to Grayson. When she was finished, Alyssa's lovely face was shadowed with concern.

"I doubt anyone told you, but before I ascended the throne, the Cunts captured me and tried to make me submit to a false ascension, which would've given them control of the planet."

The pain in Alyssa's eyes made Katelyn lay a comforting hand on the queen's arm. "How did you escape?"

A short snort of a laugh issued from Alyssa. "You described those altars perfectly. Uncomfortable as hell, aren't they?" She smiled, but it never reached her eyes. "I used my ability to manipulate energy to cause extreme arousal in all of them long enough for me to escape. I'm just glad someone else came along who knew how to open a portal. I made Stone teach me how to call one as soon as I got back." She waved her hands in the air in front of her. "Anyway, I'm not sure what all the symbols mean. You said you've seen them before. Do you remember where or when?"

Katelyn racked her brain, but the answer stayed stubbornly just beyond her reach. "I can't place it. I just know I've seen it before. Though I don't think it was quite the same, if that makes sense. And I especially didn't like the knife through the eye, for obvious reasons."

"That could be the Cunt twist on the ceremony. But don't worry, our guards are keeping Rita safe, and we'll figure this out."

Katelyn's thoughts turned to her stubborn best friend. "Do you think I could get a message to Rita? I don't want her to worry, you know?"

Alyssa smiled. "I'll get you some writing supplies after the baths."

It was time Katelyn got up off the floor and went to see this strange new world she'd ended up on. Katelyn squared her shoulders and raised her chin. "I don't know about you, but I could really use a shower."

Alyssa's laugh filled the space around them. "I definitely could. You know, I figured we would talk and get more comfortable with each other as we spent more time together. But I guess if the last ten minutes didn't break the ice between us, nothing will."

13

As soon as she stepped into the bathhouse, humid air clung to Katelyn's skin, and the soft rushing of a distant waterfall echoed softly around them.

"We're going to the private baths. I don't think you're ready for the group baths just yet." Alyssa led the way down a long corridor made entirely of the frosty-white *balda*.

"Is there something I'm missing about the group baths? I mean, other than what I would normally assume. . . ." Her voice trailed off as she caught sight of the walls on both sides of them. Erotic paintings of couples and even groups in varying stages of copulation were painted in vivid colors that managed to convey both sensuality and passion. All the participants were naked and uninhibited. There was even a painting of several naked women in a pool pleasuring each other, which reminded her of the two men at the hot springs earlier.

Before she realized it, Katelyn found herself standing in front of the last picture, mesmerized by the erotic images. Her eyes devoured the glistening female curves, taut nipples, and clean-shaven mounds of the obviously close-knit group.

Images of herself and Alyssa inside the pool with a dozen unnamed women flashed through Katelyn's mind.

A wave of energy slapped into her like an open hand, and she gasped even as slick moisture flooded her pussy. Her nipples tightened into hard buds, and her labia ached with arousal. Panic clogged her throat, and her lungs burned until she remembered Alyssa's earlier advice.

Tears stung the backs of her eyes, and she clenched her hands until her fingernails dug into the soft flesh of her palm. She concentrated and relaxed her entire body, muscle by muscle.

Don't fight the energy. . . . She chanted Alyssa's words inside her mind like a mantra.

Finally, after what seemed like an eternity, the panic ebbed as the energy flowed through her almost above her consciousness. The sensation was like nothing she'd ever experienced, like co-existing with a very powerful elemental being. Exhilaration filled every pore of her body as if she were being regenerated from the inside out. "Wow . . ."

"Apparently, because it tasted you and knows you have an affinity for it, the energy of the planet doesn't want to leave you alone." Alyssa laid a comforting hand on Katelyn's shoulder. "It's not so bad. I deal with it every day. You just need to learn how to funnel the excess energy back into the planet, and you'll be fine."

Katelyn tensed, waiting for another energy surge or even a tsunami of lust, but neither came.

Alyssa laughed. "Now that you understand how to channel it, it won't surprise you as often as it has so far."

"Thank the Goddess for that."

"Well, we'd better get you cleaned up before Grayson comes barging in here to steal you back." The queen's voice was soft and almost breathy. She smiled and tipped her head toward the end of the hallway and the waiting baths.

Katelyn kept pace with Alyssa, and a companionable silence fell between them. Thoughts of Grayson later tonight at the hot springs made the energy flowing through Katelyn swirl with pleasure and left a delicious, tingling sensation between her thighs and across her breasts.

Prince Grayson. What was it about him that kept her so fascinated? A mental picture flashed across her mind of her chasing droplets of water down that muscled chest with her tongue. "Do the men ever join you in the baths?"

A knowing smile curved Alyssa's full lips. "After the coming-of-age ceremony, men and women bathe freely together. I don't think it works the same way for humans, but if a Klatch woman is exposed to male essence before her coming of age, it can be dangerous."

"Essence? You mean come?" Katelyn stared at Alyssa in disbelief.

The queen nodded. "Come is imbued with pure energy, so it can overload the woman's system if introduced before she comes of age. It works the same way for men exposed to women's fluids before their coming of age. But the men go through theirs at sixteen."

"Sixteen?" Katelyn stopped short just before an arched doorway. "And the women have to wait until they're twenty-four? What total and complete crap is that?"

"I agree completely."

Katelyn turned toward the sultry voice that came from just through the arched doorway.

A Klatch woman about the same age as Alyssa stood before them. She wasn't nearly as beautiful as Alyssa, but she seemed more exotic somehow. Her dark hair flowed around her until it brushed the ground. Braids were sprinkled throughout, but where Alyssa's braids were beaded with lavender, this woman's beads were multicolored, catching the muted corridor lighting with each movement.

She wore nothing but a gauzy half top like Alyssa's and string bikini underwear. Her coral nipples poked against the thin cloth, and the creamy bottom curves of her breasts were visible just underneath the short top.

Katelyn glanced back at Alyssa, noting that the queen's breasts were fuller and more rounded than the newcomer's.

An urge to reach out and trace the queen's curves—to see if they were as soft and inviting as they looked—gripped Katelyn. She bit down on her lip until the pain chased back the compulsion.

The energy curled inside her howled its fury at her defiance, the maelstrom of electricity making her dizzy.

Beads of sweat broke out on Katelyn's forehead as she swayed from the onslaught until she remembered to relax and let the power flow through her.

"I'm Sasha, the queen's lady's maid." The woman's concerned gaze tracked back and forth between Katelyn and the queen.

Katelyn blew out a slow breath as her equilibrium returned. "Sorry, I still seem to be fighting with some energy." She smiled at Sasha. "It's nice to meet you. I'm Katelyn . . . the Seer."

Understanding and pleasure lit Sasha's expression. "Welcome. It's truly an honor to serve you, Seer." She linked her arm through Katelyn's and Alyssa's and guided them forward into what looked like a changing room.

A curtain hung across the far doorway, which Katelyn assumed led to the baths, as the sounds of the waterfall seemed to emanate from there.

"Seer, would you like me to summon your lady's maid, or shall I see to sustenance for both yourself and the queen?"

Katelyn took her arm back and looked between Alyssa and Sasha. "Sus . . . sustenance? As in, sex?" Slick moisture dampened the insides of her thighs, and a deep ache settled in her pelvis.

Sasha's dark brow furrowed. "Of course." The woman glanced toward the queen, confusion clouding her eyes.

"This is Katelyn's first visit to the baths." Alyssa placed a comforting hand on Katelyn's arm. "You were very patient with me when I first arrived, Sasha. I think Katelyn will need something similar."

Katelyn's nipples hardened to tight buds inside her bra as she remembered the painting of the women in the baths. "No offense to Holly, but I don't think I would be comfortable with her . . . providing sustenance."

Sasha laughed, the comfortable sound instantly relaxing the tight muscles in Katelyn's shoulders. "I understand perfectly, Seer. Holly will take no offense. There has to be a relationship of comfort and trust between a lady's maid and those she serves. It can't be forced."

"That's a relief." Katelyn brushed her hair from her face, tucking it behind her ear. "So why don't you start at the beginning and tell me what's involved in 'sustenance.' "

"Well . . ." Alyssa chewed her bottom lip.

"Allow me, my queen." Sasha smiled at Katelyn. "We'll get you undressed, take you into the baths, shave you, and then ensure you climax to replenish your energy and the bond with the planet." The maid reached out to touch Katelyn's skirt, making Katelyn flinch. "Would you prefer traditional Klatch dress or something slightly less revealing?"

Katelyn's mind was still wrapping around the maid ensuring she climaxed as part of the bath, but Sasha's question brought her back to the present. "Uh . . ." She looked at the queen's half top and boy shorts and then shook her head. "I don't think I can quite pull that off. I'd probably prefer less revealing."

"No problem at all." Sasha stepped forward and lifted the hem of Katelyn's shirt.

After a moment of hesitation, Katelyn raised her arms and allowed the maid to pull her shirt over her head, leaving her standing in her red lace bra and her skirt. Katelyn glanced over at Alyssa in time to see the queen step out of her boy shorts and drop them on the ground next to her already discarded half top.

Katelyn's gaze locked on to the queen's supple form. Alyssa's body consisted of generous hourglass curves and smooth olive skin. Her dark hair flowed around her shoulders, accentuating the proud nipples that jutted out from dusky areolaes. Just below the taper of her waist, the swell of her hips brought Katelyn's attention to Alyssa's smoothly shaven mound and the small pink hood of her already swollen clit peeking from between her labia.

Katelyn's own clit swelled in response, and her pulse hammered as anticipation curled inside her.

Sasha distracted her by yanking down her skirt over her thighs until it pooled around her feet. The maid knelt and slipped off Katelyn's shoes and then reached up to hook her fingers in the sides of Katelyn's underwear.

Before Katelyn could open her mouth to object, the maid whisked down the underwear, baring Katelyn to both women's gazes.

Alyssa gasped, and Katelyn looked up to see the queen's gaze locked on to Katelyn's close-trimmed pubic hair. "Red. It's beautiful."

Heat rushed into Katelyn's neck and cheeks as she realized what Alyssa meant. "Natural redhead. I know from the paintings, the style here is most likely shaved, but I've never felt quite comfortable going totally bare." *Besides, Gayson liked it.* Her cheeks burned as she realized his opinion mattered—even about this.

Alyssa smiled. "Whatever makes you comfortable, Katelyn."

Not sure how to respond, Katelyn unhooked her bra and let the straps slide down her arms to the floor.

Both Sasha and the queen studied her openly, their hungry gazes making her feel enticing and beautiful.

"How about that bath?" Katelyn's voice wavered, and she cleared her throat in an attempt to muster more confidence. Hadn't she said the other day that she wanted some mind-blowing, no-strings-attached sex? She hadn't specifically mentioned a man, though that had been implied, given her inclinations at the time. Now it seemed the universe was providing in abundance. Words had power and often manifested with definite irony.

She squared her shoulders. *I'm a consenting adult, for Goddess's sake.*

Alyssa's fingers closed around Katelyn's, and she led her forward through the curtain and out into the semidark bathing chamber. Flickering candles painted red and gold designs on the walls and onto the bare skin of all three women, giving everything a surreal atmosphere.

The sound of the falls was louder here but still muted enough to allow a sense of intimacy without making the bathers have to shout to be heard. The entire chamber was comprised of the sparkling *balda*.

A large pool was inset into the floor, and lazy wisps of steam rose from the gently churning water almost as though an underground hot springs fed into the pool somewhere. The faint aroma of sulfur strengthened that assumption.

Small cubbyholes were etched into the walls and held all manner of soaps and towels, along with what appeared to be purple fruits Katelyn didn't recognize. As she neared the pool, she noticed several raised platforms resting just under the water's churning surface in the shallow end. The water gurgled and rushed, and a small waterfall fell into the edge of the pool against the side so people could enjoy it from both the shallow and deep ends.

Katelyn followed Alyssa and stepped onto the first stair of

the pool, sighing as the warm water frothed around her ankles. Each of the remaining steps took her deeper, the warm water caressing her calves, thighs, mound, and belly. When her feet touched the bottom of the pool, she crouched until the water lapped lazily around her neck. Her hair fanned around her, becoming heavier as moisture soaked the strands.

The water bubbled around her in a comforting caress, and she closed her eyes and allowed the sensation to seep into her. "Mmmm . . ."

"The baths are wonderful, aren't they?" Alyssa's voice sounded content beside her.

Katelyn opened her eyes to see the queen floating a few feet away, also submerged to her neck. Her dark hair was already wet and slicked back against her head. Movement to the side caught Katelyn's attention.

Sasha had followed them into the pool but had gone to the cubbyholes to retrieve a basket filled with supplies. "Who would like to go first?"

Alyssa swam forward to hover next to Katelyn. "Why don't you? There's no need to be nervous."

Katelyn knew the queen's smile was meant to be encouraging. She swallowed her fear and made her way toward the maid. "What do I do?"

"Just lie here on this platform and relax." Sasha held out a hand, and Katelyn allowed the maid to help her up onto the raised surface.

The surface was soft and giving like some sort of thin gel mattress, and the head was slightly raised to cradle her in comfort. Katelyn flipped her hair above her head, enjoying the sensation of the strands swirling in the currents. An inch of water lapped against her body, but she wasn't cold. The warm, humid air of the cavern kept her comfortable.

However, she was exposed for both women to see. She re-

sisted the urge to cover herself with her hands and instead relaxed against the platform. The motion of the water and the
gentle sounds from the waterfall slowly soothed her, and she
could almost imagine she was at a day spa being pampered.

Warm fingers gripped under her knees.

Katelyn jumped—nearly rolling off the platform into the
churning water.

The maid's expression was apologetic. "I didn't mean to
startle you, Seer."

Alyssa placed a comforting hand against Katelyn's thigh.
"Would you be more comfortable with just me?"

Katelyn swallowed hard, and her gaze slid toward the maid.
Relief and anticipation flowed through her. She was comfortable with Alyssa and not quite ready for a group yet, apparently.

Sasha smiled and dipped her head. "Of course. It wasn't my
wish to overwhelm you, Seer. When you are ready, I will be
available if you wish help with your hair or your wardrobe."

Katelyn breathed a sigh of relief as Sasha disappeared and
left her alone with Alyssa. However, now that they were alone,
she wasn't sure what to do.

"Remember, this was new to me not so long ago, Katelyn."
Alyssa smiled. "You are welcome to bathe alone, or we can just
talk while we bathe together. It's up to you."

A surge of disappointment arrowed through Katelyn. Now
that she had been given a choice, she realized she wanted this.

The attraction for Alyssa wasn't only because of the planet.
Without the societal restrictions, Katelyn was curious and
wanted to know what it felt like to caress and kiss a woman.
The energy incident with Alyssa upstairs had only whetted her
appetite for the real thing, and she wasn't about to let her fear
keep her from this opportunity.

Katelyn sat up and scooted forward, letting her legs dangle into the water off the end of the platform. The water teased her labia just under her clit, and Katelyn squirmed until she became used to the sensation. "I'm ready. Show me what to do." Her voice sounded foreign in her ears—breathy and seductive but steady and confident at the same time.

Alyssa's face blossomed as she smiled. She stepped between Katelyn's thighs, and Katelyn was surprised to find their faces at the same height. There must have been a step at the bottom of the platform.

Katelyn held her breath, waiting for Alyssa's bare skin to press against hers, but Alyssa surprised her when, instead, she picked a fuzzy purple fruit from the basket.

Alyssa peeled back the skin to reveal what looked like purple whipped topping. The musky scent of lavender filled Katelyn's senses, adding to the sensual tension thrumming between them. "This is *ponga* fruit. It's used in most of the bathing here because of its unique properties." The queen scooped some of the fruit's flesh with her first two fingers and then slathered it over Katelyn's nipple.

Katelyn had been about to ask what properties the fruit had when the feathery touch caught her off guard. She gasped, and her nipple pebbled to a hard nub under the fleeting attention.

More was smeared over Katelyn's other peak, and she leaned back, putting her weight on her arms and hands to give Alyssa unrestricted access.

Alyssa gathered another fat dollop of the fruit and stared into Katelyn's eyes as she reached to spread it over Katelyn's clit and labia.

Katelyn's breath caught in her throat as Alyssa's fingers lingered against her, tracing the outer lips protecting her sensitive clit and then slowly dipping inside to trace the slit until it met the platform. Alyssa's finger slid easily between her lips, and

Katelyn wondered if it was from her own juices or from the *ponga*.

A slow tingling began across Katelyn's nipples and then started between her thighs. "Oh . . ."

The queen smiled. "It's the *ponga*." She set the fruit aside and then stepped close between Katelyn's legs, the heat of their bodies sizzling.

Katelyn sat forward until her breasts pressed against Alyssa's. A moan slipped through her lips as she realized she was unprepared for the sensation of the woman's soft curves against her own, the taut nipples teasing against her flesh as the tingling from the *ponga* increased.

Alyssa's fingers traced Katelyn's jaw as she slowly closed the distance between them.

Katelyn gave herself up to the moment and let her eyes drift closed. When Alyssa's soft mouth met Katelyn's parted lips, Katelyn melted into the kiss. Her arms went around the queen to trace the soft skin of her shoulders and back.

Alyssa's tongue delved into Katelyn's mouth, a gentle invasion rather than the hard demand of Grayson's. Two totally opposite sensations but equally erotic.

The queen tasted like vanilla, and her faint scent of honeysuckle threaded through the lavender from the *ponga*. The two women's tongues tangled, a soft assault against Katelyn's senses. As she grew braver, she traced her fingers over the queen's gently flared hips to the rounded flesh of her ass. Katelyn pulled her closer, and Alyssa's smooth mound ground against Katelyn's clit, zinging a bolt of arousal through her and stealing her breath.

When Alyssa reached between them to lightly pinch Katelyn's still tingling nipple, the energy inside her howled to life, expanding to fill every inch of her. Katelyn gasped and nearly fell backward but caught herself, bracing herself again with her arms and hands behind her. Alyssa's hot mouth closed over one of Alyssa's nipples, sending another powerful surge of energy spinning through Katelyn. She arched her back, thrusting her aching breast into Alyssa's mouth and letting her head fall back in surrender.

Alyssa sucked the puckered peak hard while her fingers tickled a teasing path down Katelyn's rib cage to her navel and then farther down to comb through her short-cropped, red curls.

"I love your curls. I've never been with a woman with pubic hair." Alyssa's hot breath feathered over Katelyn's wet nipple, making her shiver—but not with cold. She laughed. "Not that I've been with any other woman besides Sasha."

Before Katelyn could think of a response, Alyssa lightly grazed her nipple and then soothed it with her tongue before licking a wet line over to the other breast for the same treatment. Katelyn began to shake as the tension inside her grew. The queen touched the slit between Katelyn's swollen labia, avoiding her aching clit, and dipped one finger just inside the rim of Katelyn's pussy before tracing the slow path once more.

Katelyn bucked her hips, silently begging for those soft fingers to tease her clit, but Alyssa only continued her slow torture against both Katelyn's breast and pussy. The queen sucked one nipple hard, making Katelyn cry out as pure pleasure flooded through every nerve ending. Alyssa released the hold with an audible *pop* and then kissed her way down Katelyn's gently rounded stomach to her short curls.

Katelyn laid back on the platform, her legs spread wide, shamelessly offering herself to Alyssa's attentions. She bit her lip to keep from begging the other woman to taste her, to plunge her tongue deep inside Katelyn's pussy.

The queen's warm tongue traced Katelyn's slit as her finger had done earlier, and Katelyn raised her hips, silently begging for more. Alyssa's movements were more timid than Grayson's had been, but her movements were also much softer and more sensual.

"Please . . . Alyssa, please . . ."

Alyssa's rumbling laugh against Katelyn's swollen flesh nearly drove Katelyn over the edge. She gripped the sides of the platform until her fingers hurt.

Finally Alyssa's lips closed over Katelyn's clit, sucking and then lightly flicking the underside of the sensitive bud with her tongue. The tension deep inside Katelyn's body built and built as the sensual assault against her clit continued. She thrashed her head back and forth on the platform, silently begging for release.

One soft finger traced her aching slit from the bottom of her clit all the way back to the sensitive ring of muscle at her ass. Katelyn gasped at the light pressure around and around her tight pucker. Then the tip of the finger teased the opening, which shot intense sensations straight to Katelyn's core.

No one had ever touched her like this before Grayson had today, and a vivid picture of Grayson slipping his cock inside her ass pushed her over the edge.

Katelyn screamed as the orgasm slapped her and the energy exploded outward from her body, the release—both inside and outside of her body—a decompression of tension, an expulsion of energy, and an answering flood of pure, raw pleasure.

A second strangled scream echoed hers, and Katelyn gasped as Alyssa slumped forward, her soft curves pressing against Katelyn's sensitive flesh.

The energy sated and curled, sleeping inside Katelyn once more, her head lolling to the side as she slowly opened her eyes.

Grayson and the king stood beside the bath, watching with hungry interest.

Katelyn yelped and sat up, her arm automatically covering her bare breasts.

Her motion dislodged Alyssa, and the queen sank into the water to her neck.

Katelyn gathered the last shreds of her dignity and glared at the men. "Is there anywhere on this fucking planet a woman can have an orgasm without an audience?"

14

———————

Katelyn peered around the archway of the dressing room and jumped when she found Grayson watching her. The intensity of his gaze made her nipples pucker and her clit swell with anticipation.

Terrific—so much for avoiding him until my ego recovers. Apparently, my body bounced back fast, and it's ready for dessert.

After Katelyn had escaped to the dressing area, her self-esteem in tatters, Alyssa had finally explained that she often had a problem projecting her fantasies to King Stone. However, everyone was surprised that Katelyn had projected hers to Grayson. Apparently, both men had received very vivid visions of the activities taking place in the baths and had come to investigate.

So much for any private fantasies on this freaking planet.

She was oddly offended that they all had doubted her abilities, but then she reminded herself that those "abilities" were what had brought Grayson to the pool.

Can't have it both ways!

"Good afternoon, Seer. Are you feeling better?" Grayson's

rumbling voice caused a flurry of tingling sensations deep in her belly, and she remembered what it felt like to have him talk to her in that deep voice while he was buried inside her.

"*Better* isn't quite the word I'd use." Once again, her thoughts had centered firmly in her crotch before she'd even realized it. She gritted her teeth and wrestled them back under control.

A glance up at him only made things worse. Not only did the devastating smile cause her insides to go all gooey, but the man actually had the gall to stand there looking scrumptious as if he hadn't caught her naked with the queen's face between her thighs.

Her cheeks burned, and she wished she could rewind the morning and lock the king and Grayson out of the baths until she was dressed and recovered.

What does that say about me? That I have no desire to erase my experience with the queen?

She fisted her hands at her sides, fighting a fresh wave of embarrassment. She raised her chin and raked her gaze over Grayson, taking in the long, dark hair pulled back and fastened against the back of his neck and his muscular bare forearms where his tunic had been rolled up nearly to the elbows. His dark trousers lovingly caressed powerful thighs, and, of course, the outline of a very impressive cock she'd experienced first-hand earlier.

Get a grip. The last thing I need today is another public orgasm!

Katelyn stepped fully into the hallway and steeled herself against the attraction she knew would pull her toward Grayson even if they were on Earth. She knew better than to think it was only the planet causing all this.

Maybe that accounted for her sudden penchant for kinky sexual encounters with women. But one look at Grayson told her that he would rev her libido into high gear no matter what planet they happened to be on.

"Look," she said with a sigh. "It's been a long day already, and, in addition to you, the king, the queen, and a lady's maid have all seen me naked. I'm feeling a bit . . . exposed, right now."

Grayson's expression turned almost sheepish. "I am sorry for embarrassing you. I've never received a vision from anyone before, and when Stone and I saw them at the same time . . ." He shrugged. "We just found our way to the baths."

Katelyn rolled her eyes and shoved her hair over her shoulder. "I'm not saying I wouldn't have done the same exact thing in your place. I'm just saying I need a few hours without anyone seeing me naked, with no public orgasms, and without the pink crystals having their way with me."

Grayson raised his eyebrows. "What happened with the crystals?"

Katelyn sighed. She'd forgotten he didn't know about that yet. "It's a long story. Suffice it to say, they liked me a little too much."

Grayson was making a valiant effort not to smile even through his curiosity, but the corners of his lips quirked up anyway, which threatened to make Katelyn smile back. "I thought we could take some dinner to the hot springs—without Ryan this time. However, if you're still feeling exposed . . ."

A warm tingling fluttered deep inside her belly, and a happy buoyancy filled her chest. "Are you trying to get me alone, your highness?"

His amethyst eyes darkened, sending the tingling into high gear. "Most definitely."

"Queen Alyssandra, please see reason. The Seer is obviously unstable."

Alyssa clenched her jaw to keep from blurting out exactly what she thought of Valen and his group of twenty or so Klatch who had asked for a special audience. Their leader, Valen, was the same man who had spoken out against the triangle at the council meeting. He also happened to be a self-righteous pain in the ass, if Alyssa's limited exposure to him so far was any indication.

She stood and waved Stone back to his seat.

The energy from her husband's anger vibrated along her back like small electric shocks, and she took a deep breath to center her own emotions. "Valen, reports of what happened at the hot springs already reached me well before you requested this audience." She crossed her arms and struggled for her most logical and diplomatic voice. "We have no other Seers on Tador at the moment, so I'm sure you're not familiar with how their gift affects them. Visions drain the Seer's energy, and some visions will obviously cause an emotional reaction. None of that suggests she is unstable."

"So we are to rely on someone who might break down at any moment, to maintain a third of the planet's energy?" Condescension dripped from Valen's words, and Alyssa bit her tongue to keep from lashing out in anger. His eyes narrowed and his nostrils flared as he smacked a fist into his open palm.

The rest of his group stayed in a close huddle near him, showing Alyssa that not only was he the leader, but that most of the people with him would let him do their thinking for him—a fact that only made them more dangerous, in Alyssa's mind.

Jaseen, a petite woman with generous curves, whom Alyssa suspected was one of Valen's consorts, snorted. "The queen has always maintained the symbiosis alone on Tador, regardless of whatever fiction has been written in the journals. We can't afford to dilute the bloodlines any further."

Again, Alyssa bit back the sharp reply that tried to spring

from her lips, and she took a deep breath to calm her emotions before she replied. "Jaseen, show me proof that the journals are fiction."

The woman's mouth opened and closed like a fish too long out of water, and Alyssa plowed forward, her point proven by the woman's pained silence. "Think what you will, but the Klatch are not as pureblood as everyone would like to think." She stared the little woman down until, reluctantly, Jaseen dropped her gaze, allowing Alyssa to turn her attention back to Valen. "And the Seer's emotional state is not at issue here. In fact, I don't remember anyone asking me to submit to an emotional evaluation before I ascended the throne as the sole provider of energy for Tador. My show of power seemed impressive enough that no one asked any other questions."

Valen's lips thinned into a hard line. "I know you are reluctant to admit that your decision in the matter of the triangle was faulty, but a true leader would consider the well being of the people before her own pride— I urge you to consider that before you doom our entire race. How ashamed your parents would be if they were here to witness your heresy."

Stone shot to his feet behind her, the energy from his rage nearly suffocating her. At the same time, the four members of the royal guard stationed around the room took several steps forward, their eyes narrowed, their hands open and ready to cast spells to protect the queen.

Valen and his followers stiffened, their eyes darting toward the guards and the angry king. All of them kept their arms at their sides, obviously unwilling to show any aggression other than their barbed words.

"I'll rip out his tongue, and if your father and mother were here, they would help me." Her husband's angry voice sounded inside her head—telepathy between the ascended queen and her king was one of the perks of this job.

"I appreciate the sentiment, my love, but after growing up

with Sela, Valen doesn't provide much of a challenge for me. I'll take care of him."

Stone's searing energy receded to tolerable levels, and he remained behind her like a protective sentinel. Alyssa glanced toward Gavin, the head of her royal guard, and with a small smile let him know she could handle the situation.

Gavin nodded in return but didn't move back toward his original station, and neither did any of the other three guards.

The queen smiled serenely at Valen and his followers, who still stood stiffly as if expecting her to have them all put to death. "If you're hoping to shame me into following the path you prefer, Valen, you're sadly mistaken." She refused to bring her parents—the previous king and queen—into this conversation. The fact that her parents had agreed that the triangle was a necessity wouldn't sway Valen anyway. Instead, Alyssa lifted her chin and pinned the man with her intense gaze. "I had nothing but the people's best interests in mind when I made this decision. If I recall correctly, all of you were content to let both my mother and the planet slowly deteriorate until we were left with only the current choice. So you have very little room to complain, now that I'm taking action to save our way of life."

Valen's jaw clenched, and his eyes blazed with fury. Several of his followers' hands fisted at their sides, and a few low mutters drifted from the group. "You refuse to see reason. With all due respect, your *majesty*, you force me to rally the people against this folly. Mark my words, this triangle will never happen."

Alyssa stepped forward, invading Valen's personal space. The air around her crackled with her energy as her anger leaked through her calm facade.

Valen's eyes dilated, the black center nearly eating the outer lavender. Otherwise, his expression remained defiant even as his face lost a little of its normal color.

"You forget yourself, Valen." Alyssa kept her voice low, relieved it came out sounding even and unconcerned, because her stomach roiled with anger. "Tador is not and has never been a democracy. You have all willingly entrusted the care of the planet to me. Tador attracts what it needs—which includes the Seer and, eventually, a Healer. If you do anything to endanger the successful completion of the triangle, it will be considered an act of treason."

Valen's eyes widened, and a quick look of surprise flashed across his face before his features settled into the previous angry mask. "You would silence any dissenters by sentencing them to death? I caution you to think of how you will be remembered, Alyssandra de Klatch. A queen has never been asked to step down, but that doesn't mean it couldn't happen."

His group seemed to constrict into a tighter cluster; only Valen stood slightly apart.

Alyssa's gaze bore into Valen's until the man flinched under her scrutiny. "This is a free society, and dissenters aren't persecuted. However, those who undermine the well being of the planet are terrorists and will be dealt with as such. So, save your threats."

She shook her head, suddenly very tired with this entire conversation. A few steps took her closer to the group, though they nearly flinched away as she walked past. The way their gazes tracked her movements assured her she had their full attention.

"Let me lay it on the line for you all. There isn't another royal princess and prince pairing powerful enough to ascend the throne. Too many died in the attempt before Stone found me, so now we're stuck with each other. I've made the best decision for the situation and for the planet, and I'm done discussing it." She sliced the air with her hand. "I've tried to be patient and let everyone have their say, but now it's time for all of you to either jump on the bandwagon, or go find a place to live on Earth where you don't have to accept my decisions. Do we understand each other?" Alyssa made sure her gaze touched each person in the group as a tense silence filled the room. "This discussion is now officially closed."

Tension in the room mounted as the group digested the full import of her words. Alyssa stood stock still, unwilling to be the first one to move. She allowed her gaze to roam over the faces of the Klatch before her. Some appeared angry, while others looked stunned, but without Valen's guidance, none of them seemed to know what to do.

After several minutes, Valen finally spoke. "You have made yourself perfectly clear, my queen." He gave a curt nod before he turned to leave. After a definite pause, the rest of the group trailed after him.

One of the guards closed the door behind them firmly, and Alyssa slowly blew out the breath she'd been holding. Her entire body began to shake as the adrenaline flowed out of her like water down an open drain.

Stone captured Alyssa's hand to brush a kiss over her knuckles. His warm tongue darted out to leave a hot, wet line across her skin, which pulled a sharp gasp from her.

A small tendril of energy snaked from that point of contact to every erogenous zone in her body, making her shudder.

"You're weak, beloved. Let me replenish your energy." Concern laced Stone's words and a crease had formed between his dark brows.

Alyssa opened her eyes and smiled up at her husband. "Before you take it upon yourself to distract me, we need to decide what to do about Valen and his group."

"My queen." Gavin stepped forward, dressed in the dark purple livery of the royal guard. "If I may offer a suggestion?"

"Please do, Gavin," Stone offered. "I don't think Alyssandra has much more energy to spare for this right now."

Alyssa forced her lips to curve into a smile at her husband's understatement. Her limbs felt as if they weighed a thousand pounds.

Stone laid a comforting hand on Alyssa's shoulder as he finished addressing the guard. "You have more experience in security matters than we do. As always, we appreciate any advice you can offer."

The man's expression didn't change, but she thought she noticed a glint of appreciation in the man's eyes. "If we were to assign someone to follow each of the . . . dissenters . . . we would most likely be able to head off any threats before they happen." He pursed his lips. "We would, of course, be discreet."

A short laugh bubbled up in Alyssa, even through her exhaustion, and she let it free. "Gavin, if it weren't highly inappropriate, I would kiss you on the lips right now." She sighed. "I would give you a raise, except for that pesky part of Klatch culture where we don't use money."

Gavin grinned—the first actual grin she had ever seen from the stoic man. "We require no recompense for performing our duty, my queen. As you know, everything we could need is already provided for us. However, perhaps when you are recovered we could discuss a few things that might make the lives of the guards more . . . pleasant?"

Stone smiled, and Alyssa knew her brow furrowed with confusion. Sometimes the Klatch penchant for beating around the bush could become trying. The thought had never occurred to her that the guards were unhappy in any way. They all appeared perfectly content, and she had never met one who hadn't acted totally loyal.

"My wife hasn't been on Tador long enough to understand what you're asking, Gavin. However, knowing her as I do, I think she would be open to the discussions you're suggesting."

"*Damn it, Stone,*" she projected inside his head. "*I know this is a matriarchal society, but you're the king, for God's sake. If there is something that needed to be fixed, why didn't you tell me?"*

"*Beloved, it is not my place.*"

She glared at his familiar answer and vowed to try to bring it up again when she had the time.

Stone only smiled at her unspoken thought, which, from experience, she knew he had heard. "*It's a long-standing restriction for the guards to be unable to enter into a relationship. They may provide themselves sexual sustenance, of course, or provide it for another guard, but no emotional attachments are allowed.*"

"What?" Alyssa sat up in her chair, her anger at past queens burning hot in her veins. She looked between Gavin and Stone. "Are you telling me that in this sexual society, they are essentially treated like priests? No wives, no girlfriends, or boyfriends? What a total crock of—"

"Don't get me wrong, my lady." Gavin dipped his chin to avoid meeting her gaze—a royal-guard habit that still irritated her. "We willingly choose to become part of the guard and are honored to serve the royal family—"

She pushed to her feet and chopped the air in front of her with her hand. "Bullshit." At Gavin's surprised expression, she added, "Bullshit that you have to give up having any type of fulfilling relationship to go into this line of work."

"Your majesty." The sides of Gavin's lips curved up slightly—probably at her language.

She would bet he'd never heard her mother say "bullshit" as queen.

"The purpose," Gavin said, "was to ensure the guards had no distractions from their duties and would not be afraid to give their lives for their charges."

Alyssa frowned at him. "Whatever—I don't buy it. The Secret Service back on Earth doesn't have rules like that, and they are still able to protect the President—with very few exceptions." She raised her chin. "So, as of right now, that old rule is banished."

"However, beloved," Stone added, "if any two guards on the same team are involved, I would suggest one of them transfer to a new team."

"Fair enough, my lord," Gavin added before Alyssa could comment. "I can assure you none of our number will object to such a stipulation."

Several of the guards exchanged quick looks, excitement about the change in rules evident in their expressions.

Stone clapped Gavin on the back. "As soon as we have the triangle in place, we should convene to discuss the rest of the guard's concerns. But, for pity's sake, man, once your shift is done, go find a willing maid or whoever strikes your fancy."

A wolfish grin appeared on Gavin's face. "Thank you, your majesties." The guard opened his mouth as though he wanted to say more, but then he closed his lips.

Alyssa raised her eyebrow and pierced him with a questioning look. "As my loyal guard, I expect you to keep me fully informed on everything, Gavin. It's too late to hold back now, and I don't want you to."

Gavin dipped his chin. "Regardless of what anyone says, my lady, I see a great leader in both you and King Stone. With very little preparation, you have made difficult decisions that might be painful for the people to accept but are definitely in their best interest. You are both fair and caring leaders, and I'm proud to serve in any capacity I may." He raised his gaze to meet Alyssa's—a rare gesture she appreciated. "And, also, regardless of what Valen said, your parents are extremely proud of you. The entire guard feels the same and will stand behind you, no matter what."

Thick emotion tightened Alyssa's chest. The comment had blindsided her—in a good way. How often over the past few months had she wondered if she was the worst ruler in the history of her planet? What a nice change to hear that someone thought she was doing a good job—especially the guards who had been privy to the ruling decisions on Tador before she had taken over. Granted, those rules had been her parents', but they had shown faith in her by deciding to relocate to a home in the country as soon as Alyssa had ascended—most likely to let her carve out her own niche as queen without feeling as though she was constantly in their shadow.

She swallowed hard. "Thank you, Gavin." Her voice shook as tears threatened. "That means more than you know."

15

The sensation of someone watching her made the hairs on the back of Rita's neck prickle. The same feeling had dogged her every day since Katelyn had left on her cruise.

Rita had decided to come into work early today because the new pendant shipment was due. But now, walking along the sidewalk in the early morning sunshine, the churning in her gut made her feel like this area was a dark, deserted alley at midnight on a moonless night.

Rita quickened her pace, her purse clutched tight to her chest, and her gaze darting all around to ensure no one could sneak up on her. She rounded the corner and immediately froze.

The front door of the shop stood open, shattered glass from the side window scattered over the sidewalk.

Her heart pounded, and she swallowed past a huge lump of fear that had gathered inside her throat.

She pulled her cell phone from her purse, flipped it open, and dialed 9 . . . 1 . . . and then a man stepped through the doorway. Rita willed her finger to hit the last digit, but for some reason, she hesitated.

He held up a badge and said, "I'm Detective Damien, ma'am. Are you the owner?"

She would have to trust that it was a Phoenix police badge he flashed because she hadn't been able to tear her eyes off his face.

By all that's holy, I'm dead, and this must be heaven.

The man before her could only be described as mouthwatering. His coloring reminded her of the hottie Katelyn had run off with—not that Rita could blame her friend one bit.

Hair so black it had blue highlights flowed down to the best set of shoulders Rita had ever seen. She spared only a quick glance for the rest of his body, making sure it was also the stuff of wet dreams, before her gaze flitted back to his face.

He had deep purple eyes framed with long, inky black lashes any woman would kill for, a patrician nose, and high cheekbones covered in dusky, olive skin. His sensual mouth, curved up at the edges, made Rita think of hot, sweaty nights with lace teddies and silk sheets.

"Miss?"

His voice was a perfect, clear tenor, and she had a sudden urge to ask him to sing, but she was afraid that beautiful voice might give her on-the-spot orgasms. "Uh . . ."

"Are you Rita Eldridge?" he asked in a way that said he already knew the answer.

She managed to close her mouth and nod while she mentally gathered her scattered brain cells. "Yes, I am Rita." *Good job, maybe he'll just think you're mentally challenged instead of an insane idiot around men.*

"We responded to an alarm. Could you come inside and let us know if anything is missing?" He reached into the back pocket of his black jeans, which seemed like they had been lovingly painted on, and pulled out an envelope. "Oh, and this was on the floor just inside the doorway, as though it had been slipped underneath the door."

Rita's brow furrowed, and her logic cut through several, but not all, layers of the lust in which she was caught. "We have tight weather stripping on the bottom of our front door. There's no way anyone could've slipped anything underneath it while it was closed. Otherwise, during the monsoon season, we'd be inundated with dust."

He crouched and examined the bottom of the door, his long fingers tracing the weather stripping until it seemed erotic. He pursed his lips before standing. "You're right." He handed her the letter. "Can you tell me who the letter is from? It may give us a clue as to who broke in to your shop."

Rita turned the envelope over in her hands and immediately recognized Katelyn's writing on the front. She carefully tore open the envelope and pulled out two pages covered in Katelyn's chicken scratch. "It's from my partner. She's out of town on a cruise. I'm not sure how the letter got inside, though."

"She does have a key?"

"Of course, but as I said, she's on a cruise, which would make it difficult for her to unlock the shop, drop a letter on the floor, and then relock the shop before someone broke in."

He nodded but not in agreement—more like an acknowledgement that he had heard her. "Can you come back inside and check to see if anything's missing?" he asked again. "The apartment above the shop seems to have been the focal point—it has been ransacked."

Panic clawed through Rita's stomach as she headed straight through the shop and toward the stairs along the back wall, Detective Damien's voice trailing behind her. Katelyn's apartment was the only thing up there. Something was going on with her roommate, and it wasn't good, if the roiling in her gut was any indication. "Nothing was disturbed downstairs?" she asked without turning as she took the stairs two at a time.

He must have followed her, because his answer came from close behind her. "It's pretty bad up here." His voice held a gentle warning.

Rita stepped onto the top landing, and her breath caught. The sapphire-blue door to Katelyn's apartment was shattered along one side where the deadbolt had been forced by someone's shoulder—if the shape of the indentation in the door was any indication. The door stood half open, which gave Rita an unimpeded view of the devastation that now comprised her friend's apartment.

Broken crystals and vases lay scattered across the floor, along with scraps of paper and chunks of foam that had probably come from the couch and torn clothing.

"Oh, Katelyn . . ." Rita pulled the door all the way open and stepped inside, careful not to step on anything sharp. She walked from room to room, her anger growing brighter with the sight of each new act of destruction. When she reached Katelyn's bedroom, tears pricked at the backs of her eyes, and her throat was so tight she wasn't sure she could speak.

The mattress had been shoved off the bed, and the chest of drawers had been pushed over, some of the drawers broken, their contents littered across the floor. Pictures had been torn off the wall, the glass and frames smashed, and there were dark smudges along the wall that looked like char marks.

Tension radiated through Rita, and she fisted her hands at her sides. Her gaze swept the room and finally stopped on Katelyn's cedar chest, which sat at the foot of her bed. The dome-lidded box was made of thick cherry wood and was an antique Katelyn had found and lovingly restored. It appeared to be the only piece of furniture in the apartment that hadn't sustained any damage. The dome lid was open, and several small journals spilled over the top and out onto the surrounding floor.

Rita stooped to pick one up and then flipped the book open.

A child's loopy cursive writing filled every line of every page. The dates, as well as Katelyn's name written on the front, confirmed they were hers. Rita leaned over to look inside the chest and realized that it was full to the brim with these journals. She flipped through a few more and found them much like the first.

"I never knew Katelyn kept diaries, especially this far back."

"Do you know why anyone would break in here? Did your partner have any enemies?"

A strangled squeak escaped Rita as she nearly jumped out of her skin.

The sight of Katelyn's ransacked apartment had chased all thoughts of the hunky detective from her mind.

"My apologies." He dipped his chin, almost an abbreviated bow, which made her wonder where he was from. "I didn't mean to startle you."

She swallowed hard and willed her heart to slow to something resembling normal. "I forgot you were following me. I can't believe someone would do all this." She gestured to encompass the room. "Katelyn doesn't have any enemies or even family." She pursed her lips as she glanced around the room again. "Were these diaries open like this when you found them?"

"Yes. Is there anything in there worth taking? Information that can be used for blackmail? Anything?" He pushed his hair away from his face, the movement making the sculpted muscles in his forearms bunch and move.

A desire to run her tongue along the bulging vein in that perfect forearm ran through her, and she bit her tongue to keep from embarrassing herself. Instead shook her head to answer his question. "From the dates, these were written when she was very young. Day-to-day happenings of a child. I can't see what value they would offer anyone."

Damien's gentle smile made her suspect he knew what she'd been thinking about his arms, which flamed heat up her neck and into her cheeks. "Either of you have jealous ex-boyfriends, fiancés, or husbands who don't like you being in business together? Anything like that? The damage here seems very personal, since they didn't touch the shop downstairs."

Aedan. Damn, I'm engaged to Aedan, and here I am ogling the local police. She glanced at her engagement ring as if surprised to find it still on her finger. "I'm engaged, but my fiancé and Katelyn have never met—although Katelyn doesn't like him. She says she gets bad vibes every time I mention him."

Damien nodded as though he understood completely, which confused Rita, because she didn't understand. "Do you ladies have insurance on the shop?"

Rita frowned at the quick subject change as she tried to figure out why he had asked. "Of course. Why?"

He gestured to the char marks along the wall.

Her temper snapped as she realized what was behind his question. "I have no idea what those are from." She crossed her arms and glared up at him. "If we were going to burn down our building for the insurance money, we would be smart enough to actually set fire to the building instead of just charring the walls!"

Damien only smiled at her outburst. "No offense intended. You realize I have to ask these questions, and, of course, we'll investigate further."

Her brow furrowed. "Yes," she said, still angry.

"I'm going to have some plainclothes detectives frequent your shop for the next several days. You'll never know they are here, but they should keep you safe. Do you have a friend you can stay with in the meantime, in case this is personal against one of you?" His purple gaze captured hers, and Rita had the distinct impression he could see all the way into her soul and liked what he saw.

A deep shudder ran through her body, and she inhaled a shaky breath.

"Take a look around the shop and let me know if you find anything missing or disturbed. I'll be back later."

Before she could form a coherent reply, he disappeared through the ruined door of Katelyn's apartment.

Rita furrowed her brow, and she chewed her bottom lip as she gazed around the walls at the char marks that were probably the marks of something else.

"Wait—I've never met a detective with long hair, and he didn't leave me with a phone number to contact him or anything." She growled low in her throat as she berated herself for thinking with her crotch and not with her head when it came to Detective Damien.

She raced down the stairs and searched the shop, but he was gone. The front door of the shop she'd found shattered several minutes earlier was now boarded up and had been locked tight behind him—without the key. "What the hell?" she demanded of the empty room.

Sela paced the length of the basement and back; the *click-click* of her strappy sandals echoed off the walls with each step. She raked her gaze over the finished basement that had the holding cell on one side, the full bar along the far corner, and, of course, some of her favorite torture devices displayed in the center.

This was usually her favorite room, but today it brought her no pleasure. She wasn't sure if it would cheer her to hear the screams of some poor human or even of a Cunt who had displeased her.

Her stormy mood billowed around her like a large, dark cloud. Guards and servants scattered to stay out of her way, much to her annoyance. If one of them pissed her off, maybe it would break this funk she found herself in.

It was all Aedan's fault!

She'd played with fire, and now she'd finally gotten burned.

The pleasant ache between her thighs and even between her ass cheeks reminded her of Aedan's domination the night before— all night.

Why had she ever given in to her fantasies and let the man dominate her?

She sighed. She knew exactly why.

It was tiring to always be the one in control, to always have all the power. She had tried with other men to give them the illusion of control, but it hadn't been enough to fulfill her fantasy, and, worse, Aedan knew it and exploited that embarrassing fact.

A shudder ran through her, and her nipples tightened against her soft cotton tank top. Her slit slicked with moisture, and her clit pulsed at the thought of how Aedan had made her beg him to drive his cock inside her tight ass while he fisted his hands in her hair.

She ground her teeth as need rose up bright and hot along with the knowledge she would submit to him again and again. Maybe she should kill him and save herself the humiliation of her people finding out about this chink in her armor. Maybe—

"My queen." The guard's voice was soft, as if he thought she might kill him for speaking.

Kill a few guards out of anger in the past, and they think you're ready to do it all the time. "Speak," she said through gritted teeth, almost glad he had interrupted her tortured thoughts.

The man never flinched, but she sensed that he braced for her attack, which irritated her further because she wanted to do just that. However, attacks weren't as satisfying when the victims were ready for them, so she resisted.

"My lady, Aedan has returned with a report and a prisoner and humbly asks if you will see him."

Sela clenched her jaw as she searched the guard's face for any sign that he knew her weakness. Or that she craved that weakness like a drug, even as self-loathing and terror at such an admission clawed at her insides.

The man kept his gaze down, as was proper, which gave Sela no chance to see if the knowledge of her shame shone in his eyes.

Rage boiled inside her, and she let her power build as she backhanded him, sending him flying against the wall.

As he slumped to the floor, dazed, the plaster from the wall crumbling around him, a great emptiness filled Sela. The usual rush of adrenaline and even sexual satisfaction she usually found by causing others pain had paled.

Only her new drug of choice would do. Damn.

She closed her eyes and took a deep breath, holding it for several seconds before blowing it out slowly. "Tell Aedan to meet me in my bedroom in an hour." *Let him wait.*

One hour later, exactly, Sela walked through the doors to her bedroom, anticipation curling inside her stomach like a hungry dragon.

Aedan stood next to a very handsome Cunt warrior, who wore only loose-fitting jeans, which hung low on his trim hips. His wrists were manacled and suspended above him, attached to a chain hanging from the ceiling that had been installed for Sela's sex swing and activities just such as this.

The chain was just a few inches short, so the man balanced on bare tiptoes to keep his entire body weight from centering on his wrists.

Sela walked a slow circle around her new captive, carefully keeping her gaze from colliding with Aedan's. "Report." She continued to circle the bound man and trailed one manicured fingertip over his pale skin, enjoying the gooseflesh that rose in the wake of her touch.

"This warrior has failed you, and I brought him as a gift."

She narrowed her gaze and finally met Aedan's. "How has he failed me?" *And what did you have in mind for my gift?*

"He broke into the Seer's shop as instructed, but just as he found the journals, a team of Klatch found him. He escaped but without the journals. However, at least we know our intelligence is sound."

"There were six of them, my queen—" The man's voice cut off in midsentence when Aedan punched him in the face. Blood spurted from the cut on his lip, and his head lolled a bit on his shoulders.

Obviously, Aedan wanted him alive for whatever Sela's "gift" happened to be. She nearly moaned as her labia swelled around her clit with arousal.

"As I was saying, my lady, he found journals that seem to be in a child's hand and have many of the ascension symbols on them—both Klatch and our versions of the ceremony." His eyes blazed with passion, which nearly made her whimper. Then he whispered, "They are the Seer's journals, and he was able to draw the lost power symbol for us."

Sela stared at Aedan a moment to make sure he was serious and then grabbed the man's chin between her fingers and squeezed, making sure he looked her in the eye. "Are you sure you drew it exactly? I'll peel your cock like a banana and feed it to the rats if you've brought me the wrong symbol."

"I remember it exactly, my queen. I swear it." His lip had started to swell where it had split, but she detected only truth in his words.

A small bubble of triumph surged through Sela, and a smile slowly spread across her face. She laughed, the sound filling the entire room. The power symbol for the triangle ascension had been lost when she had killed her successor. How could she have known she needed to divulge the woman of her secrets before Sela slit her throat?

The split between the Cunts and the Klatch had been a long time coming, and the Cunts hadn't stopped at just wanting enough energy to rule Tador—they wanted to rule Earth, too, because a large energy supply existed here. However, the weaklings that ruled Tador saw no need for greed. Sela sneered at their shortsightedness.

"The Seer has foreseen our success, Aedan. That means we no longer need that pretender queen to take back what's ours." Tador was a living entity that had a drive for survival, and even though the planet had an affinity for the throned queen, if that queen couldn't supply the planet with the energy to thrive and survive, Tador would find another way to continue to exist. Sela rubbed her hands together with satisfaction. "As long as we perform our ceremony before the triangle ceremony is complete, the planet is ours."

"I promised you I wouldn't disappoint you again, my queen."

"You've pleased me." She darted her gaze from the prisoner back to Aedan. "Now, what about my gift?"

Aedan smiled, but the gesture looked more like he had bared his teeth. "Would my queen do me the honor of a private audience in which to enjoy your gift? I promise I have wonderful things planned."

Heat seared through Sela's entire body, and she somehow managed to say, "Very well."

The guards left without a word, and as the door closed, she turned toward Aedan, only to see his smile had turned feral.

"So?" she demanded, glad her voice didn't betray her. "Show me." She gestured toward the captive man, enjoying the way his muscular shoulders bunched as he struggled to keep his weight off his wrists.

"No—you show *me*." Aedan's low voice sent a tendril of excitement snaking through Sela.

"What—"

The back of Aedan's hand struck Sela hard across the cheekbone, which blossomed pain and sparks of light just behind her eyelids as she fell to the floor.

She landed on her hip, and the taste of copper along with a

sting inside her mouth told her she had bitten her cheek on the way down. Her tongue glided over the cut even as her body cried out for more.

"Show me, Sela." Aedan's gaze bore into hers. "I want to see you on your knees sucking his cock like the good little whore you are."

Sela's pride balked even as a dark flood of erotic excitement surged through her. "You—"

Pain blossomed again as Aedan's fist caught her in the same cheek, throwing her backward and causing her pussy to throb.

"Do as I say. Now." Aedan loomed over her. "Suck your gift's cock, Sela."

When she didn't move right away, Aedan grabbed her by the hair and dragged her toward the man, whose eyes had widened.

No one had seen the queen of the Cunts treated this way.

Which is why Sela would make sure the prisoner died before he could pass on the information.

She pushed to her knees, the hard floor uncomfortable under her capris.

The man's low-slung jeans were easy to unbutton and unzip, and they took only a small tug before they fell around his ankles to reveal a long, thick cock with pearly pre-come gathered in the slit. Sela wrapped her fingers around his length and leaned forward so she could dart her tongue out to lick away his salty essence. The tart, musky flavor burst over her tongue, and she made an "mmm" sound in the back of her throat.

When she sucked the swollen head between her lips, the Cunt warrior moaned as his cock hardened further. Sela swirled her tongue over the smooth skin and then teased the indent of the slit.

She took his length as deep as she could until it bumped the back of her throat, and she sucked hard, making the man hiss with pleasure.

Aedan moved away, but Sela didn't pay attention, more intent on the cock in her mouth she stroked with her hand while she sucked, licked, and played.

The man lurched and then stood flat on the floor, and she had to adjust her position. She wasn't sure why Aedan had set him free, but she wasn't concerned, because she could use her magic to kill both men in an instant if needed.

Rough fingers grabbed the back of her hair, pulling her away from her cock treat. "Grab her hair like this and then fuck her mouth hard. Give her no mercy—she likes it hard and dominant." Aedan yanked on her hair until she whimpered—with need. "Don't you, Sela?"

"Yes. . . ."

"Yes, what?" Aedan tightened his grip, holding her neck at an awkward angle. "Tell this commoner what you want, and if you're good and you please him, I'll reward you." He let go of her hair so fast she nearly toppled over.

More moisture flooded her slit, and the still tender ring of muscle around her ass tingled with anticipation at Aedan's mention of "reward." She bit her lip, her dark desires overriding her pride. She stared at the stiff cock still bobbing in front of her face and licked her lips. "I want it hard and dominant." The words tasted like ashes inside her mouth, but she reminded herself the reward would be worth a small concession.

A depraved smile curved the man's lips, and he stepped forward, grabbing the sides of Sela's hair like handles and thrusting his cock into her mouth, nearly gagging her.

Sela opened her throat and adjusted to his rhythm until she could breathe through her nose and suck him with each hard thrust. Her fingers found his balls, and she rolled them in her hand, enjoying the way they tightened against his body with each pump inside her throat.

She constricted her lips around him.

He stiffened and cried out.

His balls contracted in her hand, and he arched his hips as his hot come spilled down her throat.

His rapid breathing sounded harsh in the sudden silence of the room.

The man slid his softened cock out from her lips and then yanked her by her hair to stand. As soon as she stood, he pulled her close, capturing her mouth with his.

"Lie on your back on the floor." Aedan's voice sounded strained, and Sela wasn't sure if this directive was for her or for the man. But when Aedan's piercing gaze wasn't aimed at her, she stepped away, waiting for the man to comply.

Aedan crushed her against the long line of his body almost gently and took possession of her mouth as if he owned it. His tongue dipped inside her mouth, and she was sure he could taste the other man's come mixed with her blood from when she'd cut the inside of her cheek. She tried to wriggle away, uncomfortable with this sudden lack of violence and heat. What had happened to his anger and his possession?

He bracketed his arms around her, keeping her in place. "You're not willing to give me whatever I desire, whore? Only obedience brings rewards."

Not sure what to answer, she shook her head. However, Aedan must've taken the action as something positive because he brushed his lips over hers before claiming her mouth again. When she relaxed against him and let him lead the kiss, he bit her bottom lip hard.

A gasp tore from her throat at the unexpected sensation, and then the gasp turned into a long, low moan. Maybe letting Aedan lead did have more advantages than she had thought.

He grabbed the neckline of her tank top and yanked until the sound of the cloth ripping echoed inside the room. The ruined top bared her breasts to his hungry gaze, and he tossed the top to the floor.

Sela stumbled back and then caught her balance, unbutton-ing her capris and sliding them off until she stood only in her sandals and her red lace thong.

Aedan growled and stalked forward to slip one finger under the red triangle at the front of her thong to tease her aching clit. "I can smell your arousal. Ask me for what you want, Sela. Ask me."

Her hips arched into his hand, and small jolts of arousal zinged straight from her clit to every pore inside her body. She licked her lips, but words still eluded her.

He leaned to capture one of her nipples in his mouth. He clamped on to the sensitive bud until she cried out, and another rush of moisture coated the finger that still traced her slit. With his teeth still worrying her tightened nub, he said, "Ask me."

"I . . . Will you fuck me in the ass?"

A groan of satisfaction emanated from Aedan, and he scooped her up, turning her and setting her on top of the man who was now lying on the floor. She straddled him, his cock teasing her slit where Aedan had just touched her.

A quick rip came from behind, and her thong fell away, leav-ing her bare.

Aedan stripped and knelt behind her, his warmth burning through her as his heavy cock lay against the crack of her ass like a promise of things to come. He didn't speak, but he raised her and then positioned the other man's cock at her core. "Don't move," he ordered. Then he bent her forward so her palms rested on the other man's chest and her breasts swung under her. He spread her ass cheeks and positioned the tip of his cock at her rear opening.

Her thighs trembled as she obeyed his directive not to im-pale herself, and now with two cocks positioned ready to thrust inside her, it took all her willpower to keep her hips from arch-ing to take them both.

Aedan reached around her, his arm bracketed low across her

stomach, and then suddenly he thrust inside her while he pushed her down onto the other cock.

Sela cried out as they both filled her, the sensation almost too much for her body to take. Before she could recover or grow used to the feeling, Aedan had both lifted her off the other man and pulled out of her, leaving her empty and bereft.

Then he filled her from both sides again, thrusting into her while slamming her down, using her body for his own pleasure. She wondered briefly if he could feel the other cock so close to his own and yet separated by her inner muscles.

Aedan set up a punishing rhythm, and all Sela could do was hold on. The sounds of flesh slapping flesh filled the room along with the pungent smells of sex and sweat.

Her inner muscles tightened and pulsed as she neared her peak, and just before she shattered, Aedan barked against her ear, "Kill him," and then thrust inside her again.

Sela exploded. Her orgasm fueled her magic, and she poured it down into the man's chest even as he spurted his come deep inside her.

16

"Gray." Alyssandra stopped Grayson in the hallway. "Where's Katelyn?"

He studied Alyssa for a long moment, noting the furrows between her dark brows and the shadows in her liquid lavender eyes. "She's changing. We're going back to the hot springs—without Ryan this time."

"Ryan told me about this afternoon. I guess he does have horrible timing." Alyssandra smiled. "Though I remember you being unapologetic about things like that when it came to me and Stone in similar situations."

Grayson shrugged and resisted giving Alyssa an answering smile since he knew he was guilty as charged. "What's happened? You look like you're bearing bad news."

"Some good, some concerning." She shrugged, which jiggled the full globes of her breasts that peeked from under her half top. "One of the guards we assigned to Rita's shop just gave us a report. They caught a Cunt ransacking Katelyn's apartment above the shop. He escaped before they could find out what he was after."

Anger and a strong need to protect Katelyn—and Rita, because Katelyn cared about her—rose into Grayson's chest.

The queen held up a hand, forestalling his outburst. "We pulled some strings and had Detective Damien assigned to the case. Nothing seems to be missing, but Rita is suspicious."

Grayson nodded. He had met the half-Klatch detective. In fact, he remembered the man's mother had used to visit Grayson's family when Grayson was small. Many years ago, Damien's mother had moved permanently to Earth, where her son wouldn't bear the mark of a half breed. Grayson had heard she had died recently.

"What would they want with Katelyn's apartment?" He rubbed his chin with his fingers, noting the beginnings of rough stubble. "I thought Rita would be more a target than Katelyn's personal things."

"We did, too. However, the guards found these." She held up two journals covered in rich burgundy leather. The bindings were worn and the pages wavy as though they had seen heavy use.

He opened the first journal and noticed Katelyn's name written in childhood cursive along with dates that would've made her about eight years old.

"Look at the fourth of July. I haven't read all of it, but that entry caught my attention. There may be more of interest."

Wednesday, July 4
There's a Fourth of July party today, but of course I'm not invited because I knew Jenny Warner's grandmother would have a heart attack and die on that cruise last month. It's not my fault she died, but that stupid Jenny told everyone I cursed her gran. She said if they talk to me, their families will die, too. I thought Jenny was my friend, and I only wanted to warn her. Now she hates me. Just last month we were having sleepovers at each other's

houses, and now she's turned all the kids at school against me. It's so unfair! Why do I have to have these stupid visions anyway?

Mom said we can go watch fireworks when she and Dad get home from work, but I'm still never speaking to Jenny again! And I won't waste my time telling anyone else anything I see either. The only people I can trust with that are my parents and Prince.

So, while Jenny's party was going on, I stayed home and went to play with Prince in the castle. It was raining there today, so not many adults were around to see us. We played tag in the big maze made out of plants next to the huge waterfall.

Prince always cheers me up. He doesn't seem to mind my visions. I told him I saw him in a vision where he's all grown up, marrying a pretty blond lady with big blue eyes. Prince just laughed and told me all his people have dark hair, and marriage was too far away to think about. I wonder where he got that scar in my vision though. It looks like it had to hurt!

I was a little disappointed that he didn't like red hair, because he's not so bad for a boy. Maybe I'll marry him myself someday since we like the same things. Besides, redheads have to be better—that stupid Jenny has blond hair. Ick!

It seems to me people should like each other before they get married, but Prince says the marriages are arranged for them. I don't think I'd like that too much. What if you get stuck with someone totally gross?

Anyway, this is the best part! When we were playing hide-and-seek, I found an old alcove that was totally closed in and all walled off by hedges around the base of the waterfall. It didn't look like anything would be back there, so I was surprised to see it. It was the first time ever Prince hasn't found me! Ha!

It was a little hard to get to, and I ripped my new green shirt, but it was worth it. There was a three-sided statue that was all grown over with vines and moss, but when I cleaned it off, it turned out to be pretty and white like all the rocks in Prince's world. All three sides of the statue were really pretty women with big boobs, and I even think they were naked! It's a good thing I didn't show Prince—boys shouldn't see that stuff. Anyhow, the ladies all had funny triangle drawings on their stomachs, and I really liked the side with the eye. I wonder if she is a Seer like me? Wouldn't that be cool!

Gotta go! Time for dinner. When I'm done I'll get my colored pencils I got for my birthday and draw the cool triangle.

Grayson swallowed hard as emotions he couldn't name made his chest and throat tight. What would it have been like to know Katelyn as a child? He winced against the sudden pain of lost time with her and then glanced back at the drawing, studying it for several minutes, trying to picture what Katelyn had seen that day.

He shook his head and glanced up at Alyssandra, only to see his own confusion mirrored in her eyes. "Why wouldn't she remember something like that if she remembered Ryan?"

"It was one day out of a little girl's life. I doubt she thought it was important—just an interesting discovery." Alyssandra ran her fingers over the journal as if she could discern its secrets through touch. "But if we could find that statue, it would prove the triangles actually existed, although I'm not sure if the symbols have any significance or not. None of the journals in the queen's archives describe the ritual in detail—they just allude to different elements of it."

Grayson glanced at Katelyn's lopsided writing and ran his thumb over the words. He again wished he could've known Katelyn as a little girl. Reading her innocent words had given him insight into the vivacious woman he had already come to care for. What would all the other journals hold? "The area she talks about—there's nothing there but brambles and then solid *balda* at the base of the waterfall."

"Obviously, a small child found something we haven't. We may have to have some of the Klatch children help us look." Alyssandra sighed. "Maybe you and Katelyn could take a detour on the way to the hot springs and see if she remembers the area." She handed him the other journal, and he trailed his fingers over the worn leather. "I think it's time to tell her everything and see if she's willing to help us."

Grayson nodded. "Her birthday is tomorrow. If we are going to do the coming-of-age ceremony, it needs to be done tomorrow night." He ran his hand through his hair, pushing it back over his shoulder. "I just hope it's not too late."

Alyssa bit her bottom lip. "I haven't shown Ryan. The journals, I mean. I'm not sure what to make of him marrying a blonde. The people are upset enough with a human, but a blonde . . . Even a human blonde will go over like condoms in a convent."

The analogy made Grayson smile. "You never know. Some of the nuns—er . . . people—might be excited by that prospect." He kissed her cheek. "It will all work out, Alyssandra. Have some faith." *And hopefully, Katelyn won't feed me my own bollocks for keeping this from her.*

Katelyn bounded up the stairs and into her room. Funny how after only a few days, she thought of this as *her* room. She smiled as she recognized the familiar feelings of comfort that had brought her here as a child. No wonder she had such an affinity for the place and its people.

Happiness infused her, and she realized she had never felt so light and buoyant in her entire life. She couldn't describe it and was afraid to analyze anything too closely for fear of losing it.

She missed Rita and even her shop, but nothing else seemed to pull her back to Earth. Phoenix had been her home her entire life, and while she enjoyed the gorgeous summers, the breathtaking scenery, and the mild winters, Tador made Phoenix pale in comparison. Eventually she would have to quit her impromptu vacation and return home, but for now she wanted to enjoy Grayson and this place for as long as she could.

I wonder how long that will be . . . " I'll have to ask Grayson if they found out why those blond guys attacked me."

"My lady?"

Katelyn nearly jumped out of her skin as Holly emerged from the side dressing room. With a hand over her heart, Katelyn willed it to stop galloping, and she sucked in a lungful of air. "Sorry, Holly. Just talking to myself."

Holly bobbed her head, but concern clouded her pale lavender eyes.

"Is something wrong?" Katelyn stepped closer to the smaller woman and opened her senses. Agitation and fear streamed off the lady's maid in thick waves. "We don't know each other that well yet, but I can tell something is bothering you."

Holly's large eyes filled with tears, and her energy was tinged with fear. "I could get into a lot of trouble."

Katelyn pulled the woman down on the bed and sat next to her. "I'd like to help if you'll let me. I'll do everything I can to keep you from getting into trouble."

The maid's voice came out as a watery whisper. "I'm not supposed to tell you why you're really here."

A hard stab of dread settled firmly inside Katelyn's stomach, and her hands became clammy. She wiped them on her skirt and swallowed the large lump that had formed in her throat. "What are you talking about? I'm here because Grayson saved me from an attack."

The little maid winced at Katelyn's hard tone. "Yes, ma'am. But the prince was looking for you to bring you back for the triangle when the attack happened."

The crudely painted triangle on the wall of the ceremony chamber in her vision loomed large in her mind's eye. Her temples began a slow throb, and her stomach roiled, threatening to bring up what remained of her lunch. "Tell me what you know about the triangle." Her voice came out flat and dead, which matched how she felt inside.

"To keep the planet from deteriorating further, the queen, king, and princes Ryan and Grayson decided to institute something called a triangle. It involves mating the two princes with two humans with special gifts—a Seer and a Healer—who would then share the job of supplying energy to the planet with the queen."

"Mating?" She knew her mouth dropped open, and she couldn't seem to close it. "The word sounds archaic and absurd!"

"Yes, my lady, heirs would be expected." Holly scrubbed at her wet face with her hand.

"Heirs?" Shock hit Katelyn. She cared for Grayson—a lot. She might even be a little in love with him, but children? She wanted children someday, but she didn't like the idea of being a brood mare. "Was that the only reason Grayson brought me here?"

The maid bobbed her head. "A Seer is needed for the triangle, and—"

"And I happened to be handy." Katelyn's voice came out as a low growl.

"If the coming-of-age ceremony isn't performed on your twenty-fourth birthday, they will have to find another Seer who meets the criterion."

Katelyn bolted to her feet, her hands fisted at her sides as boiling rage seared through her veins. "Criterion?" It wasn't bad enough that she had been convenient and fit the bill, but now it seemed that if she didn't work out, they would toss her aside and find a suitable replacement. "I'll kick his balls so hard he'll be searching for them for weeks!"

She thought about everyone she had met here—Alyssa, Ryan, Sasha, and even King Stone. They were probably all laughing at her. Looking her over like livestock they were considering for purchase. Oddly, Ryan's betrayal hurt most of all—he had tainted the happy memories of her childhood, which was something she could never get back.

She suddenly felt as if she'd been stabbed through the heart. If only this had killed her instead of leaving her with this searing pain.

A sob welled up through her anger, and she held it in by sheer willpower.

"My lady, there is more." Holly's tears had stopped, and she finally met Katelyn's gaze.

"You might as well tell me the rest." Katelyn's voice shook, and she couldn't muster the pride to care. "It will save me killing him twice." Grayson's smiling face loomed inside her mind, and she shook her head to clear it. "Bastard!"

"Your friend Rita—the one who is engaged to the Cunt?" The maid looked at her for confirmation, but Katelyn's blood had turned to ice.

"Say that again." Katelyn gripped Holly's shoulders so hard the woman winced.

"Your friend Rita—the one who is engaged to the Cunt." The maid's voice came out as a mere whisper, but the words finally penetrated Katelyn's anger and turned into icy fear.

"I knew Aedan was no good. But what does he want with Rita?"

"He wants you. The Cunts want control of Tador, just as Grayson and the royal Klatch families do. If the Cunts can't have you, they will punish your friend instead. And if they can have you, they can use her as a blood sacrifice."

Katelyn let her legs buckle, and she sat hard on the bed next to Holly. A large gulf of helplessness weighted her limbs. "What the hell do I do now? I have to get to Rita, but I can't fight the Cunts." She thought back to the whizzing beams of energy the night they had attacked her shop.

Holly brightened. "I can take you through the portal and get you safely to your friend. You and Rita could leave town until your birthday is past and they all look for another Seer. If you don't complete the coming-of-age ritual, you can't be the Seer in the triangle. You would be of no further use for the Klatch or the Cunts."

No further use . . . The words burned through Katelyn in a painful rush.

Thoughts of losing Grayson and Tador tore through her,

shredding her emotions and tightening her stomach. A drop of wetness splashed against her hand, and she realized she was crying—large, fat tears flowing freely down her cheeks.

Another Seer meant that Grayson would belong to some other woman. A sob broke free as she imagined Grayson in the arms of anyone but her.

She wished she hadn't heard any of this until after their night in the hot springs. What would she give for just one more night of ignorance? One more night of being the center of his attention?

Too much, she was afraid. "What the hell has happened to me?"

She shook her head in an attempt to stem the tears. "Why tell me all this? Aren't you loyal to Grayson and the royal family?"

Holly dropped her gaze. "I have served the royal family faithfully since I was a girl, like my mother and ten generations before." She raised her chin to look at Katelyn, her eyes still watery with tears. "However, the queen refuses to listen to the will of the people. We disagree with the institution of the triangle. It will dilute the bloodline of the Klatch, which is the same thing that created the race of the Cunts. No offense meant, my lady, but mixing human blood with full-blooded Klatch is very dangerous."

Katelyn wasn't in the mood to poke holes in Holly's argument, but Holly sounded a bit like a zealot. However, if Holly could help her get to Rita in time to save her friend from becoming a pawn, Katelyn would have to overlook Holly's political views for now.

"Let's go. I'll deal with Grayson later."

17

"We have to hurry."

Katelyn followed Holly to the end of a long hallway where a huge tapestry hung. People made of thread laughed and cavorted in a brightly colored, lush landscape, and Katelyn averted her eyes, unable to look at their smiling faces.

Holly lifted the side of the tapestry and gestured for Katelyn to follow.

A few steps forward brought Katelyn close enough to see the lady's maid push open a door that blended so well with the wall, Katelyn would have missed it even without the tapestry blocking her view.

"Mind the steps, my lady. It's dark, but there's a door to the outside at the bottom."

Her mind numb, Katelyn stepped inside and nearly gasped as the door swung shut behind her and plunged them into inky blackness. The smell of rich earth filled her senses, and chill air licked at her skin until she shivered. "Shit."

"Trail your hand down the wall and keep moving, my lady."

Holly's footsteps moved away, much faster than Katelyn was willing to move without the benefit of her sight.

She stretched out her arm until her fingertips brushed smooth, cold stone. After bracing all her weight on her left foot, she stretched out her right foot, searching for the next step. When she found purchase, she stepped down carefully and then repeated the entire process.

The steps were smooth and clear of debris, and the passage didn't seem to be dusty or unused. She wondered how often the servants slipped through these passages and outside.

Minutes dragged by as Katelyn's breathing echoed around her and she made slow progress.

Soft moonlight spilled in through an opening door.

After enduring the inky blackness, Katelyn blinked several times to allow her eyes to adjust. Pristine white walls, absent of crystals, surrounded her, and she found herself halfway down the flight of large stone steps. More confident, now that she could see, she rushed down the remaining steps and followed Holly out into the night.

The half moon cast silver light over them, and the velvet warmth of the night, along with the pungent odor of growing things, enveloped them.

They followed the outside wall of the castle until they reached a statuary that blocked their path. Holly grabbed Katelyn's hand and pulled her through a narrow hole in the giant garden maze off to their right.

Because of the tight fit, Katelyn would bet this wasn't the maze's main path. Maybe it was something only the servants knew about and used?

Abundant foliage crowded around them, rising so high Katelyn knew Grayson wouldn't be able to see over the top.

At the thought of Grayson, Katelyn's heart constricted, and a fresh wave of betrayal and pain tore through her, quickening her steps. She hugged herself and concentrated on following the little maid as they wound and curved. Occasional branches snagged at Katelyn's hair, and she had to stop several times to free herself to keep from ripping chunks of hair from her scalp.

"Holly, Grayson, and Alyssandra said all the portals were being guarded. How are we going to get through without them seeing us?"

The maid continued forward but answered over her shoulder. "This portal isn't in common use. In fact, there are only a few people who know about it." She held a branch back to let Katelyn pass. "They rerouted parts of the maze when my parents were young—it's done every sixty years or so to keep it fresh and interesting. This portal was inside one of the new walls of the maze, but my father kept the path trimmed and used it like a private doorway to Earth."

For some reason Katelyn hadn't imagined the mousy little maid with parents and a family. Ridiculous, she knew, but the woman had seemed to blend into the background until tonight. What other things had she missed because she hadn't bothered to pay attention?

Grayson. . . . Her mind had to add.

Damnit! Why hadn't she asked more questions? She was a reasonably smart and savvy woman, but she had walked into this situation blindly and gotten comfortable. And, worse than that, she'd grown to care for him.

She abruptly closed off that train of thought as her throat tightened. Rita was in danger, and that's what she needed to concentrate on right now. Aedan had to have targeted Rita just to stay close to the needed Seer. "I'll emasculate the bastard if he hurts her," she mumbled under her breath.

Wasn't there anyone besides Rita who didn't want Katelyn only because she'd been born with this gift that had been both a blessing and a curse all her life?

Katelyn took a deep breath and willed her mind back to the issue at hand. "How will we find Rita? Can you control where the portal opens on Earth?"

"Only to a point, Seer. They are at specific points here on Tador, but they can be opened to most places on Earth as long as we don't let the humans see. Unfortunately, coming back from Earth isn't as easy." Holly stopped at a dead end in the hedge and drew a circle in the air with her open palm. A shimmery circle formed and then grew until it was an oval large enough for them to step through. "Brace yourself, Seer. The *between* is uncomfortable even to those who have been through many times. Keep moving, no matter what. It sucks at your energy, and if you stop, you will die."

"Terrific." Katelyn wondered what she had gotten herself into. But thoughts of saving Rita pushed her forward after Holly.

A bone-deep cold closed around Katelyn, stealing her breath. The taste of dank mold sat heavy on the back of her tongue as she pushed forward through the still air. With each step, her energy leached out into the void, and a quiver of panic started deep in her gut and slowly traveled up her throat.

Katelyn clamped her lips together, refusing to give in to the impulse to scream. That would waste energy, and she wanted to ensure she had plenty of reserves to get out of this awful place. Obviously, the Klatch used this mode of travel quite often, and they'd grown used to it. Even though she was a mere human and not a Klatch witch, she was determined to make it through without incident.

She trudged after the maid, forcing one foot in front of the other for what seemed like hours. Small spots began to dance in front of her eyes, and she felt light-headed.

Holly stopped and waved her open palm in a circle, again forming the shimmery oval that grew until it was large enough for them to walk through.

Katelyn wasted no more time and nearly dove through the portal, landing on her hands and knees against hard ceramic tile just behind the maid. She sucked in lungfuls of air as warmth slowly returned to her limbs.

"Please forgive me, my lady." Holly's voice was filled with genuine regret. "I did what I thought best for my home world." Holly backed away and disappeared inside the portal.

Katelyn's head snapped up, and only then did she notice she was surrounded by nearly a dozen pale blond men and one woman. Icy fingers danced down her spine.

"Welcome, Seer." The woman's voice slid over Katelyn like an oily caress—all condescension and sex. "My name is Sela, Queen of the Cunts. Welcome to my home."

"She's vanished along with her lady's maid, my lord."

Grayson's gut clenched as the guard told him what he had suspected for the past several hours. Grayson cursed and paced away, looking for something to throw or break. "Have you rechecked all the portals?"

"Yes, my lord." The guard's weathered face looked as grim as Grayson felt. "All the portals are guarded, and no one was seen entering or leaving who wasn't known to the guards."

Grayson fisted his hands at his sides as fear wormed its way through him. Somehow, he knew his Seer had gotten herself into trouble. He only wished he knew where she was so he could bring her back safely.

Shouting sounded beyond the doors to the throne room, and then the heavy doors banged open to reveal four guards dragging Valen and Holly forward. Sasha, Queen Alyssandra's lady's maid, brought up the rear.

Valen's chin was held at a proud angle, while Holly refused to meet anyone's gaze.

The king and queen chose that moment to rush into the

throne room through the side door, probably having heard the noise. "What's happened?" they asked together.

"I'm about to find out." Grayson strode forward and towered over Holly, which made the young maid cower. "What have you done with Katelyn?" His voice boomed through the room, and she winced.

The woman squeaked and then stared up at him, wide-eyed, her mouth opening and closing, but no sound emerging.

"She did what any loyal Klatch would do," Valen offered in a quiet voice.

A few steps took Grayson inside Valen's personal space, but the smaller man didn't back down. "And just what, in your warped opinion, would that be, Valen?"

"What I warned the queen we would do. Stop the triangle. And we have."

"My lord," one of the guards spoke up. "We noticed Valen sneaking around the grounds, and we followed him to a path that has been cut into one of the maze hedges. There's an old portal hidden there. Apparently, Holly told the Seer about the triangle and the fact that her friend is engaged to the Cunt, which made her run. Sela has the Seer."

Grayson's gut churned, and he turned to see Stone and Alyssandra looking pale and grave.

"We'll gather some guards and get her out of there," Stone said immediately.

"We don't know where they're holding her," Grayson reminded the King. He thought about dragging Holly back with them, but concentration was needed to set a portal destination, and she could very well lead them into a trap, or worse yet—a portal with no exit.

Alyssandra stepped forward to lay a comforting hand on Grayson's arm. "From reports, we know Sela no longer uses the house I grew up in, but I know of several other places they could've gone. Don't forget, I lived with her for the past two decades."

"It's too dangerous," Grayson said, only to be interrupted by Stone, who said, "Absolutely not."

The queen rounded on both of them, her anger causing her hair to float and spark around her like a living thing as the energy in the room increased until it was hard to breathe. "We don't have much time to waste. I'm going, and that's final. Gather your guards or stay behind."

She whirled toward Valen and Holly and stalked forward with murder in her eyes. "You will be tried as a terrorist and put to death, just as I promised, Valen. Make no mistake."

"No!" Holly struggled against the guards. "Let Valen live. I told the Seer everything, and I delivered her to the Cunts."

Alyssa glowered at Holly. "Believe me, I understand the things a woman will do for love. But betraying your people and endangering the well being of us all is way over the line." She leaned forward until she was nose to nose with the little woman. "Don't worry, Holly, you'll be tried and put to death together." Without taking her eyes off Holly, she said to the guards, "Lock them up separately. I don't know if this place even has a dungeon, but if we don't, we need one."

"Alyssandra." The king's voice was low with warning, and Grayson took a step back. He didn't blame Stone for being protective—he would've done the same. But this wasn't his woman—and besides, she was a damned powerful witch who could knock him on his ass, pregnant or no.

She turned, her eyes still blazing fire. "This planet is my responsibility, Stone, and I'm the only one who knows enough about the Cunt property holdings to give us a starting place to look."

Stone's jaw clenched, and he threw a glance at Valen that promised pain and agony if anything happened to his wife. In the end, Stone nodded. "Once we find where they are holding her, you stay back and let the guards do their jobs."

Rather than answering, Alyssandra raised one eyebrow and walked out through the open throne-room doors.

"Witch," whispered Stone, the affection and grudging respect obvious in that one word.

"You were supposed to pick me up, Aedan." Rita gripped her cell phone so hard she was surprised it didn't crack in her hand.

"It can't be helped, darling." His voice sounded normal, but Rita got the distinct impression he was lying through his teeth. "Why don't you just grab a cab and meet me at the following address." He rattled off an address that would take her at least an hour cab ride to get to—after she called one.

Phoenix wasn't like New York or Boston. There wasn't a cab sitting on every corner waiting to take you where you wanted to go. Things were so spread out in Phoenix, everyone needed their own car—or a reliable fiancé who remembered he told you he would pick you up!

Rita rummaged for a pad of paper and a pencil in the cubby behind the display case and scribbled down the address. "You still haven't told me why we are going way out there. There's nothing but farmland and private homes out that far."

"You'll have to trust me, love."

Was that a woman she heard in the background? Her gut twisted, and she had a sudden irrational desire to run home and lock the door.

What the hell?

"I promise you, Rita, it will be worth it."

Click.

Rita's eyes widened as she realized he had hung up on her.

She flung her cell phone on the counter with a curse, glad she hadn't broken the thick glass of the display case.

One of the three dark-haired male hunks Detective Damien had left to watch her—if he even was a detective—glanced over at her, and she ground her teeth.

She had called the Phoenix police department to check on Damien and had received reassurances that he was legitimate, but something still didn't feel right.

Did everyone in her life right now think she was an idiot, or was she truly losing her mind? Her patience had run out.

She closed her eyes and sighed. "Damn, I'm turning into Katelyn, trusting gut feelings rather than logic."

"Using a balance of both has always served me best," said a deep voice.

Rita started, and her eyes flew open to see Detective Damien standing in front of her. His long hair had been pulled back and fastened at the back of his neck, and his strange purple eyes held amusement.

"You scared the crap out of me!" she said.

He didn't smile, but there was definite amusement in his eyes. "My apologies. That was not my intention." He gave a sharp nod, which once again reminded her of something out of regency England rather than modern day. "Are you all right? I think your cell phone is repentant for whatever it has done." He picked up the phone, tracing one long finger across the crack that had blossomed in the faceplate.

His calm, slightly amused voice irritated her somehow. "I'm just frustrated with all the people lately I know aren't telling me the entire truth." She fixed him with an intense glare. "But who'd expect me to accept what they tell me without question."

Now he did smile, just a slight curving of the lips that made his handsome face devastating and nearly stole her breath. "I'm sure you can't be referring to me, because you already checked my credentials." He raised his eyebrows in question and then shook his head. "I see." His amusement only seemed to increase. "You do need to keep in mind that detectives are secretive by nature."

Rita crossed her arms, enjoying the banter despite her anger and suspicions. "Uh-huh. I think there's more to it than that, but I have other men to worry about right now who confuse me much more than you do."

"I couldn't help but overhear. It sounds like he's left you without a ride." He rubbed his fingers over his chin, where the faintest shadow of dark stubble had begun to appear, and glanced at the pad of paper on which she'd scribbled the address Aedan had given her. "I would be more than happy to give you a ride. I live out that way."

Rita was surprised to find she wanted to accept, though she wasn't so sure she wanted to see Aedan tonight. Her gut roiled at the thought of meeting him, and yet she wanted to get to the bottom of whatever he was hiding from her. If she might murder someone, who better to take along than a cop? She nearly laughed.

"I'm perfectly safe, you know." He grabbed his badge off his belt and held it up. "Detective. Cop. Good guy." He grinned, and she smiled back before she could stop herself.

"Doesn't driving me around go against department regulations or something?"

His expression turned sheepish. "Technically. But I am off duty. I was just checking in on my way home." He cocked his head to one side, which made him seem more approachable somehow. "So are you in?"

She did laugh this time. "All right. I'd appreciate it," she said before she could change her mind.

"Great. Have you found anything else missing from your shop?"

Her brow furrowed as her thoughts turned back toward the break-in. "Nothing from the shop. And I can't say for sure about anything inside Katelyn's apartment until she returns."

"Let me know."

A friendly yet awkward silence fell between them until they both laughed.

Rita ripped the page with the address from the notepad to give her hands something to do. "Give me about fifteen minutes to take care of some things and get one of the cashiers to lock up for me?"

"I'll be waiting in the café. I have to feed my caffeine addiction." His deep purple gaze bore into hers, and her heart did a funny little jump as she looked back at him.

She dropped her eyes and instantly felt the loss. "We have great gourmet coffees. Oh, and you might want to let your guys know they can leave. Though I have to say, having some tall, dark, and hunky men around has really raised the frequency of our female business."

Damien glanced over his shoulder at the nearest dark hunk, who had four attractive women all trying to catch his eye.

"Pretty rough duty." He turned back to her. "But I prefer mine right now."

Heat flared into her cheeks and also between her thighs. Aedan never made her feel like he could eat her for dessert in the middle of a roomful of people. Maybe there was something to this gut-feeling thing after all.

18

Katelyn pushed to her feet, her knees and palms still stinging from landing so hard on the tile at the Cunt queen's feet.

She might have been stupid and allowed herself to get into this situation, but she would face it standing tall. "What the hell do you want from me?" A quick glance around the room at what looked like a holding cell and some type of kinky-looking S and M device didn't calm her at all. Neither did the half dozen mean-looking guards stationed around the room looking at her like she was their new toy.

Sela tsked as she looked Katelyn up and down. "Such a nice body to waste on fucking one of those Klatch bastards—even the royal ones. You're curvy rather than fat like that ungrateful cow I raised. I'm sure you'll soon appreciate the superiority of the Cunts in that arena."

Cold marched up the back of Katelyn's neck. This was the woman who had raised Alyssa? She still remembered the look of anger and hatred that had burned in the queen's eyes when she had spoken of this woman.

Goddess help me. . . .

Was she going to be raped? She bit back her fear and instead let her anger shine in her eyes. "I have no intention of fucking anyone I don't choose to. You obviously wanted me for something, because evidently you paid off the lady's maid to bring me here. So what do you want?"

Sela circled her, and Katelyn turned to keep the woman in her line of sight. Sela may be the queen here, but to Katelyn she looked like Malibu Barbie—but with evil glittering in her clear blue eyes.

Psycho Malibu Barbie takes on Freddie Kruger in a cage match. Katelyn couldn't even muster a smile at her own joke. Although she felt sorry for Freddie in that match up.

"I only want you to fulfill your purpose, Seer." Sela spread manicured hands wide, showing off very tasteful but expensive gold rings. "We'll help you complete your coming-of-age ceremony, and then you and your business partner will help us perform our own triangle ceremony that will give us power over our home planet."

"I would rather die than help you take over Tador." Katelyn suppressed a shudder at these people having rule over the planet that had brought her so many happy memories.

Sela ran a manicured nail down the side of Katelyn's cheek, and Katelyn flinched. "You mistakenly think we are asking your opinion. You *will* help us one way or another—and then you'll die."

Fear snaked through Katelyn.

She had no idea how to answer that, so she kept silent.

"Besides," Sela continued, "you had your chance to be part of the triangle on Tador and stay with those weaklings who hold my planet. Obviously, you ran away of your own free will."

Katelyn scowled because she couldn't dispute this. Damnit! Why hadn't Grayson been straight with her and explained the triangle earlier?

She acknowledged she would've run fast and far, but who knows? After she'd had a chance to think it through, she might have chosen to help.

But he hadn't given her the chance.

If Katelyn had it to do over again, she would confront Grayson with Holly's information and hash it out.

In hindsight, she knew he wouldn't have left Rita on Earth if he'd thought she was in danger. Katelyn remembered the guards he'd said were watching Rita and the shop and wanted to smack herself in the head.

If she ever got a hold of Holly, she would rip the little manipulative bitch limb from limb.

It was ironic, now that she saw the situation clearly and wanted a chance to fix it. Now she might not ever get to.

Her hair fell into her face, and she brushed it away. "What does Rita have to do with this?"

"My lovely fiancée has been chosen to be your blood sacrifice." A tall, pale man she recognized from the attack at her shop stepped into the room.

Katelyn's blood chilled further. Clammy moisture dampened her palms and her forehead. *Blood sacrifice?* A quick flash of the crudely painted red symbols in her vision made her pause.

The symbols were painted in blood. . . .

"I don't believe we've met." The man smiled, revealing even, white teeth. "I'm Aedan, Rita's fiancé. Though, due to current circumstances, she won't be alive long enough to plan a wedding."

Damien glanced over at the woman in the passenger's seat and couldn't help but smile. The setting sun shone off her short brown hair and made her blue eyes shine.

This was one of the easiest favors he had ever done for the Klatch.

He was only half Klatch, but he'd grown up listening to his mother tell stories about her home. He hoped one day to visit, but there was a definite bigotry against non–full bloods, even though there were a lot of Klatch half breeds walking the streets of Earth.

However, Damien's mother had several friends and relatives within the Klatch Royal Guard, and once he joined the police force, he often did favors for the guard to help keep the Klatch activities off the human radar, so to speak. He knew they only told him what was necessary and no more, but if his mother were alive, this would have made her happy.

"I really appreciate you driving me out here."

"I told you I live out this way anyway." Sort of—as in, the totally opposite direction. His Klatch favor only entailed keeping an eye on Rita and making sure no Cunts returned to her shop, but something about this situation told him there was more, and he couldn't help but dig deeper. He wasn't sure if it was cop instinct or infatuation with the woman sitting next to him—or both.

Her brown hair was cut into a short bob that made her look like a pixie. Large blue eyes almost too big for her face, and Cupid's bow lips, fascinated him. Damien's cock hardened as he thought about exploring those enticing lips.

Normally he wouldn't allow himself such thoughts about an engaged woman, but for some reason he couldn't get this woman out of his mind.

"So how long have you been engaged?"

Her expression darkened, and she sucked her bottom lip inside her mouth as she glanced down at the diamond ring on her left hand.

"Only a few days." She shook her head. "I was so excited to get engaged, but now . . ." She turned to look out the window as if the passing scenery held some answers. "It seems like once I said yes, Aedan turned into a different person. Distant, secretive. I can't explain it, but it's just not right." She huffed out a breath and rolled her eyes. "Sorry. Didn't mean to unload on you there."

"No problem. You should always listen to your gut—it's saved my life more times than I can count." He sped up to make it through a yellow light. "Cops aren't exactly bartenders, but I like it when I don't have to beat confessions out of people."

She laughed as he'd hoped. "What about you? Are you married?"

He shook his head. "No. I've had several long-term relationships, but none of the women want to share me with my job, so the relationships haven't lasted."

Rita nodded. "I hope you find someone. You're too much of a nice guy to be alone."

Damien's brow furrowed, and he passed a slow-moving SUV before he turned to look at her. "How do you know I'm a nice guy?"

"Well, all the hotties you stationed at my store respect you, and they've told me several stories to back that up. Also, not many men would drive an hour in the opposite direction from where they live to take me out to Arizona farming country." She grinned. "But I do appreciate it."

He laughed. "Busted."

The "hotties" were actually full-blood Klatch guards, so it meant a lot to him to hear he had earned their respect. "How did you know?"

"I plied the guards with brownies and coffee when they first arrived, and they told me about you." She grinned. "I wasn't going to get into a car with a complete stranger—even if he *is* good-looking."

Damien winked over at her. "So . . . you think I'm good-looking. I think that's a good start."

She laughed. "Where were you a few weeks ago before I got engaged?"

He slowed and turned into the neighborhood the address indicated. "Look at it this way. Maybe I'm the temptation put before you to test if you made the right decision or not." He glanced over at her again. "I'd *looove* to help you decide."

"I'll just bet you would." She faced forward, but there was a wide grin on her face.

He stopped at a four-way stop and gazed out over the cotton fields thick with greenery. It always amazed him that just a short drive out of the city there were lush farmlands and pastures. The houses this far out tended to be fewer and farther between, due to the fields or horse property, and several of the roads weren't paved.

He waved a Toyota 4x4 through the intersection and then turned left, wincing as the now-dirt road kicked up gravel against the bottom of his car. "Should be just past these next fields on the right."

A large, yellow, two-story farmhouse stood in a crisply manicured yard, which seemed totally out of place with the rest of the houses in the area. Six cars of varying makes sat in the driveway and in the side yard, and Damien noted some serious surveillance equipment on the roof—cameras, floodlights, motion sensors, etc.

He slowed as they neared the house, flipped open the phone on his belt, and hit speed dial for one of the Klatch still guarding the shop.

Rita's brow furrowed, but she remained silent.

Zack picked up on the first ring. "Damien."

"My internal cop alarms are going off like crazy. This farmhouse out in Litchfield? It looks out of place, with some extremely high-tech surveillance equipment. I want someone to know where we're at in case there's a problem."

"I'm sending two men, just to be sure," came the gruff voice on the other end.

Damien gave Zack the address and hung up as he pulled into the long cement driveway—another rarity in a neighborhood with gravel driveways. "You sure you want to go in there?"

Rita must've felt the bad vibes, too, because she shook her head. She stared up at the house and rubbed her hands up and down her arms as though cold. "No. This doesn't feel right at all."

Damien put the car in reverse just as a sizzling blue bolt of energy cracked against the hood.

Sparks flew inside the car as systems shorted, and the car died.

Rita screamed, and Damien reached for his Ruger while hitting REDIAL on his phone and then dropping it to the floor. At least Zack would know to hurry.

Blue beams hit from several directions, and the smell of burning wires rose around them.

The car's window shattered, shards of the safety glass flying. Damien lunged over Rita to shield her the best he could.

When the worst of the explosion of glass passed, he sat up, bringing his Ruger into firing position and looking for a target.

Another energy beam snaked out and connected with the barrel of his weapon. The electricity surged through the firearm and singed his fingers.

He cursed and tossed the gun away. It skittered over the charred hood of his car before falling on the ground.

"Damien!" Rita sounded panicked but not hysterical.

A tall blond man jumped onto the hood of the car and knelt to look inside the now broken windshield. "Well, it's the half-breed detective. Thanks for bringing my fianceé."

Blue energy filled Damien's vision, and then . . . nothing.

Grayson slammed his fist into the wooden bookcase in the queen's archives and cursed in frustration. Sharp pain lanced through his knuckles as his skin split open, and the impact jarred his entire arm.

"Did that help?" Alyssandra asked with a raised eyebrow.

He scowled at her, but she only motioned for Sasha to tend to his hand. "No," he said as he flopped down in an empty chair. "I've never felt so helpless in my entire life."

Stone and Ryan shot sympathetic glances toward him, but remained silent.

Grayson winced as Sasha smoothed some *ponga* over his injury. He knew it would disinfect the wound, but it would also cause arousal to generate the sexual energy his body needed to heal. That only brought home the fact that Katelyn was gone. "Maybe there are some places we haven't checked—"

The queen interrupted him. "About a gazillion, but we went to every single place I knew the Cunts owned when I lived among them. We have to find another way to pinpoint where they've taken her."

Ryan rubbed his thumb absently over his scar. "Too bad you two don't have a psychic connection like Alyssandra and Stone, Gray. That would at least let us talk to her."

Gray cursed under his breath as his cock hardened uncomfortably inside his breeches from the *ponga*. He shifted to find a more comfortable position.

"Wait." Alyssandra sat forward in her seat, her lavender eyes snapping with barely suppressed excitement. "Maybe we do have a way to contact her."

"How?" Grayson tried to sit forward, but his aching cock protested being bent at that angle.

"Do you remember when you and Stone caught Katelyn and me in the baths?"

The memory of that scene rose up as if seared into his mind. Katelyn's pale body laid out on the platform, her waterfall of red hair streaming down to be teased by the roiling water,

Alyssandra's face buried between his Seer's thighs, Katelyn's pink nipples tight and straining as she moaned out her orgasm.

Grayson's balls tightened, and he knew the tip of his cock would be leaking pre-come. He nodded, not sure if he could speak past the surge of heat pulsing through his body.

"And didn't you say you entered her dreams, and that's how you healed your shoulder and helped her heal her wound?" Alyssandra's voice shook with eagerness.

"Yes, but how can we combine those two things to help us now?" This came from Stone, who had followed the conversation with a scowl.

The queen huffed out a breath, frustrated with them all for not keeping up.

"Wait." Ryan smiled and pointed toward Alyssandra. "I get what you're saying. But if you're right, they are going to try to perform her coming-of-age ceremony. And if they do it their way, she won't ever be able to participate in the triangle with us. She'll be bound to them."

Anger, laced with fear for Katelyn, ran a line of cold through Grayson's body, quieting his unruly cock. He started to protest, but Ryan held up a hand.

"Give me a second to explain before you turn into the protective Neanderthal."

Grayson scowled, but remained silent.

"Have any of you ever seen the Cunt version of the coming-of-age ceremony?" When everyone shook their heads, Ryan smiled. "My mother told me about one she saw before the Cunts were banished from Tador. Their ceremony is a perversion of ours, and their coming-of-age ceremony combines some of the same elements from our ascension, but it's almost backward. They always start with the contribution small contribution of blood, then of essence, and then they move on to the blood sacrifice as they consummate."

Grayson glanced at his hand, not surprised to see light scabs already forming over the injuries. His cock throbbed, and he knew he needed to come soon, and he didn't relish the thought of doing it here while they were discussing how to save his Seer. "I'm not getting how this is going to help us."

Alyssandra gazed directly into his eyes.

An extremely vivid, full-color vision of the scene in the baths rose up inside his mind's eye, though this time Ryan and Sasha stood beside him as well as Stone.

Katelyn's hips arched off the platform, and her fingers gripped the gel-covered sides as she screamed out her release.

The pressure inside Grayson's balls broke, and he grunted as he came, his eyes slipping closed as the very intense orgasm ripped through his system.

When he opened his eyes, he found himself staring again into the queen's smiling face, and the front of his breeches was soaked with his come.

"Damn." Ryan's voice sounded strained, and his erection was obvious, tenting the front of his breeches. "That was one of the most erotic things I've ever seen." His voice held awe and wonder. "If we get to see things like that for this triangle, I'm totally in."

Grayson swallowed hard and stood, cursing as the warm wetness stuck against his skin. "Point taken, my queen."

She inclined her head. "That should heal your knuckles. We have about a half hour until the sun has fully set on Earth and they'll start the ceremony. Let's go to the private baths to try to connect with the Seer. The water as well as the *balda* is more conductive and might help us funnel energy better."

"Group sex with the queen," Ryan said with a smile. "I think I'm going to like this."

Grayson could only agree—especially after that reminder of what he'd seen.

Stone still scowled.

"That's what the triangle will be anyway, Stone." Ryan stood, entirely too pleased with himself. "Get used to sharing."

Grayson shook his head. "Wait until it's *your* woman you're sharing, Ryan."

Ryan's face clouded as that last point hit home. He looked at Stone and then at Grayson. "You may have a valid point there."

Fast, heavy footsteps pounded toward them, and Grayson tried to hide his wet breeches with a nearby book.

Gavin, the captain of the Royal Guard, looked flushed as though he'd been running. "Zack knows where they're being held, and now the Cunts most likely have Rita and the detective. It will take Zack and his men about an hour to get there."

Everyone started moving toward the door except Stone. "Wait."

When he had everyone's attention, he continued. "If she completes the coming-of-age ceremony with all our energy and then decides not to go through with the triangle, we won't be able to replace her with another Seer." He glanced at each one of them in turn, and Grayson's heart constricted inside his chest.

Leaving Katelyn to the Cunts wasn't an option—it would give the Cunts power over the triangle. Even worse, he would lose her. He tried to imagine another woman in his arms, another woman taking her place by his side in the triangle, and he winced against a sharp pain that felt as if someone had stabbed him through the heart.

"If Katelyn doesn't choose the triangle . . ." He looked at each of them in turn and spoke his feelings even though they burned his throat, "then I can't either." He shook his head. "I'm so sorry . . . I can't—"

Stone smiled grimly. "You know I understand." He placed a comforting hand on Grayson's shoulder. "I wasn't suggesting we leave her. I only wanted everyone to be aware what's on the line if we do this."

Ryan spoke up. "Tador is a part of Katie-Cat. I'm willing to take the gamble."

Alyssandra smiled. "We're wasting time. It sounds like we're all agreed. Let's go before Grayson's breeches dry to his thighs."

19

Katelyn's awareness slowly returned, but she couldn't seem to will her eyes to open or her limbs to move. She expanded her senses, but even those were sluggish and slow. Her steady heartbeat echoed in time with her throbbing head, but it seemed as if her blood had become too thick to move fluidly through her veins.

A fuzzy thought occurred to her that she must've been drugged.

Her mind told her she should be terrified but apparently her body had no surplus energy to entertain that emotion.

A cold breeze fluttered across her bare skin, and she realized she was naked. A small trickle of panic broke through her haze. With supreme willpower, she moved her fingertips on one hand, and they brushed against rough stone.

The altar!

Shit! Katelyn would bet that if she were able to open her eyes, there would be a large, crudely painted triangle on the wall—the one she had seen in her vision.

Just as she decided that she should muster enough energy to

feel some despair, she sensed a familiar tickle at the edge of her consciousness.

It felt like . . . Grayson . . . and Alyssandra . . . and others.

Those must be some strong drugs they gave me!

She suddenly found herself in the private baths on Tador where she and Alyssandra had been caught together. "Wha—"

Grayson's arms closed around her, and she groaned at the feel of his naked body pressed against the length of hers. "Don't talk, Seer. The Cunts still have you. We've come to you in a vision."

"How?" she whispered.

"Shhh," he soothed, and she collapsed against him, her chin resting on his shoulder while he held her.

Her eyes fluttered open, and she noticed King Stone, Alyssa, and Ryan, also nude and inside the baths.

The queen smiled at her reassuringly. "Don't speak or they'll hear you. Just nod."

Grayson nipped her earlobe, causing a fresh surge of energy to snake through her body, which chased back the lethargy swimming inside her a little. "You have to trust us, Katelyn. Do you trust me?"

She nodded. "Sorry . . ." she said so softly she wasn't sure he heard it.

"It's all right. I should've told you earlier." He tightened his arms around her, and she pursed her lips together to keep from speaking again. "None of that matters now. We think we can get you out of this if you trust us. You'll have to go through the coming-of-age ceremony, but the choice of the triangle will be up to you."

He pulled back and took her chin in his hand, his gaze locked with hers until she thought she might drown in the amethyst depths of his eyes. "Do you understand?"

She opened her mouth and then snapped it shut. If she could speak, she would tell him how angry and hurt she was. But for now she would settle for whatever it took to get out of this situation—even if it meant sleeping with the entire planet of Klatch.

Grayson brushed a kiss over her lips, causing another surge of energy to snake through her. "Just like in the dream vision you and I had the first day you were here, we can complete your coming-of-age ceremony with just you and I. However, because you aren't physically here, Alyssandra is going to pull everyone inside that chamber inside one of her visions. They will think they are carrying out their own ceremony, but I promise you it won't be real."

"We'll use the energy of Tador to power the vision so you'll be linked to the planet and its effects, but by the time the Cunts figure that out, it will be too late for them to do anything about it," Alyssandra added.

"Remember, love, it's not real, but try to act as if it is." Grayson's thumb feathered over her cheek, but she barely felt it. "No matter what you see. All right?"

Warmth curled around her heart, and her eyes widened. Had he just called her "love"?

The word resonated inside her and took root. Was that what she felt for Grayson?

She studied him. His eyes held a possessive warmth she had never noticed before; along with concern, and, if she wasn't mistaken, a trace of terror.

At least, that's what she was feeling at the thought of never seeing Grayson again. The intense emotion nearly ripped her in two.

When had it happened? Somewhere in the last handful of days, it had snuck up on her and captured her unaware.

Love . . . that's what she felt for Grayson. She was in love with him.

"Are you ready?" he asked.

Katelyn nodded and hugged him tight. She took a last glance

around, only then realizing that at least twenty hunky Klatch men also sat in the private pool with them. Her brow furrowed in confusion. What exactly did this ceremony entail?

The scene abruptly changed, and she was strapped naked to the altar she had seen in her previous vision. The crudely painted triangle symbol marred the wall at her feet. She stiffened.

"Remember . . . not real." Grayson's deep voice feathered against her ear, and she instantly relaxed, trying to appear as if the drugs hadn't worn off at all. A few naked Cunts milled around the room, and the entire scene had a surreal feeling, like a nightmare of being strapped to a dentist's chair—antiseptic and impersonal, yet invasive.

The woman who had introduced herself as Sela filled Katelyn's vision, her blond hair falling over her forehead and into her face, obscuring large blue eyes.

"Finally awake, Seer? It's time for your coming-of-age ceremony—the correct version—not that archaic bullshit the Klatch still cling to."

Katelyn allowed her head to loll to the side, as if it were a struggle to make even that small movement.

Sela smirked and ran one manicured finger through the curls on Katelyn's mound. "Save your strength, Seer. Between the energy blast we knocked you out with and a nice cocktail of something to help you relax, you'll not be able to do more than lie back and enjoy our attentions."

Katelyn recoiled from the finger and only then realized she didn't feel it touching her. However, the stone altar did dig into the sensitive skin of her ass, and she tried to wiggle to find a more comfortable position.

She focused her mind and started to understand what Grayson and Alyssa had meant. The Cunts had her in the altar room, which meant she really was strapped naked to this uncomfortable hunk of rock. But if the queen pulled everyone into a vision, their brains would tell them what Alyssa wanted them to see.

Terrific—I'm laid out like an erotic meal on a platter. This plan of yours better work, Grayson! She knew he couldn't hear her, but she hoped screaming it inside her head would convey the general idea to him.

Sela's evil laugh echoed around the room, running stabs of icy fear down Katelyn's spine despite what her logic had just worked out. Sela cast an imperious glance toward the back of the room. "Aedan, bring your human bitch and the spare. We're ready to start."

Katelyn stiffened and tried to struggle against the haze that still lay over her mind.

Grayson's warm lips grazed over the sensitive skin at her neck, and she shivered, but relaxed against him. "*It's not real. Relax.*"

Easy for him to say—he wasn't the one trussed up on this rock watching this!

Sela returned her attention to Katelyn, and evil glee glittered inside the woman's eyes as her oily gaze raked over Katelyn, making her feel unclean.

Katelyn tried to flinch away, even though she couldn't feel Sela's touch.

"She's attractive enough that I just might take her myself when the ceremony is complete." Sela licked her lips in anticipation.

Aedan edged into her line of sight with Rita tossed over his shoulder like a bag of dog food.

Katelyn bit back a gasp as she saw her friend, her vision suddenly too real. "No," slipped through her lips as a soft whisper before she could stop it.

Aedan dumped Rita on the other altar like a rag doll, and her head cracked hard against the unforgiving stone.

Katelyn winced.

"*Not real.*" Grayson's deep voice sounded softly inside her ear, and she held her breath, trying to convince her pounding heart.

"Your friend has been kind enough to volunteer to be the blood sacrifice for your ceremony." Aedan smirked. "It worked out perfectly. There's such a close attachment between you, the energy from her blood will give a nice boost."

Sela pulled off her tank top to reveal small, pert, pink-tipped breasts. Her nipples were large and nearly overpowered the small mounds of her breasts. However, her body was tight and muscled like an athlete's. She skimmed her pants down her hips and kicked them off, leaving herself bare.

A ripping sound off to the side brought Katelyn's attention back to Rita. Aedan tore her clothes off in violent tugs, yanking them out from under her until she lay naked on the altar, just like in Katelyn's vision.

She screwed her eyes shut, internally chanting, *Not real. Not real. Not real.*

A sound she couldn't identify startled her.

She opened her eyes to see an unconscious, dark-haired man on the floor between the altars. A Cunt warrior kicked him hard in the chest before retreating.

Sela clapped her hands twice, making Katelyn jump.

A long line of pale blond men filed into the room and stood naked at the feet of both altars. She recognized a few of them as the men who had attacked her and Grayson in her store that first night.

Katelyn couldn't help but notice that some had large, thick cocks that jutted out proudly from a pale nest of curls, while others' cocks were long and thin like a pencil or short and stubby like a Vienna sausage. But all of them stood as alert as they were able to—the cocks as well as the men.

Katelyn couldn't remember if she had ever seen so many cocks on display at one time before. If the circumstances weren't so dire, she might have enjoyed inspecting them.

However, none were as good as Grayson's, whose was thick and long with dusky skin and seemed to be made specifically for her.

Aedan walked in front of her, now totally naked.

He carried an empty goblet and a wicked-looking, curved knife—the blade looked almost like the letter C.

"Get on with it," Sela snapped and took the goblet from him. She wedged it between Katelyn's thighs, tight against her clit. Katelyn expected the metal goblet to feel cold, but it might as well not have been there.

"The Cunts start their ceremonies with blood from the participants and then offer a blood sacrifice to cement the ritual," added Ryan.

Katelyn resisted the urge to answer, but she appreciated his voice, which reminded her that she wasn't alone inside the most surreal vision of her life. How many Seers had ever had an en-masse vision?

Sela placed the wicked blade against her palm, and with a quick motion sliced open the skin. She made a fist and squeezed several drops of blood into the goblet between Katelyn's thighs.

Aedan accepted the knife and repeated the process. Then he dipped his first two fingers inside the liquid and reached out toward her.

She flinched from his reach, but couldn't escape.

His fingers traced the same triangle pattern from the wall onto her stomach, and then he held out the dripping fingers for Sela, who sucked them between her lips and licked them clean.

She released them and then turned toward the twenty naked men at the foot of the altars. "It's midnight. Let the ceremony begin so we can celebrate the Seer's birthday."

Something cool and smooth feathered against Katelyn's nipples and then between her legs, and she frowned, trying to see where the sensation had come from.

"It's ponga, love. Relax."

As though triggered by Grayson's words, her skin began to tingle, and a slow burn of energy flowed through her, chasing back the haze. Her nipples tightened into hard buds, and her clit swelled and throbbed for attention.

The twenty Cunts surrounded her, their cocks all seeming to strain toward her. She tried to look at Rita to see if there were men surrounding her as well, but she couldn't see past the wall of male flesh.

Sela's voice started chanting words Katelyn couldn't make out, and then the others joined in. Over and over they chanted until Katelyn felt like some sort of ancient sacrifice in a book.

The men started stroking their hard cocks, and her eyes widened as she realized what could come next. *You've got to freaking be kidding me! I'm either in a gang-bang, or twenty men are going to come all over me.*

"Close your eyes. See the reality. Keep them closed. Trust me," Grayson said.

Unwilling to watch either of the possibilities, Katelyn closed her eyes, and immediately she was back inside the baths with Grayson holding her. He stroked a large hand over her hair, and she sighed against his familiar touch.

His dark, amethyst gaze burned into hers, and he slowly lowered his mouth to hers.

His lips were hot and demanding, and she instantly opened for him, his tongue dipping inside to possess and explore.

Katelyn gave herself up to the sensations as waves of energy pulsed through her body in time with the throbbing between her legs. She snuggled closer to Grayson, using her position straddling his lap to trap his cock between them and to rub her folds against him.

He hissed with pleasure and with one large palm cupped her ass and pulled her snug against him.

His dark chest hairs rasped against her nipples, intensifying the sensations, and he buried his free hand in her hair as if he were afraid she would dissolve in his arms.

Her labia throbbed, and she craved Grayson's cock inside her more than she had ever wanted anything in her life. She reached for him, and he broke the kiss to shake his head.

"Not yet, love." He rested his forehead against hers as if stopping had cost him a great deal of control. "We need more energy before we join."

The twenty Klatch men stood and moved forward in the pool to surround them. The water level licked their thighs—or for some of the shorter ones, teased the undersides of their balls—and all of them had impressive cocks straining from dark nests of curls. "Much better," she whispered and then stiffened when Grayson chuckled in her ear.

"In such a sexual society, most are blessed with very impressive equipment. The Cunts have diluted the bloodline and done so much inbreeding, they don't always see those same benefits." His voice sounded strained, but his words were patient as though it was important to help her understand.

The men surrounding them gripped their cocks in one hand and began to stroke themselves.

Every direction she looked, there was a dark wet dream stroking an impossibly large cock, and there were balls of nearly every shape and size she could imagine. Pre-come already glistened on the tips of some of the cocks, and a few beads of water streamed from muscled abdomens and down well-toned thighs covered with dark hair.

Her pussy throbbed, demanding to be filled, and she wriggled against Grayson, hoping to break through his chains of control until he fucked her hard and fast.

He took her face in his large hands and pierced her with an intense gaze. "We need their essence to give us enough energy to make this vision real—to link your coming of age with the Klatch and not with the Cunts. Do you understand?"

She furrowed her brow and she squirmed against him, relief from this intense sexual frustration the only thing on her mind.

"Trust me?"

He repeated those words again as though to assure himself more than her. She stared into the dark, swirling depths of his eyes and wanted to drown in the deep passion she saw.

She nodded, and a slow smile spread across Grayson's face as if she had given him the best gift in the world.

He lowered his face to hers, capturing her lips, his thumbs feathering over her cheeks, his palms hot against her skin. Their tongues dueled together as her nipples and slit still tingled and nearly burned with urgency.

She traced her fingers down over the muscles of his back and shoulders, enjoying how his body fit so perfectly against hers.

A whirlpool of energy slowly churned inside her as Grayson pleasured her mouth and held her tight.

Their breathing quickened, and they gasped for air between deep kisses as they devoured each other. The sounds of splashing water and flesh slapping against flesh filled her ears, and her body screamed for Grayson to drive inside her and add their own flavor to the cacophony of noise.

One of the men growled, and a sizzling burst of hot energy hit her shoulder. Katelyn cried out as her body absorbed it like a greedy child with candy. The foreign energy swirled with her own and intensified every sensation.

Grayson swallowed her cry and delved back inside her mouth, teasing, tracing, nipping, and then soothing.

Four more hot bursts of energy hit her back and shoulders

in quick succession, and she arched against them as she actually felt her skin suck the offered essence inside like nourishment.

Grayson held her tightly as more and more of the sizzling deposits hit her skin.

She lost track of all reality—there were only Grayson's lips on hers, anchoring her, and the growing energy swirling inside her. It howled faster and faster, until she was afraid her body would never be able to contain it all. A quick fear of her body shattering into a million pieces flashed through her mind, but then was lost as the wave of energy engulfed her, pulling her under, threatening to drown her in the overwhelming sensations.

Fear and panic combined, and her eyes flew open, thrusting her back into the room where she was tied to an altar. Aedan stood between her spread thighs and thrust his long, thin cock inside her.

She flinched against the invasion, a scream starting in the back of her throat. The sound came out only as a strangled squeak because she felt—nothing. "That's it?" she asked out loud before she remembered that this wasn't real. Aedan wasn't inside her and would never be.

However, Aedan, who was caught in the vision, scowled, and thrust harder, trying to punish her for her comment.

"*Come back to me. Close your eyes. . . .*" Grayson's voice pulled her back, and she allowed her eyes to slip closed.

His handsome face formed before her. "Let's hope I don't get the same reaction." Without warning, he drove into her, pulling her down hard onto his lap, burying himself deep inside her aching heat.

Katelyn couldn't contain the shaky gasp that spilled from her throat or the long moan that followed it.

His mouth slanted over hers, and she was plunged back inside the swirling vortex of sensations assaulting her.

She was dimly aware of Alyssa crying out—ecstasy plain in her strangled shout—and then Stone's voice and Ryan's joined the fray.

Grayson drove inside her mercilessly, filling her impossibly with each rough thrust.

Her pussy pulsed around him, dragging her over the edge and into an orgasm that contracted her entire body and rolled huge waves of pleasure through her until she was afraid she wouldn't be able to bear any more.

Grayson thrust hard once more, crying out as his hot seed spilled inside her—causing the vortex inside her to explode once more.

Colors flashed behind her eyelids, and energy sizzled over her skin, making every hair on her body stand on end. Finally, she floated back into her body and made the mistake of opening her eyes in time to see Sela thrust the curved knife deep into Rita's bare stomach.

"No!" She tried to sit up, but her arms and legs wouldn't obey her commands. Tears sprang to her eyes and strangled sobs broke from her lips.

Sela and Aedan shouted with joy, and the other Cunts joined in. "She is ours!"

Sela stalked forward, the knife still dangled from her hand, dripping with Rita's blood. Little splatters of crimson marred her pale skin.

Katelyn tasted bile on the back of her tongue and swallowed hard.

"You are ours to control, now, Seer. You can't fight us. You've been infused with our energy." Aedan stepped behind Sela, a smirk on his face as he laid a possessive arm around her shoulders.

"Listen to me carefully, Seer." Sela leaned so close to Katelyn's face small droplets of spittle sprayed forward. "You will return to Tador, and you will kill the queen. Poison her, stab her, I don't care. Just do it." She bared her teeth. "Our spy will be watching and will tell us when it's complete."

Then all hell broke loose.

The room exploded around her.

Shards of wood and plaster rained down over everything, and angry shouts filled the air.

Sizzling beams of blue and pink seared through the room, leaving the smell of burning ozone in their wake.

A blue beam bore down on her—directly toward her face.

She winced, ready for the painful impact, but just before it reached her, it bounced off some unseen barrier and hit the wall in front of her, piercing the crude triangle drawing.

Katelyn clamped her eyes shut. "Grayson!" Her shout echoed through the room, blending with the riot of noise.

"*Katelyn, I'm here. The Klatch are there to retrieve you.*" "*Sleep.*" She noticed Grayson's voice was heavy with languor.

She tried to speak, to ask questions or figure out what was happening, but the suggestion was too strong, and a comfortable blackness sucked her under.

20

Sela groaned and sat up. She rubbed her shoulder, where she'd been hit by a Klatch energy beam, and glanced around at the ruin and stench that used to be her altar room.

Her warriors groaned and slowly stirred around the room, a few lay totally still, their open eyes unseeing. She hoped they didn't start to stink before they had a chance to dispose of the bodies.

The Seer, the sacrifice, and even the spare were nowhere to be seen. The damned Klatch who'd destroyed her house must've taken them.

A laugh slowly built inside her throat, and she let it out, even though every small movement hurt. "It's too late. She is ours now."

She lay back against the floor and let the warmth of victory flow though her.

Waiting had seemed like an eternity, but now it was so close she felt as if she could reach out and touch it. Soon, very soon, she would sit on the Tador throne where she belonged.

* * *

Grayson knocked lightly on the door to Alyssandra and Stone's private rooms.

The door cracked open, and Sasha beckoned him inside. Immediately, the scent of lavender that always clung to the queen filled his nostrils and made him smile.

"I came to check on Rita and the detective."

"Grayson." Alyssandra rushed forward to envelop him in a quick hug. "They're both sleeping. It will take time for them to recover from the energy blasts, but other than that, they seem fine. Sasha is watching over them." She gestured toward the lady's maid, who smiled in recognition.

"I'll bring refreshments if you'll watch over my charges for a few minutes, my queen."

Alyssandra nodded her agreement and returned her attention to Grayson. "How is Katelyn? I'm assuming you just came from there."

"She hasn't stirred at all since we brought her back." He paced away and shoved his hand through his hair, pulling much of it from its tie at the back of his neck. "I'm concerned. She sleeps so deeply I can't even reach her with a vision. How can we be sure she's all right?"

The queen pulled him down onto an overstuffed chair and sat beside him. "She's been through a lot. Let her rest. Her energy is strong, and I remember sleeping a long time after my ceremony." She shook her head. "Even though she didn't ascend the throne, this was the most bizarre ceremony I've ever heard of, and it took quite a bit out of all of us, but especially her."

Grayson swallowed hard, unease roiling his stomach and making him uncomfortable. He hoped Alyssandra was right. "What of Sela's demand that Katelyn kill you?"

The queen smiled, but it didn't reach her eyes. "Let's just hope our vision worked."

"I know it did." His voice came out harsher than he'd intended. "Can't you feel the energy from Tador flowing through Katelyn more freely now?"

Alyssandra laughed and shook her head. "I meant I hope the vision worked on Sela and her crew. At least this way we have a way to flush out the spy Sela mentioned." She chewed her bottom lip as she thought. "If the vision didn't work, we might never find them until they strike."

"How do you plan on flushing them out?"

She grinned up at him. "Keep up, Grayson. I'm going to let Katelyn kill me."

Katelyn's eyes fluttered open, and she stretched like a cat, enjoying the small aches that always came after an intense bout of very good sex. She yawned and then relaxed back against the soft pillow with a large sigh. A low thrum of energy seemed to exist between her and the planet itself, grounding her and nourishing her.

She frowned in thought and turned toward the window.

What appeared to be midmorning sun spilled through the open patio doors of her room on Tador. A gentle breeze teased the long white curtains that hung at the edges of the doors and brought her the scent of gardenias, roses, and several other flowers she couldn't identify.

For a quick moment, she thought she might have dreamed following Holly through the *between* and the vision on the altar with Sela and Aedan.

Choppy memories of being carried back through the *between* and Grayson rocking her in his embrace filtered back to her, shattering her quick illusion that it hadn't happened.

The door banged open, and Grayson rushed in. Joy and relief brightened his expression, and he sank down on the bed next to her and enveloped her in a crushing hug.

She sank into his embrace, enjoying the heat and energy radiating between them as emotions welled up bright and thick, clogging her throat and making tears prick the backs of her eyes. She tightened her arms around him, and she buried her face against his chest, inhaling Grayson's scent—spicy chai and man. The combination made her smile.

She couldn't imagine not having this man in her life. This man, this world, this race of people felt more a part of her than Earth ever had. There, she was an outcast. Here, she was accepted for who and what she was.

Grayson kissed her hair. "You scared me, my little Seer."

She laughed and loosened her grip, pulling away so she could see his face. His amethyst eyes were shiny with unshed moisture he blinked away when he realized she'd seen. "I'm so sorry, Grayson. I should've confronted you when Holly told me about the triangle." After she blew out a long breath, she glanced down at her fingers. "Running is what I seem to do best, and I not only got myself in trouble, but all of you, and Rita. . . ." Her voice trailed off as the memory of the large blade plunging into Rita's bare stomach surfaced inside her mind.

"Rita is fine, as is the detective who drove her to the house." Grayson brushed her hair back from her face and then with a single finger lifted her chin and raised her gaze to his.

"Detective?"

In answer, Grayson closed his lips over hers in a gentle but firm possession of her mouth. All questions about the detective and everything else scattered at the feel of his lips on hers. She opened for him, and he delved inside, stroking and sucking her tongue and exploring each crevice of her mouth.

Her body came alive as if trained to respond only to Grayson's touch. The energy she had felt earlier, running between her and the planet, growled like a hungry dragon waking deep inside her. It wanted to be fed, and Katelyn had no objections.

Her nipples hardened, straining toward Grayson, and slick, liquid heat dampened her pussy.

Grayson groaned into her mouth as he threaded his fingers through her hair at her nape. "Dear God, I can smell your arousal."

She nipped his bottom lip, making the energy howl faster in delight.

They tore at each other's clothes until they were bare, their bodies pressed together as they writhed to close any space between them. In a quick move, Grayson rolled her beneath him and thrust inside her.

She gasped at the sudden invasion, but then widened her thighs, hooking them around his waist and raising her hips to take him more fully.

Grayson buried his face against her neck, driving inside her hard and fast, claiming her. With each thrust, he drove her higher and higher until she screamed as her orgasm slammed into her.

Grayson never slowed his pace, pounding into her as the walls of her pussy clenched around him in rhythmic waves and her toes curled with the force of her pleasure—which only served to prolong her climax.

She bit his shoulder, and he hardened further inside her.

He paused only long enough to push her legs upward to drape them over his shoulders before he drove inside her again.

She gasped as his thick length filled her, this angle making it feel like he penetrated all the way to her soul.

He palmed the globes of her ass in his large hands, tilting her and deepening the angle even further. Two more deep thrusts, and another climax slammed into her and then another, as if they came in a constant wave.

"Look at me." Grayson's voice was a demand. Katelyn's eyes fluttered open and he captured her gaze.

"I love you. . . ." The words spilled from her lips, surprising her. She hadn't known she'd planned on saying them—especially not in the middle of sweaty sex with Grayson pistoning inside her.

Her words seemed to trigger his release. He stiffened, a feral and possessive smile curving his lips before his face contorted with the force of his orgasm.

His hot come spilled inside her, and she felt every spurt as the energy roared through both of them in a searing rush and then exploded outward to shatter the mirror and sizzle along the face of the *balda*.

When her senses returned, Stone stood just inside the door to her chamber. He looked embarrassed at finding them. "My apologies. I was passing and heard the mirrors shatter and smelled the burning. . . ." His mouth snapped shut, and he backed toward the door. "My apologies."

The door closed behind him, and Grayson and Katelyn giggled like children caught being naughty.

"Say that again." Grayson's vulnerable gaze seared into hers.

Katelyn didn't pretend to misunderstand him. She took a deep breath and said, "I love you."

A smile blossomed across his face, and he kissed her hard before pulling back to look down at her again. "How did I get so lucky to fall in love with a woman who actually loves me back? That's unheard of in royal marriages, you know. Other than with Stone and Alyssandra, that is."

She laughed, happiness and sated energy curling inside her. "Is that your way of trying to get out of saying it?" She punched him in the arm. "It won't work."

He grabbed her wrists and pressed them down into the pillow on either side of her head. "I love you, Seer. Now what are you going to do about it?"

She bit her lip and took a deep breath before answering.

"Why don't you tell me about this triangle, and we'll go from there?"

He cocked his head, studying her to make sure she was serious. "Are you sure? Once we find the Healer and she goes through the coming of age, there is a triangle ascension ceremony with all of us. You'll be bound here to help provide the planet and the other participants with energy."

"I love you, and I love this place. I'll do whatever it takes to save both." Katelyn was surprised to feel no doubts—only a deep knowing that she had chosen the right path.

Where the hell was that a few days ago? She smiled and shook her head. "So, what's next?"

They gazed into each other's eyes for a long moment as a comfortable silence settled between them.

"If you're sure, then you marry me—as soon as you kill the queen."

Katelyn took a deep breath and slipped inside Alyssandra's large bedchamber. It was open and airy with crystal white walls. The color purple was everywhere in varying shades, and open books lay scattered about the room as though the queen liked to read several books at once.

Katelyn pressed her hand to the front pocket of her jeans, reassuring herself the small vial was still there and hadn't broken.

A quick glance showed her where to find her goal. The queen would return from her evening bath in a few minutes and would have hot tea as she did every night.

Katelyn made her way toward the small round table next to the huge four-poster bed. The table held only a steaming ceramic mug and another book, lying facedown and open.

Thank the Goddess Grayson and Stone had told her when the maid had gone to deliver the tea. Espionage didn't seem to be one of her strengths—especially since her hands already shook.

With silent steps, she crept forward and glanced around to make sure no one had seen her, but everything seemed calm and quiet. She squared her shoulders for courage and then worked the cork out of the top of the bottle until it came free with a small *pop*. She took a deep breath and tilted the dark vial of liquid into the mug, watching it disappear into the depths of the dark beverage.

Footsteps sounded in the hallway, and Katelyn panicked and slipped inside the large walk-in closet. She had hoped to be able to hide out on the balcony to watch, but she would have to make do. She huddled next to a large hanger full of diaphanous cloth inlaid with small crystals. She had no idea what occasion there would be to wear it, but she was glad it was large enough to hide behind.

She peeked out, careful not to be seen, and watched the queen close the door behind her and walk forward toward her nightly tea.

Alyssa picked up the mug, audibly inhaled, and took a healthy sip. She made a soft "mmm" sound and then took another big drink of the tea before opening her book and reading as she crossed the room, the mug still in hand.

Halfway to her dressing table, the queen groaned and clutched her stomach, her face contorted with pain. Her mouth opened and closed as though trying to speak, but unable to form the words.

Alyssa crumpled to the floor in a heap, her arm flung outward, her eyes glazed and staring. The mug broke into several pieces, the remaining tea spilling against the throw rug.

Immediately, a small, curvy woman Katelyn didn't recognize ran into the room and looked around. As soon as she was sure no one was around, she relaxed, and a smile stretched across her lips. She walked slowly toward the queen's still form and looked down on her, her hands fisted on her full hips.

"You shouldn't have threatened Valen, my lady. You overstepped your bounds and had to be stopped. Your mother can heal the planet, now that she's had some rest."

Anger surged inside Katelyn, and bile rose in the back of her throat. This woman would've gladly watched the queen die. Before Katelyn knew what she planned, she stepped out of the closet and started forward.

Grayson and Ryan stepped in through the open balcony doors, surprising the woman as well.

The woman gasped and started to back away.

Katelyn had already closed the distance, her hand balled into a fist, which she drove into the center of the maid's face. "Bitch!"

The sound of bones crunching sounded loud inside the room. Katelyn barely felt the pain that shot through her knuckles and wrist as blood spurted from the woman's nose.

The woman wailed and cried, her hands pressed to her face.

Gavin and some royal guards burst into the room and took the sobbing woman away.

Only then did Katelyn turn to look at Alyssa, who had rolled onto her back and stared up at Katelyn in surprise.

"Damn. Remind me never to piss you off." Alyssa held up an arm, but before Katelyn could reach out to help her up, Stone rushed forward and picked up his wife in his arms, depositing her gently on the bed.

The adrenaline drained from Katelyn's body, leaving her shaking and weak. Before her legs buckled, Grayson led her to the sitting area and settled her in an overstuffed chair. She mumbled her thanks, and then a hysterical laugh rose in her throat. "Who the hell was that?"

Alyssa sat down across from her. "Jaseen. She's one of Valen's consorts."

"And," Stone added, "was one of the group who threatened Alyssandra to drop the triangle or else." He propped his hip on the chair in which his wife sat. "I am a bit jealous you got to punch her."

Katelyn smiled. "Did I do a good job as an assassin?"

Grayson kissed her abraded knuckles. "You were wonderful. What did you put into the queen's tea?"

"Chai I took from your rooms." She smiled. "But you'd better hide your stash, I think she liked it."

"I did," answered Alyssa. "I just can't believe she thought my mother could reascend the throne. It would kill her even to try."

"Jaseen was a private cook for your parents," Stone said, disbelief thick in his voice. "What could have moved her to want your death?" He glanced over at his wife.

Alyssa shook her head. "Instituting this triangle has done strange things to everyone. Maybe now that Katelyn has heard everything, she could help us find both the statues and the Healer."

Katelyn examined her sore knuckles. "I would love to spend some time reading back over those journals I wrote growing up. I think, with everyone's help, I can figure out where I saw the statues. And who knows, maybe I wrote something more about Ryan's blond wife."

"I guess it's too late to marry you myself." Ryan gave a mock pout and then laughed when Grayson shot him a murderous look. He held his hands in front of him in surrender. "I was only kidding. Katie-Cat is a handful, and I wish you all the luck in the world."

"Hey!" Katelyn protested and then laughed with everyone else.

Grayson moved to sit next to Katelyn, his arm draped around her possessively. "This woman has agreed to marry me, and I want it done quickly before she comes to her senses." A smile played at his lips. "*After* the wedding ceremony, *and* our trip to the hot springs that keeps being interrupted, *then* she can try to trigger a vision about the Healer and find the statue."

She elbowed him and shook her head with a smile. "We aren't even married, and you're already bossy."

21

Sela glared down at Aedan, whose throat was trapped under one of her new designer boots. "So, let me get this straight, you've lost contact with your informants? All of them?"

Several guards stood around the edges of the room with small smirks on their faces.

Aedan opened his mouth, but only a small gurgle escaped.

Sela arched an eyebrow and huffed in impatience. But she finally took some of the pressure off his throat.

Aedan coughed and gasped for breath.

"Well?" she demanded.

"I . . ." His voice sounded like a hoarse croak. "I went to meet with them last night, and they never showed up."

Anger snapped and sizzled through Sela's body. "What did I tell you I would do if you failed me again, Aedan?"

He struggled to swallow under the pressure of her boot. "I'm valuable to you, Sela. Don't throw that away for a small setback."

Sela's fury bubbled and exploded from every pore of her body.

Power slammed into Aedan as well as into the guards.

Sela raised her arms, enjoying the surge of energy flooding through her, uncaring if anyone in the room survived.

Only when every guard slumped to the floor unconscious and Aedan went limp under her boot did she let her power flow away.

Sela stretched her neck from side to side, enjoying the small pops of her vertebrae realigning. She turned and kicked Aedan in the side with all her strength, enjoying the loud crack of bone in the now silent room.

"A good power surge is almost as good as an orgasm. If you live, we'll discuss more later."

Katelyn gritted her teeth and walked down the front steps of the castle, the gentle breeze playing against her bare skin.

"Are you ready?" Alyssandra asked from beside her, fully dressed—or at least as fully as the Klatch ever were.

"Why do I have to be naked again? I feel like I'm stuck inside a *Star Trek* episode at one of those nude weddings."

"I wouldn't mention that to Grayson," Alyssa offered. "I don't think he would get the reference. Just remember, my wedding involved sex in a vat of oil and burning all the reception food to crisps. You've got it easy—for now."

Katelyn cringed. "Don't remind me." She had heard all about the queen's ascension ceremony, her wedding, and all the public sex and nudity involved. Some of those same things would be involved in the triangle ceremony, but Katelyn at least had until they found the Healer to worry about that.

The area between the base of the stairs and the large fountain had been cleared for the ceremony. There were no flowers arranged or pews set up as she was used to seeing at a wedding—but, then, the area was so beautiful it didn't need any decoration. The large, two-story fountain made entirely of sparkling *balda* gurgled happily in the background. A gentle breeze brought the scents of a variety of flowers and other blooming things and gently teased the full boughs of the tall trees—not to mention the hardening of Katelyn's nipples into tight points.

Weddings were rare on Tador, because usually only the royal family married, so a large crowd had gathered to watch. Katelyn tried not to be self-conscious about her full hips or her bright red curls at the apex of her thighs.

She wondered briefly how many in the crowd disapproved of her being here and of Grayson marrying her. But a quick glance assured her that royal guards were scattered throughout the crowd.

Her foot touched grass at the base of the stairs, and she looked up—straight into Grayson's intense amethyst eyes.

Everyone faded to the background—everyone except Grayson. This was why she was here. This man who had taught her to trust and to open her heart. He was worth any amount of embarrassment. And after this he would be hers. Wholly and totally hers.

He took her hand in his, his cock hardening into a thick length as soon as he touched her. "Damn. I don't think I'll ever get enough of you."

"You mean *you* won't, or *he* won't?" She stroked his cock, and he hissed with pleasure.

Through gritted teeth, he said, "I think it's safe to say both of us will never tire of you." He crushed her to him, capturing her lips, and she kissed him back.

When cheers erupted from the crowd, she stiffened, remembering they had an audience.

"Prince Grayson, Seer, if you are ready?"

Katelyn turned to see an elderly woman dressed in the normal Klatch gauzy clothes, braids sprinkled throughout her long gray hair.

Grayson led Katelyn forward to stand in front of the

woman. Rita stood off to the right side—Katelyn's maid of honor. Katelyn stopped to give her a quick hug, accepted an encouraging smile, and then moved so Alyssa could take her place next to Rita.

It had taken quite a bit of explaining for Rita to wrap her mind around Tador, but because both she and Detective Damien would be in danger from the Cunts back on Earth, they had temporarily moved to Tador and were staying with Alyssandra's parents in the country.

And as for the shop, Ethel Harding had agreed to run it in their absence. She was still grateful that Grayson had pointed her toward her newest husband-to-be, so she was feeling generous.

Ryan and Stone stood off to Grayson's left, their expressions unreadable.

"Let the ceremony begin." The elderly woman's gravelly voice rang out over the clearing. She clapped her hands twice, and the crowd quieted and turned their attention toward her. "I am Annara, and as the eldest princess of the second house of Klatch, it falls to me to officiate." She held out her hands to both Katelyn and Grayson.

Katelyn stepped forward to take the proffered hand, and Grayson mirrored her movements. Annara brought her hands together, keeping them cupped over hers and Grayson's.

"Katelyn Hunt, Seer, do you willingly come forward to be permanently joined with Grayson de Klatch, the Seventh Prince of Klatch? To share your life, energy, and responsibilities with him? He stands before you today stripped of pride and material barriers." Annara glanced down at Grayson's substantial erection, and a small smile played across her lips before she raised her gaze to Katelyn. "Do you accept him?"

A herd of butterflies fluttered inside Katelyn's stomach, and she placed her free hand over her abdomen to soothe them. She had never thought she would have a long-term relationship, let alone get married. And certainly not naked in front of a crowd. However, here she was, jumping with excitement to do just that. "I do."

"Grayson de Klatch, Seventh Prince of Klatch, do you willingly come forward to be permanently joined with Katelyn Hunt, Seer? To share your life, energy, and responsibilities with her? She stands before you today stripped of pride and material barriers. Do you accept her?"

"Yes," Grayson said quickly, just as impatient as Katelyn.

Katelyn smiled at him, and he winked.

"Turn and face the castle as you receive your wedding mark."

A quick sizzling jolt against Katelyn's hip told her it was complete. *Damn, that was an easy way to get a tattoo!*

She smiled. The Klatch didn't do something as potentially temporary as wedding rings, but rather something permanent and lasting—just like her feelings for Grayson. Katelyn glanced at Grayson's hip and then at her own. They each bore a tiny, curved sword criss-crossed with a red rose—the same emblem that graced the flag that flew over the castle.

Annara stepped forward, raising her hands over her head. "I officially declare them wed."

Before the cheers of the crowd died down, Grayson grabbed Katelyn around the middle and flipped her over his shoulder, carrying her back toward the castle.

"Grayson!" She caught herself just before her face hit the muscled plane of his back, but she did reach down and pinch his gorgeous, tight ass, earning a renewed cheer from the crowds.

He jogged up the steps, his large hand on her ass to keep her in place.

She tried to twist around to see where they were headed, but he slapped her ass, sending a jolt of excitement and energy through her.

"Patience, Seer. You're mine now to do with as I wish."

She bristled. "Do I have to remind you that you're also mine to do with as I see fit?"

Grayson growled low in his throat. "As long as we have the same thing in mind."

A laugh spilled from Katelyn's throat and turned into a giggle when he jogged into his room and dumped her unceremoniously on the bed. She bounced, and before she could push herself up on the pillows, Grayson was on top of her, spreading her thighs and driving into her.

She groaned as he filled her. Before he could pull out and thrust again, she locked her legs around him and rolled him over so she was on top and Grayson's legs were dangling off the bed.

A quick flash of surprise rolled across Grayson's face and then dissolved as she began to ride him.

Katelyn braced her hands on either side of Grayson's head, her full breasts swinging in front of his face as she impaled herself again and again. The energy inside her woke in an instant, filling her and causing every part of her body to burn with need.

Grayson lifted his head and captured one breast in the hot cave of his mouth, sending shivers across her skin. He laved and nipped her, and Katelyn adjusted her movements to allow him more ready access to her breasts.

His large hands cupped her hips, pulling her more snugly against him with every thrust.

Her internal muscles gripped him, tighter and tighter until the first tingling sensation of her orgasm tickled deep inside her belly. She continued to ride him, his mouth hot on her breasts, the breeze carrying the sound of laughter and talking from the crowd below.

He bit down hard on her nipple, and she shattered, her muscles milking him, and the energy howling through them both with the force of gale winds.

Grayson cried out and stiffened underneath her as his hot come spilled inside her.

When most of her spasms had stopped, Katelyn collapsed on top of him, his softening cock still inside her. Her limbs felt like lead, and his warmth seeped into her, making her smile.

"Are you having a vision, my Seer?" He nuzzled her neck.

"Mmmm." She let her eyes drift closed. "No, but if you give me another five minutes to recover, I'd like to have one about making love to my new husband until he walks funny."

Grayson's cock hardened inside her, making her laugh.

"Well, at least, *wife*, I can tell we're thinking the same thing."

Turn the page and you'll be
ADDICTED!

From Lydia Parks,
coming soon from Aphrodisia!

1

Jake Brand tipped his chair back on two legs, wrapped his hand around a glass of whiskey, and took in the sights as though he had all the time in the world. In a way, he did. At least, in the foreseeable future, he had a decent shot at eternity.

The young blonde leaning over a table, shaking her backside in his direction, was another matter. In a few short years, her firm breasts would start to sag and her tight ass would droop. If she were lucky, some lonely trucker would offer her his life savings and a ranch-style home in the outskirts of Albuquerque before that happened.

But tonight, Jake planned to entertain the sweet young thing in exchange for dinner.

"You sure are taking your time with that drink," the blonde said, frowning at the five-dollar bill on his table.

Jake plucked a folded fifty from his shirt pocket and dropped it on top of the five. "I've got nothing but time, darlin'."

The young woman's eyes widened and her red, full lips

stretched into a greedy smile. She snatched the bill from the table and stuffed it into the back pocket of her denim miniskirt.

She winked at him. "I'll be back for you in just a minute."

"I'll be right here," he said, grinning. He watched her hurry to the bar, toss her towel under it, and whisper something to the bartender.

The burly redheaded bartender glanced over at Jake and nodded, and the blonde started back for Jake's table, swinging her hips as she tapped out the background song's rhythm with her high heels. He liked the way the shoes made her legs look a mile long. The thought of those legs wrapped around him caused a pleasant reaction, and he moved to adjust his tightening jeans.

She didn't stop at his table, but continued forward until she stood straddling his thighs, her hands locked behind his neck as she swayed back and forth in time with the music. "My name's Candy," she said, her voice soft in his ear. "You like candy, don't you?"

"Hmm," he said, inhaling her scent, weeding out vanilla shampoo, cheap perfume, stale cigarettes, whiskey fumes, and sweat. Yes, he definitely had the right dinner partner. "I can eat candy all night long."

"Oh, baby," she whispered, "You make me hot."

He chuckled at the insincerity of her words. Undoubtedly, few of her many customers cared if she meant them or not, and he didn't, either. Before the night was over, he'd get the truth from her, and she'd be more than just *hot*.

Jake ran the tips of his fingers up the backs of her exposed thighs.

She stepped back to frown down at him. "No touching. That's house rules."

He grinned again, enjoying the way her simple emotions played across her face.

He lowered his voice a notch. "I could bring you to a quivering climax without touching you, but it wouldn't be nearly as much fun."

One corner of her mouth curled up in cynical amusement. "You think so?"

"I know so." Jake used the Touch to retrace the paths of his fingers with his thoughts, remembering the warmth, the smoothness, the soft hairs on her upper thighs.

"*Hey*." She took another step back and stared into his eyes.

Jake pushed a simple concept into her simple mind. *Pleasure like you've never known.*

She swallowed hard, hesitated, and then moved forward to straddle his thighs again. He could smell her excitement as she sat on his legs and wrapped her arms around his shoulders. "I don't know how you did that," she said softly. "And I don't really care. You wanna go in the back room?"

"I think we should go up to my room."

She nodded, then turned her head to kiss him. Her warm breath caressed his skin before her lips met his, and he closed his eyes to enjoy the heated tenderness of her mouth. Her tongue slid across his lips, moving precariously close to the razor-sharp points of his teeth. Jake let a groan escape as he enjoyed the way her heat enveloped his growing erection, in spite of the clothes between them.

Candy ended the kiss and stood, drawing Jake after her with her small hand in his, leading him upstairs. The noise of the saloon-turned-strip joint faded below them as they climbed, leaving only a bass vibration in its wake.

"Which room?"

He nodded toward the door at the end of the small hallway. "Six."

"The best." She raised one eyebrow. "You rich or something?"

"Something."

"Oh, I see." She tossed her head, sending her blond waves into a dance around her shoulders. Candy knew exactly how attractive she was. "So, you're a man of mystery. Your name isn't *John*, is it?"

"No, it's Jake." He withdrew the key from his pocket, unlocked the door and pushed it open, then stepped aside as his young visitor entered. She didn't look around; she'd seen the room before.

"Jake." She turned in the middle of the room and smiled as she surveyed him from head to toe. "You know your fifty bucks don't buy you much. You want a blow job, or straight sex?"

Jake laughed then. "How do you know I'm not a peace officer?"

"A cop?" Candy grinned. "I know cops. Half the force comes in here after their shift. You're different, but you ain't no cop."

He nodded as he crossed the room and sat on the foot of the bed. "You're right about that. I'm different."

Candy tugged at the hem of her shirt, her head cocked seductively. "For twenty more, I take off my clothes just for you, baby."

Jake pulled off his boots and dropped them onto the floor. "I've got a better idea. How about a wager?"

The young woman straightened and narrowed her eyes. "You tryin' to tell me you ain't got no more money?"

He withdrew a hundred from his pocket and dropped it onto the bed. When she reached for it, he covered her hand with his own. "Not so fast there, sweet thing. Don't you want to hear my proposal?"

"*Proposal?*"

"For a wager."

Candy withdrew her hand slowly, then folded her arms across her chest. "I'm listening."

Jake stretched out on his side, studying the girl. "How long have you been at this?"

"At what?"

"Hooking."

Candy frowned. "You ain't some kind of preacher or something, are you? If you think you're gonna convert me—"

Jake silenced her by raising one hand. "You've got me all wrong, sweetheart. I'm definitely not a preacher."

She waited, her hands now on her hips.

"I'm willing to bet you one hundred dollars that I can bring you to a screaming climax in the next half hour."

Her eyebrows shot up and then she burst out laughing.

Jake watched her, enjoying her amusement.

"Right," she said between guffaws. "A *screaming* climax?"

He nodded.

When she managed to regain control of herself, she dropped down onto the edge of the bed, extending her hand. "You're on, Jake."

He took her hand in his, enjoying the warmth. Then he sat up and raised her hand to his lips.

"But you gotta wear a rubber."

Jake looked into her blue eyes. "Do I?"

Candy nodded. "Safe sex or no sex, that's how I stay alive."

"I promise we will run no risk of infecting you with anything."

Jake rose and drew Candy up to stand in front of him. Watching her face, he ran his palms slowly up her sides, peeling her shirt off over her head.

She stared at him with calm resolve, but goose bumps rose

on her skin where he'd touched her. "Your hands are cold," she said.

"You'll just have to warm them up for me, darlin'."

He unsnapped her skirt and pushed it off in the same manner, sliding his palms over her rounded buttocks and down the backs of her thighs. As she stood before him in her high heels, he stepped back to drink in the sight of her.

Her breasts were full and firm, with large, dark areolae. As he studied them, her nipples puckered, and he knew she liked to be watched.

Her waist, narrow with youth, led his gaze down to her partially shaved pubic mound, the line of dark brown hair giving away her true color.

Then there were those legs. Damn, they were long.

"Oh, yeah," he said, aloud but to himself. "This will be fun."

Jake stepped closer and eased his hands down from her shoulders to her breasts, memorizing the shape and warmth of them, twisting the nipples playfully before moving on to her waist and then her ass. *Nice.* He nuzzled her neck to get more of her scent, then pressed his lips to the top of her shoulder. The sound of her heart beating drowned out the hum of the room's air conditioner, and he let himself enjoy it for a few moments before turning back to the task at hand.

He moved his mouth to hers, covering her lips with his own as he eased one hand into her soft blond hair. His other hand he slid down her back to the smallest point and pulled her gently to him.

Her hands rose to his chest for balance.

He opened her mouth then, and ran his tongue around hers, catching the taste of whiskey and tobacco, as he moved his hand around her hip and eased it between her legs. Her swollen vulva parted for his fingers as he slid them back and forth, hinting at entering her, stirring her juices.

Her hands flattened against his chest.

Jake eased one finger deeper, stroking her clit, and her fingers curled. She drew on his tongue, and he continued to stroke, enjoying the way her hot little bud swelled.

Candy tore her mouth from his. "You said . . . a *screaming* climax."

"Yes, I did," he said, his mouth near her ear.

Her hips began to rock to the rhythm of his hand, and she gripped the front of his shirt in her fists. "Damn, you're good," she said, "but I don't scream for no man."

Jake chuckled as he slid his hand out from between her thighs. "Good, darlin', 'cause I don't want this to be too easy."

Candy rubbed against the front of his bulging pants. "Even if I ain't screaming, you don't have to stop."

"Don't worry, sweet thing, I'm not about to stop." He reached down with both hands, cradled her ass, and lifted her from the floor.

She wrapped her legs around his hips and her arms around his neck.

Jake carried her to the bed and eased her down as he kissed her. The girl knew how to kiss, and he felt his erection hardening to the point of discomfort. He unbuttoned his pants to relieve some of the pressure, then he withdrew from her.

Her eyes blazed as she looked up at him, partly with passion and partly from whiskey, no doubt.

Jake parted her legs, knelt at the edge of the bed, and kissed the insides of her thighs as he drew her to his mouth.

Her cunt was hot, salty, and wet, and he slowly licked the length of her, savoring the taste. Her legs opened more in response, and her ass tightened. He continued with long, slow laps as he listened to her suck air between her teeth, and he enjoyed her quickening heartbeat. Not long now, and he'd have her ready, sweetened, primed for him.

Jake pushed his tongue between her cunt lips and lashed at her clit, then drew it carefully between his teeth and sucked.

Candy's back arched, and she moaned as she neared an orgasm.

He moved away, nibbling at her thighs.

She grunted in frustration and he smiled.

Closing his eyes, Jake pushed his thoughts out then, moving the Touch up the length of her body like a hundred butterfly wings, caressing every part of her at once, flitting across her nipples and stomach, as he slid his fingers into her cunt.

Her hips rose up off the bed and she cried out in joy. "Oh . . . God . . . that's good," she said between panted breaths.

She clamped down on his fingers and flooded them with her juices as he moved in and out of her, traveling across her damp skin with his thoughts, feeling the conditioned air blow across her breasts, finding her pulse in a hundred spots at once.

His burgeoning cock emerged from the front of his pants as he enjoyed Candy, pulling her to the edge of her resistance, then pushing her away.

She cooed, and then groaned, and then growled with disappointment.

Continuing the Touch, Jake rose and removed his clothes. He loved the feel of heated flesh against his own when he drank. Letting the Touch drift lower now, he stretched out on top of Candy and kissed her neck, her jaw, and her shoulders.

She wriggled under him as the treatment intensified. His thoughts rolled over her cunt, then dipped in and out.

"Fuck me," she said, digging her fingers into his back. "Please. I'm on fire."

"Yes," he whispered, easing his cock between her legs.

She thrust up into him, taking him into her all at once, and he almost lost her.

"Oh, no, you don't," he said, drawing back.

She locked her legs around him before he could withdraw. "Good lord, get on with it."

Jake glanced over his shoulder, surprised to find Thomas Skidmore standing beside the bed, pale hands fisted on his narrow hips.

"Go away," Jake said.

"Why do you insist on doing it this way?" Skidmore waved dramatically with one arm, his style mimicking the British theater of years gone by. "I've never known anyone who felt they had to get permission. You are strange, dear boy."

Jake returned his attention to Candy, rocking against her in time with her growing need. She hadn't noticed the intrusion.

"Just hurry. We have places to go." Skidmore closed the door behind him as he left.

"Oh, God," she said, louder now. "Don't stop. Fuck me. Harder."

Jake turned his head to speak softly into her ear. "I need more than your cunt, sweet thing. I need your blood."

He felt her tense as fear crept into her fevered excitement.

"I won't hurt you," he said. "We'll come together."

After a moment of hesitation, she turned her head, offering her neck to him as she writhed in anticipation, her hands fisted against his back.

Jake pressed his lips to her neck, thrilling to the pulse rising and falling beneath the surface. He let loose of the reins then, thrusting into her sizzling cunt as his cock hardened to steel, pushing deeper, needing release nearly as much as he needed to feed.

His fangs lengthened, and he opened his mouth. Trying to hold back, savoring the anticipation, he smelled her approaching climax. Yes, she was ready.

Jake pressed his fangs into her neck and she screamed. He closed his eyes as her orgasm flooded him, first biting down on his pulsing cock, then flowing through his veins and exploding in his brain. He drew hard as he pumped his seed into her, letting her fill him with need, fulfillment, dreams, wants, desires.

He knew her arousal as she danced for hungry eyes, her smug disgust as sweaty men humped her for money, her euphoria as she lay alone at night with a vibrating orgasm rolling through her narcotic haze. And he felt her ecstasy as his own. She came again as he thrust harder, longer, until he'd taken all he could, and given all he had.

Jake held his mouth to her neck for a moment to stop the flow, then moved it away and slowed his thrusts to nice, easy strokes.

Her grip changed to a shaky hold on his shoulders, and her cries softened to weak groans.

He stilled, then withdrew and rolled onto his back to enjoy the sensations of nerves popping and firing through his entire system, waking from a long sleep. After more than a century and a half, he still loved the vibration, especially when sweetened with orgasms.

"You win."

Jake turned his head to find Candy lying with her eyes closed and her arms at her sides, her body glistening with a fine sheen of sweat. Already, the small wounds on her neck were nearly healed, and her heart rate had begun to slow.

He grinned.

If not for Skidmore waiting impatiently outside somewhere, Jake might have spent a few more hours with his little morsel. But the old man was right; they had places to go.

After getting dressed, he dropped the bill onto Candy's bare stomach, then leaned over and kissed her soundly.

She hadn't moved much, and smiled up at him. "You come back anytime, Jake."

He winked at her, then tossed the room key onto the bed beside her before leaving his dinner guest and the air conditioner's buzz behind.

Downstairs, he found the tall, thin vampire in an out-of-place purple velvet suit, standing in the shadows near the door, and Jake made his way through the maze of tables, young strippers, and horny old men.

"It's about time," Skidmore said, wrinkling his nose with disapproval.

"Some things shouldn't be rushed." Jake picked up his black felt Stetson from a hook by the door and slipped it on as he stepped into the New Mexico night. Warm, clean air swept over him as if he were no more than another jackrabbit making his way across the desert, and a star-filled sky opened above as Jake strolled across the parking lot to the convertible parked near the exit.

"Will you please get a move on?" Skidmore hurried ahead, hopping effortlessly into the passenger's seat. "I refuse to spend another day trapped in the boot of this wretched beast. It'll take at least four hours to get to the mine, and that's thirty minutes more than we have."

"Don't sweat it," Jake said, trying not to get annoyed with his fellow traveler. Skidmore tended to get on his nerves after a month or two of whining. "We'll be there in three."

Jake started the Impala and pulled out onto the narrow highway, turning north. With no one else around, he easily pushed the car to ninety and they roared through the darkness.

"Oh, I nearly forgot to tell you what I heard," Skidmore said.

It was a lie; the older vampire never forgot anything. Jake waited, but Skidmore just smiled.

"What?"

"A very special friend of yours will be at the meeting. If we

get there early enough, perhaps you'll have time to get reac-
quainted."

"Katie?" Jake glanced over at his companion, whose face
seemed to glow in the starlight.

Skidmore grinned and ignored his question.